Where
The
River
Bends

By
Doug Landgraff

Acknowledgments

I owe an outstanding debt to my friends and family who were beside me (in spirit if not physically) giving guidance, encouragement and evidence that my project could become a reality. Thanks and kudos to Audrey Danaher and Molly Landgraff for being trailblazers and inspiring me to stop procrastinating and act upon a long-standing desire to author a book. I also owe a debt of gratitude to the team from my publisher, Book Marketeers. A heartfelt thank-you to the team: Anne, the team leader; Alan Berry; Ethan West; Jack Hudson, project manager; Jay Reeves, editor; Jack Matthews; Kenrick Lazarus; and Sophie Millar. I would be remiss if I failed to mention my first readers, my wife Debbie, Robin Pearson, Sharon Moynes and Trish Mauch, all of whom gave me encouragement and invaluable guidance in a kind and considerate effort to improve the finished product with my ego intact.

This book is dedicated in memory of my daughter, Amber, who passed too quickly at a tender age, succumbing to cancer.

Prologue

Since humanity's first faltering steps, we have quested for enlightenment and self-realization. This thirst for self-discovery birthed philosophical and theological explanations and a guiding algorithm for pursuing knowledge: Aristotle's scientific method. Each individual must face the quest given a set of unique personality traits and varying circumstances resulting in observations and conclusions. When considering the totality of all members of humanity, these conclusions reveal a universal consciousness.

On the path, one encounters many obstacles: non-acceptance of otherness, inequity of distribution of wealth, the specter of man's inhumanity to man, mental instability and the inevitability of aging and death. Countering these and representing the duality of our existence are good fortune, genetic markers, the communal human spirit and the statistical probability that we call luck.

The following is the record of one boy's journey to reveal the mysteries represented by the dark, seamless monolith of unknowing (as shown in the opening scenes of the movie 2001: A Space Odyssey) leading to self-enlightenment.

Table of Contents

1

Glimpses

It was a period of great expectations and hope for the future; hope tempered by the uncertainty of the new Cold War era. The baby boom exemplified this hope. It was an economic boom tied to the reconstruction of post war Europe. The chief beneficiary to the boom was the new world power, the United States of America, vaulted into the position by the success of the Manhattan project and a willingness to use this awesome power in their own interests; now shifting the focus from military use to peacetime electrical power generation. It was a time of great activity where protest, sometimes violent, arose to effect change; Women demanding recognition of their not insignificant role during the time of peril, as well as a new freedom of expression in all aspects of their lives.

Traditional powers represented by government and class systems were being challenged by more vocal youth with fading respect for the status quo.

Minorities protested for more equitable civil rights. Artists and musicians witnessed and provided a platform to encourage rapid change. It was a time of creativity, protest and a morality shift. The summer of love in 1967 brought free love and the hippy culture to the fore. Technological advances took promising leaps that seemed to progress exponentially.

In these heady times I was representative of my general milieu with some added influences unique to my situation.It was Friday evening as Vince and I walked home after a session at the pool hall at about seven o'clock one hot, humid summer evening. We were only five minutes from my place, and neighbors gathered in the street, as was typical for summer in the city. They were outside, where it was more comfortable given the heat. Some were chilling on lawn chairs, kibitzing and having a cold one, while others were strolling and chatting. Our neighborhood had few air conditioners and no personal computers or video games to grab your attention. As a result, people were more present in each other's space.

Sometimes it was a pain in the ass because of the gossip, but it could be a lifesaver in a crisis.

I was about seventeen or so, and Vince was a year younger. Because of the heat, we had on shorts and tees. Vince was in high spirits. He bounced around like popcorn popping in a Jiffy Pop container. He thought it would be fun to yell, "Hey!" at passing cars. Our street, Central Avenue, was long and straight, with few traffic lights, mostly stop signs. It was a preferred throughway, nicknamed Central Drag Way, in recognition of past late-night stunt driving with occasional accidents. Although not constant, traffic was usually brisk.

Vince immaturely called out, "Hey," at passing cars with no evil intent when a guy and a woman in a Volkswagon beetle did a U-turn and started following us, driving against traffic.

The driver harassed Vince, demanding, "What the hell do you think you're doing, insulting my woman like that?"

Vince said, "I thought she was a girl I knew." Wrong answer Vince. The guy started yelling, "That's no girl; that's my wife!"

Then his rage turned on me.

"What are you looking at, four-eyes?"

I replied, "What's wrong with you? Are you crazy? Are you going to follow us all night?" Again, the wrong answer.

The guy accelerated, pulled into the nearest side street, exited his car, and stood waiting for us.

Vince fearfully said, "Run!" to which I replied, "*We* don't run."

As soon as we got close enough, the thug grabbed me by the collar and pulled me forward so that his face filled my vision. I went into a non-aggressive stance, arms limp at my side, wary and planning my next move. I considered punching him in the gut, but that wouldn't necessarily be incapacitating. A throat punch? I waited for his response.

He said, "Do you know who I am? I'm the road captain of the Loco Perros! So why are you mouthing off at me like that?"

Maintaining my non-aggressive stance, I replied, "Well, *sir*, what do you do when one of *your* buddies gets into trouble? Do you cover his back, or do you leave him on his own?"

This de-escalation attempt that appealed to his creed was crucial. First, I saw him weighing options, and then he pushed me away, reaching for his belt.

"I wanna show you guys something," he said.

I thought, "Oh no, here comes the knife!" He pulled up his shirt, exposing his midriff swathed in bandages.

"I just got released from the hospital for this gut wound. That's what saved you."

When he was gone, Vince and I continued to my place, where we roosted on the steps of my front porch. To say that I was relieved was an understatement, but to lighten the mood, I said, "Guy probably wears that gauze around his gut all the time to get out of fights." Vince laughed, and I knew that things would be okay.

In retrospect, the whole thing could have turned out drastically different. In my bravado, I overestimated the deterrent effect of having witnesses nearby. Stabbing is fast and can be fatal before anyone can react. At least one weekend stabbing regularly occurred in any of several haunts along nearby Drouillard Road. On the other hand, the odds had been two to one in our favor. In hindsight, had I thrown the gut punch that had been my first instinct, we might have gotten away unscathed. I was just grateful that things turned out as they did.

Over the years, I've come to believe in many folklore aphorisms: guardian angels, "it takes a village to raise a child," six degrees of separation, and the idea that perhaps, like cats, we might have nine lives. I wholeheartedly believe this. There have been too many "coincidences" in my experience to dismiss it. We get forged in a crucible, where events and influences work during formative years until the finished product emerges.

Hi! I'm Doug Landgraff. Welcome to my hometown, Windsor, Ontario, Canada. Growing up in the Automotive Capital of Canada was influential in shaping me. The city has a long, varied, and unique history. Prohibition was put into effect in the States during the twenties. Alcohol was still legal in Canada, which made Windsor a hot spot for rum running (with direct connections to Al Capone's Chicago Outfit). The border town was a den of iniquity, drawing Americans over in search of alcohol and women, concentrated at Pitt Street East. An on-duty beat cop noted that it was so busy on the weekends that it was hard to walk his beat. Finally, in the fifties, the province struck a Royal Commission and dealt with the criminal element.

The iconic activist and naturalist Farley Mowat had Windsor in his background. He was only nine at the time, and it was the thirties. I suspect that era was no joke for anyone. My parents also called Windsor home and were teenagers while Mowat was a resident. My mother recounted being on welfare and having clothes made of flour sacks, while my father was silent on almost everything. The only positive comment attributed to him by Mom was that he said, "No matter what happens, we will always have food on the table." I assumed that this came from his experiences during the Depression and his wartime service in England under rationing.

Other famous people came from Windsor, too. Paul Martin Jr., Canada's 21st Prime Minister, was born in Windsor. Past Deputy Prime Minister Herb Gray and Shania Twain also had ties to the border city.

Mowat, my brothers, and I experienced bullying in school but avoided serious consequences, although twenty-some years separated our experiences. Mowat was not fond of the place, saying that Americans, to whom he referred as industrial overlords, assumed that Windsor was just a northern suburb of Detroit. Several alternate names for the city considered upon incorporation were Richmond, the Ferry, and South Detroit. His assertion that Windsor was a northern suburb of Detroit is erroneous. The Canadian city is located on the river's south shore, placing it south of Detroit, adding support for my declaration of uniqueness because it is the only Canadian city south of the USA. That fact has left me with directional dyslexia because of my persistent notion that the States are to the north.

Windsor and Pelee Island are approximately at the same latitudes as northern California, with similar climatic features. Another unique feature is that nearby Point Pelee National Park is on the migratory path for the endangered Monarch butterfly. The area in and around the city is so flat that people say, "If you want a hill, you have to build one." Furthermore, there are grasslands and savannas nearby at Ojibway Park with a prairie ecosystem. Windsor has the warmest climate among large Ontario cities.

When the first European settlers arrived in the seventeenth century, Huron, Odawa, Potawatomi, and Iroquois First Nations inhabited the region. The land along the Detroit River was part of the Three Fires Confederacy between the Ojibwe, Potawatomi, and Odawa and the area was named Wawiitanong Zibi, or where the river bends.

About sixty years ago, an accident provided a spectacle that brought thousands of tourists to the area. A British freighter ran into a barge pulled by a tug and sank under the Ambassador Bridge. The crew got evacuated to safety. The Windsor Star reported about twenty thousand spectators in Windsor and Detroit watched "the ship flop to her side in 30 feet of water." The sinking prompted boat cruises, increasing custom on the Boblo amusement park shuttle. Parents took their kids to see the wreck, and the Ambassador Bridge, which at the time allowed foot traffic, provided a unique view. I recall seeing the derelict from this perspective and thinking it resembled a beached whale.

Thinking about the wreck reminds me of a personal adventure on the river. I went with a classmate to check out a boat purchase. The ad stressed, "Bring your own motor. Unaware of the circumstances about to unfold and ignoring my non-swimmer status, I helped Randy load the engine into the trunk of his car and off we went. The owner accompanied us to prevent the theft of his property, and we proceeded onto the river. Our motor died while we were out there and we drifted into the shipping lane. After we made several unsuccessful attempts to get the engine going, the owner told us to get out of the way, and he stepped in. A laker, bearing down on us, made him anxious to get going. Typically, lakers need help seeing small crafts in the water because they tower above the surface like a six-story building. Smaller craft are wise to stay out of the shipping lanes. With the ship bearing down on us, its shadow cast a chill in the air while the small craft owner frantically worked on repairing our motor. Time was growing short. He had removed the engine cowling and in his anxiety, he dropped some hardware into the river. He scrambled to find a solution. None of us wore life jackets because we hadn't expected to be on the water for long. As the ship bore down on us, I became acutely aware of my inability to swim and began praying. At that instant, our motor roared to life; we cleared the shipping lane and headed to shore. The boat owner was livid. He yelled at Randy for not maintaining his motor. There was no further negotiation concerning the boat. This close call was one of, but not the last, examples of my poor judgment and risky behavior. It also inspired my belief in guardian angels. Someone was watching over me. Superstitiously, I felt I had wasted one of my nine cat-like lives.

****

Windsor has special status, granted by the Canadian Radio-television and Telecommunications Commission, exempting them from most of the Canadian content (Can-Con) rules since, under territorial rights, it is part of the Detroit television and radio market. Before Can-Con, the AM radio station CKLW was the top-rated station in Windsor, Detroit, Toledo, and Cleveland in the late sixties.

This special status also allowed for more T.V. channels, predominantly American, to be broadcast in the marketplace. Such availability influentially exposed me to Motown music as it evolved. In addition, my brother, Teddy, twelve years my senior, habitually followed Dick Clark's American Bandstand, which premiered in 1957. Mom, a couple of my cousins, Teddy and I practiced the twist in the living room which Chubby Checker demonstrated on the Dick Clark show. We practiced singing the Name Game by Shirley Ellis while watching the show. Stevie Wonder, introduced to the world as Little Stevie Wonder, gained notoriety through the American Band Stand. Steve Miller, The Jackson 5, Aerosmith and many more made their first appearance there. Finally, my musical influences, fueled by proximity and availability, revealed themselves while visiting my Californian aunt with Mom. My first exposure to the just released "Good Vibrations" by the Beach Boys prompted me to observe, "Our music is better."

I would not say I had an intimate relationship with death but rather a nodding acquaintance. A few months after returning from California, in October, I lost my Dad when I was thirteen. I repeated a pattern in common with Dad since he also became fatherless when he was about the same age.

A sudden, paralyzing stroke and a fatal cerebral hemorrhage brought about Dad's demise. His death was not my first exposure. Ten days before my first birthday, my brother Dennis succumbed to leukemia at age seven. I have vignettes of memory: me sitting between my parents, bathed in dashboard light while they spoke in hushed tones of the most recent update of Dennis' condition. A year later, my maternal Grandmother passed. At her funeral, Mom told me that Meme was sleeping. I exclaimed,

"She's not sleeping; she's dead!" My paternal grandparents and my second oldest brother, Gerald, passed before my birth.

Mom was pregnant before Dad volunteered for the army at the age of twenty-three, joining the Essex Scottish, one of the regiments put into action at the raid on Dieppe Beach. Gerald died of dehydration at the age of six months. Tragically, this was before Dad returned from his ordeal. Dad never knew Gerald. My eldest brother, Teddy, didn't remember Dad upon his homecoming. He thought Dad was an uncle or something.

I was the last of six boys. Mom was pining for a girl and had not considered another boy. She refused to see me at birth, even to nurse me. I was bottle-fed by the nursing staff. Eventually, the nurses cajoled Mom into providing my identity and holding and feeding me. She named me after my pediatrician. After that, there was some discussion of child swapping with my aunt, who had four girls. Each sister envied the other. Nothing came of the conversation.

After Dennis' illness demanded intensive medical care, my parents acquired a debt burden not relieved by health insurance (which appeared years later). Subsequently, Mom experienced psychosomatic paralysis and anxiety disorder that put her out of commission for a while. Somehow, she came out of it when my pediatrician urged, "Who's going to look after this little one?" Maybe, under those circumstances, I suffered from childhood abandonment syndrome and its consequences.

Mom was anxiety-ridden and feared the loss of another child. Perhaps the OCD resultant from an authoritarian upbringing had put too much pressure on her. In any case, I ended up socially stunted as a result. To facilitate ease of handling, I was overattended, dressed, shod, and even told the time, should I ask. Otherwise, I existed by my own devices, occupied and entertained in front of the television. Mom assumed that since my brothers demanded no outside interests, I wouldn't be interested either. The family finances made it a pipe dream anyway. There wasn't a lot of interaction with my siblings or my Dad due to the gender-dominated roles of the time. As a result, I became an observer of, rather than a participant in, family affairs.

Upon school entry, I remained socially challenged. Our district had no kindergarten, so my first experience with education was full-day sessions at a first-grade level. I couldn't tell time or tie my shoes until grade four. My mother handled rather than guided me. Mom spent more time washing white shoelaces and polishing shoes to comply with societal expectations than she spent with us. Her pride and OCD behavior gave the appearance that she felt superior to others, but more accurately reflected Mom's fear of falling below expected norms. This concern for keeping up appearances also involved us. She insisted that we wear peaked hats rather than toques, overshoes rather than black rubber, calf-high boots, and dress pants rather than blue jeans.

Mom's obsession with appearances rebounded on her, though. Mike constantly lost his hats. When his headgear got replaced, with the expectation of him wearing it, his different style of dress and short stature targeted him and brought out the bullies; probably the explanation for the short man syndrome he came to exhibit in adulthood.

One day, Rod came home and announced that Mike was in a fight with three guys. Mom responded with exasperation, "And you didn't help him?" Rod replied, "But Mike was winning!" So Mom sent him back to the scene, but it was all over by then.

Mike had overcome his tormentors.

My pediatrician said I trended below average height for my age and would likely only grow to the size of a jockey. He prescribed an androgenic steroid to stimulate my growth. The drug gave me a deep voice, which always surprised strangers. It also caused outbursts of anger. In my teens, I developed cystic acne on my back, chest, and shoulders and less severe facial acne, perhaps attributable to the steroid. Because of its many side effects, androgenic steroids are no longer prescribed as a growth stimulant except when used illicitly.

Our next-door neighbor, a little boy named Brian, was a year younger than me. When Brian came over for play dates, accompanied by his mother, no matter what I played with, he wanted it. To teach me to share graciously, I was encouraged to comply. Brian's behaviour was so extreme that our moms provided matching butter knives to keep us occupied rather than toys. Still, Brian wanted the knife I had. My resentment grew as this behavior continued. Whether it was because of the testosterone or my growing resentment, I plotted to get him alone in my tiled bedroom. The throw mats in my room inspired me. I remember thinking that if I could get him to stand on the end of the rug, I could pull it from beneath him, causing him to fall. I then successfully executed my plan.

On another occasion, I lost my temper with him. He started to run away. I pursued him. As I got close enough, I pushed him from behind, causing a fall resulting in severe skinning of his nose on the sidewalk. I felt like a monster after that, so I went home and wept inconsolably. After this incident, my pediatrician discontinued the steroid. I eventually gained average height anyway, despite its discontinuation.

While weeping on our stoop following the incident, I sustained a sliver under my right thumbnail that penetrated the first knuckle. The doctor removed the nail to release it. After administration of a local anesthetic, the doctor pulled my nail off, bandaged my hand and sent me home without any pain reliever. Two hours later, when the anesthetic wore off, my nerve endings awoke. In karmic retribution, I suffered intense, fiery throbbing pain simultaneously with Brian's suffering at my hands.

This incident exemplified the tone of my future, which was to be rich with lessons, opportunities, joys and losses that arguably could only be the results of my situation in history.

2

Brothers

Brothers share the bond of blood and experience. In addition, personality and proximity, forced by room or bed-sharing, contribute to the dynamics. Finally, birth order influences sibling rivalry. Being separated by eleven months of age, Mike and Rod were strongly affected by these factors. They were "roomies," which forced proximity, often resulting in friction and outbreaks of intense emotion. Like many siblings, Mike and Rod encountered problems maintaining mutual privacy and property rights. However, one particular incident intensely inflamed Mike. He had crafted an art piece that involved emptying an egg of its contents, leaving only the shell. The eggshell, pasted on red construction paper with hand-drawn horizontal rows of rectangles mimicking a brick barrier, represented Humpty sitting on his wall. On the right upper section of the background, a printed verse next to the empty eggshell explained the tableau in rhyme.

The artwork held pride of place for Mike on their bedroom wall.

Rod was compelled to alter the illusion. In selected words of the rhyme, he put an l between the letters p and t and the occasional o,p, and y to generate the following masterpiece:

Humplty Dumplty sat on a wallopy,

Humplty Dumplty had a great fallopy,

all the King's horses and all the King's men,

Couldn't put Humplty Dumplty back together again.

This flagrant violation of property rights incited an outright brawl that became representative of their relationship.

There are many examples of this "boys will be boys" behavior. One arose around the construction of an addition to our house, a collaboration between my father and the next-door neighbor, to enlarge it to one thousand square feet. They had excavated the trough for the footings and foundation. The trenches filled with water after a period of rain. They were more of a moat than anything else. Rod jumped over the ditch to the dry gravel base in the center and encouraged Mike to follow. Mike was reluctant to take the leap. Rod assured him that he would act as his spotter, even coming up with the idea to anchor themselves together with a length of rope.

Mike, now filled with confidence, tried the jump. Rod pulled the rope tight and then tugged forward. Unfortunately, Mike got pulled into the moat for an unintended dunking. Rod had not thought things through. Rod did other impulsive things that had unintended consequences too. For instance, he cut open his basketball to find out what made the boink when the ball bounced.

One of their fights ended when their shared bathroom towel rack got ripped from the wall. Knowing that they were in trouble, they instantly collaborated to repair the damage and prevent discovery. They carefully Scotch Taped the bar in place, draping towels over the damaged areas to aid with the deception. When Mom collected laundry that week, she was shocked to have the rack come away with the towels.

Mike was mechanically gifted, while Rod wasn't. Mike took great pride in his bike, meticulously caring for it. He painted it red with careful attention. Rod, however, couldn't care less and was haphazard with maintenance. His bike was black, and often, the brakes were on the verge of failure.

Once, while riding in single file, they tried to converse. Traffic noise interfered, and Mike suggested a stop to facilitate communication. Unfortunately, Rod could not hear Mike's request to parlay. His brakes were faulty, so when Mike stopped, Rod rear-ended him.

During another brawl, Rod fled to their shared bedroom, closing the door behind him. Mike pursued and tried to force entry into the room. Rod countered with force from inside, barring entrance. Soon, the dynamics of opposing forces caused the door to split down the middle.

For all of that, they still looked out for one another. Once, when Rod had a fever, Mike acted in caregiver mode. He tried to take Rod's temperature. To sterilize the thermometer, he held it under hot running water. Unfortunately, the device exploded in his hand once heated beyond its limits.

Sometimes, Rod was a self-righteous troublemaker. For example, Mike stole some of Dad's chewing gum, and Rod ratted on him. Then Rod tried to convince our parents that anyone could prove guilt using fingerprint evidence obtained by applying black pepper to the leftover gum packaging.

Rod was clumsy because a pea lodged in his ear canal long enough to affect his balance. Mom treasured her recently acquired large decorative glass urn sprucing up the living room. Rod knocked the jar to the floor two days after its acquisition with his swinging arms; bye-bye, brand new ornament. Mom said that all Rod had to do was enter a room, and things met their end.

Since Teddy and I shared the birth date, he treated me like a gift, as if I were a pet. We shared a room, like Mike and Rod, minus the discord. Teddy often demanded that I let him administer "a nibble" (a brush of his lips) to the crown of my head. He also took me for rides in the carrier of his bicycle. I got preferential treatment when Teddy was in charge, on the rare occasions when my parents went out. He let me stay up past bedtime to watch television with him. He strictly enforced lights out for the others, using fists to overcome accusations of unfairness.

We were the first family in the neighborhood to get a T.V., chiefly because it provided cheaper entertainment than other options. It also kept me occupied being an electronic babysitter while Mom did her chores. I watched my usual shows: Captain Kangaroo, The Friendly Giant, Romper Room, and Mr. Rogers. In the late afternoon, my favorite show, Boofland, came on. Boofland's host, Jingles, interacted with the puppet characters Cecil B. Rabbit, a parody of Cecil B. DeMille (I was not too fond of this character) and Herkimer Dragon (whom I loved). Memorable product advertisements appeared interspersed between these shows.

Mike and I had a closer relationship than we had with Rod; I remember Rod in caricature from that time. It wasn't until several years later that Rod and I developed our relationship. I maintained long enduring impressions of him as a scam artist, luring us into bad deals backed by contracts, which Mom enforced. Once, Rod convinced Mike to trade his birthday gift, a camera with a flash attachment, for one Rod had purchased.

Rod's offering had no flash unit, but he presented it as the superior choice considering the savings on the cost of batteries; the exchange got backed up with a signed contract.

My love of puppetry, inspired by children's television programming, prompted Mom to keep me occupied with gifts of puppets. Eventually, I had about six of them. Mike liked them, too. He coerced me to allow access by performing a voice I loved, which Mike identified as Puppy Dog. If I refused to let him play with Petey, my canine puppet, Mike said in "the voice," Puppy Dog won't like you. I always caved for that.

Mike played surgeon, with Petey as a patient. Mike faked life-threatening conditions requiring immediate surgery. No family members were allowed into the operating room during the proceedings, and tension mounted until Mike appeared with occasional updates. Poor Petey was often at death's door. It caused many anxiety-laden moments in fear of losing my beloved Petey, but he always miraculously recovered.

In the same way, Mike gained access to my birthday gifted wagon using "the voice." Mom often wondered why, after begging for that wagon for the months leading up to my birthday, she saw Mike with it more than she saw me with it. Incidentally, I found the same wagon in Mike's garage years later. Huh!

Mike had a bit of a mean streak and liked dominating me. Once, he sat on my chest, pinning me down. Holding my arms over my head, Mike experimented with the tensile strength of spit. He ominously threatened me with progressively longer hanging spit gobs. He dangled them closer and closer before sucking them back in. Eventually, he exceeded the maximum dangle limit, and I got a gob in the face.

Another common occurrence concerned my Tinker Toy creations. I occupied myself for hours, playing with things created following illustrations in the instruction booklet or some of my designs. Mike joined in the activities as soon as he returned from school. Twenty seconds in Mike's hands was sufficient to destroy a creation that had survived my handling all day. I wondered if this was clumsiness or if it was intentional.

Another time, I was trying to make Mike laugh. I practiced funny faces in the mirror until I found one I thought would work. Then I went to the kitchen to show him. He ambushed me, though. He was crouched at the entrance to the kitchen, hiding in front of the fridge. Prepared with a tablespoon of cold applesauce ready to catapult at the next person to enter the kitchen, he made me his victim, shocked with an earful of cold applesauce.

Shortly after, Mike tried to recreate this success with a slight variation. He waited in the same place with a glass of water at the ready. He intended to throw the glass of water over the victim while fake sneezing with a loud, phony "Achoo." Unfortunately for Mike, Mom was the one who entered. She reacted angrily and began to chase Mike down the hall.

She was hellbent on justice, grabbing at Mike's shirt. The floor in that hall had a high sheen and was slippery. When she got hold of Mike's collar, the mat Mike had just sprinted over started to slide, with Mom riding along. She resembled a slightly damp, careening charioteer. Taken off guard by the mental image it presented and taken in a fit of hearty laughter, her resolve evaporated, and Mike got away scot-free.

Mike teased me about my quirks constantly. He made me feel like there was something wrong with me. There was the issue of how I swallowed, which was ridiculed and imitated. When I recited memory work, he mocked how my eyes would migrate upward as I performed. He said I made funny movements with my jaw and tongue. Then there was the issue of my journal, which he found and read without my permission. He dismissed it as repetitive and boring. He also lurked nearby when I played board games with friends, coaching them to win while he ridiculed my moves. Mike teased us about how stupid he thought Rod and I were regarding bicycle maintenance. Sometimes, he would beat me up for ratting him out to Mom. He said, "And if you tell Mom again, you'll get even more." Once, this happened outside school. He wrestled me to the ground, and while he punched me, a passing classmate said, "Come on, Mike, he's just a little guy; leave him alone."

Our house was so small that furniture got moved, and new sleeping arrangements were assigned to accommodate a Christmas tree during the festive season. These changes resulted in Mike and I sharing a bed. One night, he persistently requested that I scratch his back. I elbowed him in the mouth to make him stop. The impact split his lip and made him cry. I felt proud of myself that day.

Some accidents happened, too. Mike and Rod played backyard baseball one day. I was unaware of the bat's reach, but my brothers should have been more careful. Anyway, I walked into a swing, taking a bat to the side of my head. I often wondered if this contributed to my emergent poor eyesight. One of my eyes is off-center, just enough to cause impairment.

I wasn't always the one who got hurt, though. An undeveloped lot on our street had a crab-apple tree and was our place to play jungle adventures. The older boys climbed high in the tree, launched themselves from solid upper branches, then caught a lower limb and swung to the ground. Mike had made this maneuver many times before without harm. That day, he missed the intermediate branch, fell hard and began crying. He cradled his arm, which hung at a sickeningly unnatural angle. The odd angle, his ashen face and his pained cries upset me as we drove him to the emergency ward.

Brotherly bonds may be strengthened by shared near misses and calamities. Windsor exists in a tornado alley; warnings are standard during the summer. Historically, there have been two touchdowns that caused severe damage. The first, a category F4, occurred in 1946 before I was born. The second, an F3, happened in 1974 and destroyed the curling club, causing nine fatalities.

A storm experience shared by me and my siblings threatened to be another such event. During this particular disturbance, the sky was very dark, with a faintly greenish tint, accompanied by torrential rain and teeth-rattling peals of thunder. We were gathered on our enclosed front porch when the almost ear-splitting peel of thunder reverberated through the sky. It was so strong that I felt it in my ribcage. For sure, this could be it. To our great relief, though, the storm passed without further damage.

Another shared experience concerned a well-loved pet white mouse. Whitey delighted the whole family. His habit of nestling in the breast pockets of our shirts was fun for all, even more so when Whitey urinated in the pocket of Teddy's white shirt, leaving a warm yellow streak behind.

On a different note, our mother was quite devout and insisted that the family observe daily recitation of the rosary. Once, while reciting the "Hail Mary," I was compelled to race through the prayer, finishing before the rest of the family. I tried to see how many times I could insert the name Herkimer Dragon before the rest caught up. I built up to four recitations over prayer repetitions before Mom caught on. My brothers recognized what I was doing before Mom did and started to laugh. When she finally figured it out, she became God's Avenging Angel.

3

Meet the Family

Mom grew up in a large Francophone family in Sandwich, a district of Windsor with a high poverty level. She was one of twelve children. Her parents were devout Catholics. Her father, Pipi, was a stern disciplinarian who used corporal punishment as a form of parenting. Mom was obedient, even to the point of deferral to her parent's choice for her mate. However, she was naive and high-strung, suffering from OCD. She was needy, exhibiting the learned helplessness common to many women of her era. Her parenting style was manipulative and passive-aggressive, typical of many mothers then.

Mom's education ended with primary school. She spoke only French until she started school but gained knowledge beyond the classroom in the school of life. She was so savvy with stretching a dollar that Dad was impressed by how often she could get more for less. She used credit and bargaining as financial tools.

Mom was lovely, as were her sisters, and she had a keen fashion sense. She was a bit of a flibbertigibbet, making comments about friends like, that's my friend Harriet. See how bowlegged she is? She is also obsessed with appearances and clothes, fed by a need awakened during her Depression Era childhood. Nevertheless, she liked to look good and had a prodigious memory for past paired outfits. She could tell you what she wore on long past evenings, including the matching footwear. She had fierce pride and successfully drew the male gaze.

I am not sure how many nervous breakdowns she had, but there was a hint that she had suffered at least two. I can, however, testify to multiple midnight calls to the priest, requesting the sacrament for the sick and varied hospitalizations for surgery. In addition, she took me to the appointment, where she was told, "It's all in your head." That physician was proven wrong when a surgeon discovered and removed a foot and a half of an unhealthy bowel located during surgery for gallstones.

Today, there is a diagnosis (Irritable Bowel Syndrome) and treatment for the condition she suffered. With all the attention focused on her health, Mom could command attention by relating stories of hospitalization and suffering in search of a diagnosis. Among her cronies, she held court, telling tales of surgeries past and dispensing advice for rapid recovery in her status as a survivor.

Once post-surgery, she brought home an exhibit for me. In a sterile bottle, she presented me with a half dozen of her gallstones suspended in solution. I shook them repeatedly until they dissolved. Later, she showed her doctor the result. I've often wondered if this information was discussed among the doctors and stimulated the development of shock wave lithotripsy.

As mentioned, Mom had a thing about outward appearances fed by pride and a large helping of OCD. Naturally, therefore, our home and laundry must be above reproach. With our laundry arrayed on the clothesline, Mom bragged that it was the whitest in the neighborhood. Additionally, her windows must gleam with no hint of streaking. The same standards applied to any task assigned to me. I remember repeatedly washing a single window one Saturday afternoon until I got Mom's thumbs up.

Her parenting style was manipulative and passive-aggressive, layered with the threat of corporal punishment typical at the time. There was never the threat of "Wait til your father gets home," though, as Dad was mainly an absentee father, mentally if not physically. Instead, Mom swiftly administered the punishment using a strap fashioned from a length of black plastic baseboard material acquired with the house renovation.

Bare-bottomed, we suffered the blows while Mom intoned, "This hurts me more than it's hurting you." Yeah, right!! In fairness, most of the time, rather than the strap, we were forced to kneel in prayer and contemplation, our gaze fixed upon the crucifix that adorned our living room wall.

Dad lost his father at age thirteen, just after the stock market crash of 1929 and the beginning of the Depression. Besides the fact that Grandpa had been a farmer, we knew little about Dad's life. Granny could not keep Dad and gave him up. We only ever met his cousin, Tommy, and Dad's sister. Unfortunately, there was little contact with his side of the family.

Dad somehow finished high school and became a tradesman. He was a journeyman tool-and-die maker before my birth. A veteran of WWII, he adopted the tight-lipped attitude common to veterans. Dad was a sober alcoholic, giving up the drink when his doctor told him the addiction would be his death. He was also an ex-smoker, which attests to his inner fortitude. His dedication to A.A. directed his attention to those similarly afflicted while decreasing family time. Yet, he seemed to be on a mission, his zeal revealing spirituality inherited from his Lutheran ancestor, a minister.

By the time I was born, though, he wanted some contact with his sons. He sometimes took me to meetings, holding me on his knee while dispensing helpful advice. Not all of his interactions with me were so benign. One occasion, I was put down to nap when I realized Mom was not in the house. She claimed that she told me she would be out asking a neighbor to borrow a stamp. Having abandonment issues and finding myself alone, I panicked. I ran out of the house, dressed only in jockey shorts in mid-October. I went door to door in search of my mother. A neighbor rescued me and pointed to our car, still in the driveway, indicating that someone must be home.

Unfortunately, I had forgotten that my father was home sleeping in preparation for his night shift. Then, the neighbor wrapped me in her sweater and brought me home. My Dad received me at the door. He was not a happy camper. He took me to my room and threw me in bed, bouncing me off the wall.

When Mom returned, an angry Dad chewed her out for leaving me alone. Having been on the receiving end of that tirade, she came into the room and spanked me. I felt that was unfair because of the way I got tossed around earlier. Mike later told me of a similar event during which he had disturbed Dad's sleep and had a slipper thrown at him. Mike concluded his recitation with, "Dad is mean."

Once, I came home from school for lunch and shared a pleasant conversation with Dad. We had hot dogs, then I returned to school. About twenty minutes later, I was back with the beginnings of a migraine. Dad helped me to my bed and left the room. A few minutes later, I vomited. Dad returned, cleaned me up and changed my bedding. He took the soiled bedding and put it in the bathtub, leaving further action to my mother, when she returned from work later that day. Dad only went so far in these things. Mom came home to find a mess in the bathtub, half filled with water, holding my soiled sheets and floating stomach contents, complete with pieces of partially digested hot dogs. Dad should have done more, but he needed to sleep before his night shift began.

Because of Mom's opinion that the local variety store was a hangout, we were not allowed to go there unaccompanied. Once, my Dad took us to buy a treat. He said, "Anything you want, just ask," He failed to clarify that he offered only a choice among penny candy. When we wanted regular-sized candy bars, he said, "What do you think, I'm made of money?"

Dad had some peculiar habits. He referred to a bicycle as a wheel. He often said, "He's a good (fill in the skill) if he'd leave that drink alone," about an A.A. buddy.

He staunchly believed in faith healing and watched broadcasts of the Oral Robert's Show every Sunday. Finally, he would use the phrase, "Not of I know of," rather than, "Not that I know of." Mike displayed his disrespect for Dad by mimicking him. I don't know what caused Mike's attitude because Dad treated me relatively well despite his failings. I even established a budding relationship with him, although it wasn't warm or close.

Dad was a diabetic and always seemed to be hungry. That wasn't odd, considering the disease. He packed his black lunch bucket, which resembled a small rural mailbox, to capacity with carrots, celery sticks, and in-season fruit (doing this himself because he accused Mom of being stingy with the portions). Perhaps this was part of being diabetic, or maybe a reflection of his war experiences with rationing, or even a throwback to memories from the Depression, I don't know. Unfortunately, as is typical with diabetics, he had heart issues (he endured two heart attacks before his fatal stroke). Mom often wondered why all the cookies disappeared so quickly. We hid our intake, blaming Dad for that until his diagnosis of diabetes. We got caught the first time we pulled that after his diagnosis.

Like any married couple, my parents had their share of arguments. Usually, they were limited to raised voices and flared tempers. Once, I saw Dad throttle Mom. I went with her when she visited the church rectory seeking advice about his abuse. The priest gave her the usual line about the sanctity of marriage and wifely duty predominant in those days and sent her on her way. Mom was generally critical of Dad but, after his death, admitted his good qualities.

Dad and Teddy didn't always see eye to eye either. I witnessed several fights with them thrashing around on the floor, punching each other. There was even a case when Dad connected with a roundhouse blow to Teddy's jaw and dislocated it. Unfortunately, these physical altercations rarely resulted in happy outcomes.

Memories of family life were not all negative. On Sundays, family harmony became evident as we celebrated the day of rest, starting with early attendance at morning observances. After we returned home, Mom prepared dinner; the house was filled with comforting aromas of meat, potatoes, and gravy and the sweetness of cherry, apple, or peach pie, dumplings, or homemade beans, depending on the day's offering. The family gathered around a card table in the living room to play a board game, sharing the joys and sorrows of the past week while the meal simmered. Later in the afternoon, we would huddle around the television to share the broadcast of old movies. Rounding out the day, we gathered to watch the Ed Sullivan Show. An appearance on that show could launch a career, but Sullivan's disapproval could end one. Sullivan introduced Elvis, The Beatles, and The Doors on that show. Because they crossed Sullivan during their appearance, The Doors encountered obstacles to their rise to fame. Other musicians, such as Ethel Merman and Ella Fitzgerald, also appeared. Some audience favorites were Topo Gigio and Senor Wences. Finally, there were memories of regular visits to Pipi to fulfill my mother's obligation to her father.

Years after Dad's passing, Teddy and his wife Sherry tried to recreate the ambiance, sponsoring the Sunday meal for Mom, my wife and me. Although the food was good and the gathering pleasant, it could never adequately substitute. It lacked something "homey." The Beatles' bobbleheads in their apartment offered a touch of nostalgia, but they couldn't recover the lost childish innocence.

Mom loved to cook and bake, and we benefited from her ability. I loved her rice with raisins and bread pudding desserts. She made cakes from scratch on special occasions or from a mix for a quick, tasty dessert. One Sunday, as she prepared the cake batter using Mix Master and controlling its rise up the sidewalls with a spatula, she dropped the spatula into the bowl. It got entangled in the beaters. The resultant jam launched the batter into her hair, on her face and down her front. The white kitchen walls were also covered. Stunned, Mom began to laugh, and the rest of the family joined in. We then helped with the cleanup.

Mom started a new mix, and we had a chocolate cake dessert that day despite the mishap.

I will recount our trip to Niagara Falls to close this reminiscence of family activities. This outing included Mom, Dad, Mike, Rod and me. Of course, I wanted to see everything on offer, including the Wax Museum, funicular rides and souvenirs. Dad admonished, "You don't need that." We were only allowed to do free things. We stayed at a motel overnight. Mike and Rod shared one of the two double beds. Mom and I slept in the other. We requested an extra cot delivered and placed under the window for Dad. It was a sweltering summer night, so the windows were open to catch a breeze. My lasting memory of this trip features a couple walking past our room just as Dad farted, and we boys erupted in giggles.

4

Visiting Pipi

As a sign of respect for their sacrifices, parents expect gratitude from their children. Grandparents hope to share and bask in the joy provided by grandchildren. Mom was dutiful to this obligation, and we visited Pipi often.

Pipi was illiterate but not a fool. He had many skills that found him gainful employment over the years. He was a carpenter, raised livestock on his property, and sold the rights to an herbal cough syrup he had developed. His final occupation before retirement was as a stationary engineer (janitor) at St. Mary's High School, the all-girls Catholic School. He purchased a duplex in Sandwich and raised his family of twelve children on one side while renting the other to survive the Great Depression. He resided there until his death, supported by his son Ed and family. On the other side of the duplex lived another son, Earl and his family.

The thing I remember most from these visits is the Grand Fetes at Christmas, attended by aunts and uncles in town for the season. Initially, there would be camaraderie and free-flowing booze. It deteriorated into arguments and eventually fist fights. The combatants rolled around on the floor and tried to get their best licks in before their siblings separated them. Mike even got into it once with cousin Fred in the backyard. Fred was egged on by the next-door neighbor with "You get him, Fred!" I prefer to avoid a fight but will rise to the occasion if necessary.

The most memorable event that occurred at Pipi's features Bernice, the next-door neighbor. She lingered nearby when we visited. I noticed her easy suggestive sway previously. She had an attractive face and figure and sandy-colored hair that cascaded down her back. She was a year or two older than me. One day, she lured me into Pipi's idle coal chute, where we engaged in a period of "necking." I got pulled away when Mom called out that we were leaving. To keep our secret, I broke off immediately. On the ride home, I savored the memory of soft, warm, charcoal-flavored lips.

5

American Influences

Living in a border town has certain advantages. For example, shopping in downtown Windsor required a thirty-minute bus ride, but an additional twenty minutes longer allowed shopping in downtown Detroit. A transfer from a Windsor city bus to the Tunnel bus at the downtown terminal would take you across the border to the Detroit business center.

En route, you pass the Spirit of Detroit statue, featuring a large seated human figure holding a family and golden orb aloft in alternate hands. In 1955, Marshall Fredericks received his commission from the Detroit-Wayne Joint Building Authority to create a sculpture for the city to represent hope, progress, and the "spirit of man." A twenty-six-foot bronze, patinated male figure, seated tailor style, golden orb, casting radiating rays, in the left hand counterbalanced by a family in the right. The outstretched arms bisect the torso at about a fifteen-degree angle to horizontal. There, he sits before a curved section of wall, representing the city of Detroit. The work immediately became an iconic representation of the city. On the wall behind the sculpture, an inscription reads, "Now the Lord is that Spirit: and where the Spirit of the Lord is, there is liberty," along with the seals of both the City of Detroit and Wayne County. A plaque in front of the statue reads: "The artist expresses the concept that God, through the spirit of man, is manifested in the family, the noblest human relationship."

You disembarked on Woodward Avenue and stood before Hudson's Department Store. Hudson's was the tallest department store in the world at the time, standing at four hundred and forty feet. It was the second largest department store in the world, behind Macy's at Herald Square in New York. Grand River Avenue bounded it to the north, Farmer Street to the east and Gratiot Avenue to the south. At Christmas, it hosted Santa Claus.

Mom thought that shopping at Hudson's offered a larger selection of superior- quality linen goods and clothes at a price advantage compared to offerings in Canada.

She would make quarterly pilgrimages, limited by governmentally determined caps on duty-free purchase declarations taken upon return to Canada. Of course, I always escorted her on these occasions.

I was complicit in smuggling merchandise exceeding the duty-free limits, having it secreted beneath my clothes. Mom's unwitting mule, I went across as a skinny kid in a snowsuit and returned, appearing to be a fat kid in a snowsuit. She once smuggled a pair of high-heeled shoes, one stuffed in each pocket of my outerwear.

Of course, movement around the Detroit shopping area exposed me to some vices unavailable in Windsor. You could get three brand named, regular-sized chocolate bars for a quarter as well as soft ice cream in a cone for a dime; my wages for the collaboration I got forced into.

As we passed the Empress Burlesque Theatre on Woodward in our movements around the shopping district, I got exposed to a photographic sampling of the earthly delights within. I was a good boy, however, never staring at the semi-nude photos but still curious enough to try to steal a glimpse as we passed.

Once, Mom offered to take me to see Santa at Hudson's. I was thrilled until I realized that Santa was on the sixth floor while we joined the line on the first. Two hours in a store, dressed in a snowsuit, inching slowly toward my hero was so unpleasant that it convinced me never to do it again.

Another time, as I followed Mom around in the store, I paused momentarily to examine something that caught my eye. Unfortunately, when I turned back to Mom, she was gone. I got lost in one of the biggest stores in the world in a foreign country!

This stark realization engendered immediate terror, and I began to wail like a banshee. Hearing the commotion, Mom realized I was missing and approached the cacophony. In the interim, I had recited my name, address and phone number to the security guard who came to my aid. Mom appeared at about that time to rescue me.

While shopping in Detroit, I got my first exposure to air raid siren tests at noon and to a large population of African Americans. None of that existed in Windsor. It confused me, but I kept it to myself. I accepted these differences without question.

As I aged, the differences between Canadians and Americans became more apparent. We heard Canadians characterized as polite, navel gazers who said "aboot" and "Eh."

Of course, there were also those pesky rumors that we all lived in igloos. We even heard expressions of amazement that we had advanced technology, like street lights.

There were contrasting stories of American tourists making morning crossings through Canadian Customs, asking for the best route to get to Winnipeg for lunch. I had a conversation with a guy at an American friend's wedding. He expressed in amazement, "You talk just like we do!"

6

Neighbourhood

It was a grand undertaking when the city decided Central Avenue would no longer be a graveled avenue. The Dutch Elms lining the avenue were diseased and dying, and the city took the opportunity to widen and pave the street. I mourned the loss of the cool shade provided by those trees, which had swaddled my brothers and me while we engaged in activities in our front yard. Away went the trees, and in came the heavy machinery. For the price of moving a comfortable seat to your front yard, a major entertainment event unfolded. There was all manner of heavy construction machinery coming and going for months. Even though we lost the pastoral atmosphere that the elm tree-lined avenue had provided, we maintained the quaintness of daily home bread and milk delivery from horse-drawn wagons well into the sixties.

In my preschool years, I rose early and parked before the base-board-mounted heat vents to warm up. Later, I participated in the usual neighborhood games of hockey, backyard baseball, and football with my siblings and other neighborhood kids. I had a decent batting average then, hitting the ball out of the "park" more often than not. But given the approximately forty-foot frontage of the properties, the "park" wasn't that large.

I learned to skate on a backyard rink, wearing white girls' hand-me-down figure skates. Using a kitchen chair as support, I circled the tiny rink while Mom watched in warm comfort through the kitchen window. Unfortunately, I was a poor skater, having weak ankles and no coaching.

After the war, there was a lot of immigration to Canada. Our neighborhood had representation from all over Europe. People came here to make a new start. Most of the men were blue-collar, skilled tradespeople. Immigrants resented then, as they are now; I heard the slur, damned D.P., thrown about quite a bit along with other racial epithets. Immigrant parents brought their children. There was Joe, from Italy, who spoke no English. I met him when some bullies down the street were baiting him to sing "Old MacDonald." Joe sang, "E I E I O."

Joe's father worked in construction, so Joe gravitated naturally to activities in that vein. He became a steady visitor, bonding with Mike. Joe hung around when Mike did bike maintenance. Mike painted his bike, and Joe sat, watched, and chatted. When he left, I noticed a big red spot at the rear hip pocket of his pants, caused by sitting on the paint can lid.

Joe and I were in the same grade and often hung around together. He kept my inability to tie my shoes or tell time secrets, saving me from ridicule. He filled in for Mom during school hours. I felt like a fraud when teachers said, "Your shoe's untied," because I'd reply, "I'll tie it later." I became adept at hiding inconvenient facts, going to considerable trouble to guard against exposure like an illiterate. I was afraid of being outed at all times.

We also played chase the ball with each other. We were supposed to be playing catch, but neither of us had talent, so we just threw the ball in each other's direction and retrieved it when we invariably flubbed the catch.

One day, Joe, Brian from next door, and I played backyard baseball. The other guys had their turn at bat and hit weak grounders. When I came to bat, I said, "I'll show you how to play baseball." Unfortunately, when my bat connected, the ball arched in a pop-up trajectory, soaring over the corner of Brian's roof; then, we heard the crashing tinkle of glass.

The neighbor whose window I broke didn't like me. He was upset when my mother told him our home insurance would cover the replacement cost. He was determined to make me pay for the damages myself, stubbornly insisting that I was solely responsible, so I should pay.

Joe was brilliant, but I didn't realize it then. He learned English and was fully fluent before he started school. Being bilingual, he corrected me as I followed the wrong page in the Missal. I didn't know English appeared on the left pages and Latin on the right. I thought the right-side pages were just gibberish, but I tried to follow along page by page anyway. By the time we served as altar boys together, I had become aware of Latin. The last time I saw Joe, he was about twenty and a grown man. He became an engineer, handsome and solidly built, with dark curly hair like the image of a Roman aristocrat.

Brian still lived next door and played a role in the neighborhood hi-jinx. His family and the events surrounding them drew my interest. Brian now had a little brother, Simon. His father, Mark, was a carpenter, which was good for the neighborhood because he would do repairs as a favor for us. Brian's mother, Jasmine, liked to be referred to by her first name, an oddity for that time. She was a frequent flier at Mom's coffee klatches. Besides his brother, other players on his family stage were Barney, his white and brown beagle, his Grandmother, and his two female cousins, Bonnie and Gillian. Brian's Grandmother had a goiter pressed against her vocal cords, giving her a distinctive rasp. It became apparent when she beckoned for Brian and his brother. Barney froze to death in his doghouse one frigid winter night; he should have been inside with the family. Gillian had her left thumb severed in a lawnmower accident. That incident stuck with me and made me super cautious around moving machinery. Finally, Bonnie was a subject of infatuation when she appeared in shorts and a sleeveless top, displaying her lithe, athletic build and exceptionally well-shaped, tan legs.

Brian's father was among the first adopters of the revolutionary Edsel. Touted as the perfect car, it was not a marketing triumph. It had push buttons for everything and resulted from a marketing survey asking consumers for their preference of most desired features, giving free reign over the car's design. Mark would stand beside his new vehicle, grinning and singing its praises to everyone. The car cast a jaunty figure, with the addition of the newly designed blue maple leaf flag (eventually replaced by the now- familiar red maple leaf design that got final approval), waving from its antenna.

The Sinclairs lived in the grandest house on the block. It was of red brick construction with an ample front porch with pillars and an arch. It also had a garage, a luxury in that neighborhood. The Sinclairs were a large family with seven children, presided over by a ginger-haired father. He had trained as a priest but got turned away because of his stutter. His wife was a lovely, milky-skinned, freckled blond of Scottish descent who had worked with my aunt at the head office of Ford Motor

Company before marriage. Sinclair children were either redheads or blondes, and the brood consisted of Richard, Kory, Kendra, Michael, Jimmy, Susanne and Rose.

Their home was a gathering point for children of the neighborhood. We flocked there to play marbles and games like Simon Says, One-Two-Three Redlight, or Statue. These games were presided over by their Uncle Charles when he visited. We also played basketball around the over-the-garage-door mounted net. On hot days, we sat on a picnic table inside the open doored garage playing card games like War, Poker, Fish and Rumoli.

The more adventurous boys played "paratroopers," gaining access to the roof by climbing the garage trellises and then jumping off as if in training to be commandos. It was fun, but when we hit puberty, we experienced a shock to our groin if we didn't bend our knees properly on landing. My adventure climbing the backyard tree went awry when I got stuck for fear of falling as the tree swayed in the breeze; I had to be talked down by Mrs.Sinclair.

With all those kids, there was a need for amusements to be plentiful and close to hand. Naturally, the neighbourhood benefited also as things got shared around. The availability of a basketball net was the draw in my case. I also took advantage of their wagon and comic books, sharing them with all the kids there.

The Sinclairs acted as an incubator for childhood diseases like mumps. I never got the mumps protected by vaccination, but as they spread through the neighborhood, Mark, Brian's Dad, did; in an adult, this may cause infertility. We were exposed to new ideas at the Sinclairs', too. I learned the difference between boys and girls when Tim Williams, who had a sister, exclaimed that girls are different. I was shocked beyond belief, as having only brothers, the issue had never entered my mind. I replied, " C'mon, of course, they gotta have one…!"

As a gathering place for kids, it was also a place to observe current trends in fashion, speech, or developing fads. When the British Musical Invasion entered full swing, the Beatles were trendsetters. It was evident at the Sinclairs'. Some of the kids started sporting leather caps and square-framed glasses with blue-tinted lenses. It took more to convince me because the Beatles had not yet pulled ahead of the pack to establish supremacy as composers and innovators. I predicted that they wouldn't last more than six months. As they evolved their unique presence and continued to grow, I had to reverse that decision.

As well as the Sinclair girls, there were sisters Gina and Claudia Battaglia from across the street. I played with the older sister, Gina, but I found the younger Claudia quite a piece of eye candy (although she was too young for me to engage with). Gina and I spent time together skipping and playing hopscotch, house, chess, and other board games. We often rode our bikes together. In a sense, Gina was my first girlfriend, although this was never overtly stated. Instead, she said I was the "nicest" boy in the neighborhood. However, our close relationship deteriorated after Dad died and I had less free time.

A new family arrived in the neighborhood with a two-story brick house on a flatbed truck. The house was relocated directly across the street from ours and was the home of the Grams, who emigrated from Germany. The brood consisted of Kurt, Johan, Wolfgang, and their parents. My brothers, Mike and Rod, became thick as thieves with Kurt. They had a secret club, which convened regularly, in our garden shed. Mike was Kurt's right tenant, and Rod was his left tenant. I was just part of the entourage.

The purpose of the club was to foster camaraderie and plan events. Kurt had a prodigious mind and introduced new games and ideas through the club. I became acquainted with activities involving golf balls. Whenever we got hold of one, we dismantled it. This process proceeds patiently, circumscribing the outer coating and peeling it off. After that, we cut into the rubber-bandy layer to make it unravel. It was gratifying since it was like a chain reaction. Once it began, the elastic would self-destruct, unraveling wildly and instantaneously. Then you were left with the core, a super-ball that bounced higher than anything else. These became prized possessions.

Kurt also invented a dice game involving toy castles and plastic soldier figures. First, opponents set their bases apart with a measured no man's land between them. Then, the toy soldiers navigated this area in moves dictated by the dice throw. In this way, the game advanced until one side emerged as the victor (judged by Kurt).

We also used a length of discarded copper pipe, firecrackers, and marbles to imitate mortar fire. First, the copper tubing got jammed into the ground at whatever angle was necessary to hit the target. Then we lit a lady-finger-sized firecracker and dropped that into the copper tube, followed quickly by a marble. When the firecracker went off, the marble would be launched, with some velocity, in the direction the pipe aimed. No one stood before this homemade mortar because we knew the danger that was presented.

Finally, we made bunkers from dirt and grass and destroyed them with the mortar fire.

We also practiced different techniques, like running only on tiptoes, to improve our speed by lessening the contact time of each step with the ground. It came in handy later when I got on the track team. I became an excellent sprinter.

7

Country Cousins

Family finances were significantly affected by lingering medical bills after Dennis's death. Mom told me much later that Dennis's doctors, seeing the ravages leukemia wreaked on us and Dennis, wanted to waive the expenses in a humanitarian gesture. They all acutely felt the loss of the child. Many comments were made about the little saint indeed being in heaven. In keeping with Mom's pride, though, she stubbornly insisted on holding on to the obligation. Perhaps she felt that was the best way to compensate for her inability to save Dennis from his ordeal. In any event, it took about ten years to pay off the debt. Until the obligation cleared, we delayed luxuries. Holidays were foregone, purchasing a new family vehicle was postponed, and only essentials were allowed. Vacations usually meant visiting relatives willing to host us. We stayed with one of our country cousins in Wallaceburg most of the time.

Typically, we went to Mom's Uncle Grant and Aunt Mary's farm.

Being a city boy, this was an alien environment for me. Although I toured the farm solo, I heeded Uncle Grant's warning not to disturb the bull. Fear kept me compliant. The bull weighed over a ton, muscle with horns. You didn't have to encourage me to avoid the entry of his pen, but I did want to observe, so I approached but kept my distance. I also avoided electrified fences that kept the cows from wandering.

The farm had other oddities. Around the livestock, horseflies were common. I got warned that these beasts would take a chunk of meat from you if they bit you. I hesitated to enter the main house when these aggressive bugs crowded the spring-loaded kitchen screen door. Even the door was odd. At home, our door swung on well-oiled hinges. On the farm, it creaked open in a high nerve- grating squeak, then snapped shut with a bang. If you moved too slowly, it hit you in the backside.

Uncle Grant and Aunt Mary were gracious hosts with honest country manners, but Mom sometimes crossed the lines of graciousness there. Upon our evening arrival, Aunt Mary showed us to our room.

Mom knew I loved gravy over bread, but she forewarned me not to request it there, saying it was rude. About nine years old, I obediently complied when the condiment appeared. When Uncle Grant put a slice of bread on his plate and asked for the gravy, Mom asked me, "Why don't you have some bread and gravy?" Confused, I replied, "Because you said it was rude." Uncle Grant's eyes met Mom's, and I realized my blunder, but the cat was already out of the bag.

Another difference about the farm was the extensive unfamiliar machinery. There were wheeled devices with rows of shiny, sharp discs as big as car wheels to attach behind a tractor. Even tractors (often painted red), with their elongated open engine compartment and high rear wheels, were unfamiliar. Names like threshers and seeders referred to other wonders; their purpose was a mystery to me, the city boy. The "door yard" was populated with milling hens, which yielded ground only when threatened with proximity, scratching and pecking at the ground. They would squawk and bustle away with a flurry of wings when approached.

Even the country folk themselves were a novelty. Uncle Grant's son, Finn, had an accident with a thresher that mangled his hand. There were corn cribs that stored feed for livestock, wide open spaces shaded by tall trees, unfamiliar smells and sounds, and soft sighing breezes. There were vast azure skies, the playground of scudding clouds and the domain of a brilliant sun. It was tranquility in a manner I had never experienced before.

Dad's father farmed in Maidstone, and Mom's family traced back to many farmers. Even Mom's brother (my godfather), Uncle Sly, farmed and repeatedly told Mom that if he had to take me, I would learn what hard work was. It felt like a threat or at least a disapproving judgment of me. My Christmas gifts underscored the no-nonsense practicality of Uncle Sly: a pair of pajamas alternating in cycle with a flannel shirt.

One year, we visited with Mom's cousin Enid and her husband, Clint. They had a couple of kids. Cousin Grant, about a year and a half older than me, thought I was stupid because I couldn't ride a bike yet—my attempts while there were disastrous. I rode into a shrub as I let go of the handlebars to block the hanging branches. Other than that, I liked Grant. We spent some afternoons together roaming the farm. Some of the time, we were in their expansive front yard beneath tall trees that cast a soothing shade. We swung from the tire swing suspended from their boughs. Other times, we explored the hayloft. From there, Grant indicated the manure pile below and laughed as he told me about when his brother fell from the loft and landed head-first in that pile. One day, as we explored, he sang his favorite song, On the Wings of a Dove. It was a nice tune but different from my usual rock and roll preference.

Grant had a plastic, collapsible drinking cup that intrigued me. I liked it so much that I traded one of my less favored puppets for it. It resembled the cartoon character Deputy Dawg. Because the image was trademarked and molded plastic, it was expensive, but the paint had worn off some parts, and it was never as precious as my Petey, fashioned from a faux fur material. When Mom discovered the unequal trade, she did something I had never experienced before. At home, she upheld exchanges between Mike and Rod, especially in the face of Rod's written contracts. In this case, she asked Enid to step in to convince Grant to reverse the trade, stressing the inequity of the transaction. I didn't care about that. I no longer liked that puppet, but I wanted that drinking cup. I was upset that she stepped in. Nonetheless, a higher authority blocked the trade.

Clint demonstrated the charm of country living, striding into the dooryard and grabbing a chicken, taking it to the chopping block with his axe in hand, decapitating it, and then releasing it to dance around until it dropped motionless. He then hung it to bleed at the side of an outbuilding. Later, they plucked the fowl and brought it to Enid to roast for supper.

I liked the freedom the farm represented because I got to stay up past my regular bedtime while we played games outside until well past dusk. I felt privileged and experienced a newfound pleasure.

We had corn on the cob for lunch on our last day there. After lunch, we played while the sweet and salty sensation lingered in our mouths. With all the preparations to leave made, a forgotten errand spurred the adults to drive away to rectify it. As time passed, my corn-stimulated bowel fermented gas. Its release immediately alerted me to a minor accident. Embarrassed, I made excuses and entered the house searching for fresh undergarments, only to remember everything was in the trunk of the absent car. What to do? What to do? I did the only thing I could think of. I retreated to the bathroom, removed my pants and undershorts, cleaned the skid mark away as thoroughly as possible with toilet paper, and redressed. Going commando occurred to me, but how would I conceal the abandoned garment? After the vehicle returned, we made our final farewells and departed. I never told anyone about my accident (until now).

8

Primary School

Introspection

In the recess of my mind,

I dig down, and I can find

That I am not who I profess to be;

I am a fraud.

I am lost when I say I'm found,

I'm free, but I'm bound,

I have friends, but I'm lonely at the same time.

I wonder, who can I be?

I can't find my identity.

And I'll search 'til I can see

The real me.

I was not precocious, but I had been asking Mom since I turned five why I couldn't attend school yet. Our school district had no kindergarten, so my entry was delayed until I turned six. With my midsummer birth date, I just met the age cutoff rules. I entered first grade slightly younger than some classmates.

September finally arrived, and I attended my first day of school. I remember that day vividly. Many first-timers, accompanied by their mothers, trudged along the route like they were going to slaughter. One of my neighbors, Sela, sobbed and moaned when it came time for her mother to depart. The wailing continued until mid-morning when the teacher finally lost it. She shouted at Sela, saying, "This stops now!"

At recess, I made my first school friend. Lachy MacKee approached me with an enormous smile and said, "Do you want to be my friend?" As simple as that, we became buddies for the duration. Unfortunately, Lachy had ADHD, a condition not to be classified for another decade. So why didn't the teachers realize that something was amiss? Lachy got "the strap" at least once daily. Did they think that he arose each morning and planned to disrupt the class to be rewarded with physical pain?

Lachy and I were eventually separated when he had to repeat grade five, but we still maintained contact until the end of primary school.

Lachy and I always played together at recess. A city park, with all kinds of equipment, adjoined our school grounds. All of the kids played there. There were twelve swings, a slide, a see-saw and lots of open space to run; this was where we played British Bulldog. There was even a baseball diamond and basketball court. In winter, parts of the park got flooded to allow ice skating.

One day, Lachy and I were playing on the seesaw when two older kids bullied us away. They wanted to play "bucking Broncos." It was a safety violation but was common practice. The two boys sat at their respective ends of the teeter-totter with their backs to each other, seated on the wrong side of the handle. The idea was that you could alternately come down with force and buck your partner off.

I never knew the exact sequence of events; I just heard Lachy's agonized scream as his knee got crushed under a descending seat. A year later, he reminded me of the accident by demonstrating how freely and unnaturally his kneecap moved around. He was pretty proud of it.

A couple of times, I invited classmates home to play after school. I knew them as Ricky and Billy Paul, so when they introduced themselves to Mom as Richard and William, I said, "I thought your names were Ricky and Billy Paul." I did not get the connection between given names and their diminutive forms. It marked me as "not so bright."

Several issues revealed themselves about now. First, my teacher, Miss Moses, noticed I was making mistakes and suggested I needed glasses. It was evident to her that I couldn't see the blackboard. She suggested I get tested, and her opinion proved to be accurate. I became "four eyes" from then on. As time passed, the shape of my eyes changed again, and I didn't need corrective lenses for a period. By the time I reached grade eight, I needed glasses permanently.

My recollection of grade two is spotty. I felt like a fraud while I hid my failings. Teachers would say, "You're smart, this should be easy for you." I would slouch and signal my agreement while hoping the truth never came to light.

I am a visual learner; I need to see each step for clarity, or I don't get it. It's another thing that marked me as "not too bright," along with my inability to ride a bike until I was in grade five. Seeing my kindergarten-aged cousin whizzing along, demonstrating a skill I had yet to master, spurred me to success. I was embarrassed, so I practiced on borrowed wheels until I developed the skill.

Finally, the most significant difference between my classmates and me was that I read voraciously. I became a bit of an intellectual snob, preferring to read "literature" rather than comics.

I could usually be found with a book in my hand. I initially read Oliver Twist in grade four, and I read Catcher in The Rye in grade eight, mainly because Mom forbade me to do so. I was marked as "different" because of that and endured comments like, "They give out books for Halloween at Landgraff's house." Later, my focus on reading brought my sexuality into question. Comments like "He wouldn't know what to do with a girl if he was locked in a closet with her." were bandied about. I was the butt of jokes. When I complained to Mom, she said, "They're just jealous." I felt that there must be more to it than that. If enough people make the same observation, perhaps it should be examined.

It puzzled me when Prue Grates kept asking me what grade I got on assignments. She seemed to know before my answer because if I didn't tell her, she'd *already know* and inform me. I think she snuck access to the teacher's master logbook. She seemed annoyed about my answer. I would only answer because I thought she was interested, but she always seemed jealous. She was the primary person saying that I wasn't "so bright."

Around that time, I began to question the validity of some practices of teachers. Once, the teacher left the room briefly, admonishing, "No talking while I step out." When she returned to the room, she asked, "Did anyone talk while I was gone?" I raised my hand in admission, so I got the strap. The lesson I learned here; lie to the teacher - no one rewards honesty and integrity.

After returning to the schoolyard after lunchtime, I encountered an "Ahoogah" horn on a bike, the trumpet type with a rubber ball end. It was just begging to get honked. When I succumbed to the temptation and honked the horn, the kindergarten teacher burst out of her classroom yelling, "You're going to the principal's office for the strap. I just told you not to honk that horn" (I wasn't present for that warning). I proclaimed my innocence to the principal but got punished anyway. I was thankful I didn't get strapped as often as Lachy did.

Another discrepancy between intent and result surfaced concerning Lenten observances. The teacher had a chart to track and award gold stars for self-reported attendance at daily mass. I thought the purpose of the penance was to atone for your sinful ways. Would all the attention, the chart and the gold stars negate the good deed? That doubt spurred me to a crisis of belief when other contradictions in concept and practice eventually came up. During the study of Geek mythology, I asked myself, "If we considered the Greeks to be misguided with their theology, how can we ensure that our belief is more valid?

In grade four, I gained some unique experiences. I got to peer tutor a classmate. Mick was of Irish descent, with straw-colored hair and pale skin. With freckles across his cheeks and the bridge of his nose, he resembled a leprechaun. He'd been held back a year, and the teacher felt that my influence might help.

Practicing for an upcoming English Language studies test, we reviewed some sample test questions. The questions were structured like this: Where (was/were) you last Saturday? My peer answered, "None of your damn business." He was hilarious! He influenced me more than I did him. We became good friends and walked home together regularly. That's how I met and became fascinated with his sister. She had features and coloring similar to her brother's. In truth, perhaps my relationship with Mick was based more on the opportunity to spend time with his sister than anything else. When we got to his house, he took off and I sat with Margaret. I even remember dropping in with the sole purpose of seeing *her*. It was not to be, however, as they moved away at the end of that year.

Sister Dominic had a friend who was doing his Masters in music. He needed to lead a choir as a requirement of his degree. The church, beside the school, facilitated our choir by providing space and an organ. Sister Dominic arranged that boys in her class would be exempted from Religion class if we joined his choir. All the boys volunteered. The choir director set some ground rules from the start. Each month, we started with one hundred merit points. The boy with the most merit points left at the end of the month would receive a silver dollar. Demerits were deducted for misbehavior, adjusting the total. Some of the things that warranted demerits were quite innocent by today's standards but nonetheless were quite entertaining at the time. For example, one day, we had to vacate the premises because one of the guys trapped a hornet in a wooden matchbox. He shook it vigorously, then threw the matchbox across the room while simultaneously opening it. Rehearsal was canceled that day for fear of getting stung. One of the boys repeatedly sang the hymn incorrectly. The words were, "Raise your voices to the skies," but he insisted on singing, "Raise your voices on your skis."

As you can see, we acted up. Anyway, the month that I was to receive the silver dollar (my score was negative fifty merit points), the Choir Director gave me four quarters. He said that the bank was out of silver dollars that month. I was disappointed about that, but money was money. After a while, the choir wound down and any boy in our class who sang at school got beaten by his peers.

It was my natural inclination to observe. I progressed from that to include investigation for cause and drawing conclusions from the observations.

In grade five, we had a teacher noted for taking a hard line on lavatory breaks. One day, I needed a break but put it off because of her attitude. I chose not to ask because it was only fifteen minutes until lunch break. I knew I could hold on long enough to reach the lavatory after dismissal. Unfortunately, our release was at the teacher's discretion. Because of some bad behavior that morning, she held us beyond the dismissal bell. To put us in our place, she kept us kneeling on the floor facing her long enough to prove her point. Unfortunately, this was more than my bladder could handle. Unable to contain it any longer, I felt the contents of my bladder leak out. The kids around me scattered in disgust while a pool expanded around me.

Mortified, I feared returning to school after the break because of the anticipated ridicule. Finally, I resigned myself to the prospect and trudged back to school. The feared insults never materialized. Because nobody said anything about the matter again, I concluded that my classmates resented and blamed the teacher.

Although my accident had no repercussions, that didn't mean that I never got bullied. On the contrary, a small but active group trolled for victims. The most disturbing assault came at the hands of my neighbor. As I passed his house, he called me "professor" and encircled my neck in his grip. He lifted and held me above the sidewalk while I hung limply in his hands. When he released me, I went home. There were some extreme examples of cruelty at the hands of the bullies.

One boy, Buzzy, would incite the formation of a posse just by being observed in the vicinity. The hue and cry of "Get Buzzy" echoed as the mob joined the pursuit, either on foot or on bicycles. The Police even got involved, but that only made things worse. I guess Buzzy's parents were concerned about his welfare in view of the fact that one local kid had done time at reform school.

A second example of extreme bullying arose after one of the grade seven girls suffered a stroke, leaving her left side paralyzed. In recognition of her disability, she was allowed to go inside immediately upon arrival, while the rest of us had to wait for the bell. It was a particular point of resentment during the winter months. The disabled girl was labeled a "Privileged Prick." It seemed extremely unkind, considering all the other challenges she faced after her vascular accident.

Then, an event of global importance, in the form of the Cuban Missile Crisis, arose.

9

Interlude: Cuban Missile Crisis

The Cuban Missile Crisis was an anxiety-filled thirteen days, from October 16 through 29, 1962, during which the United States and the USSR played a game of chicken. It was the closest the Cold War came to starting a nuclear war.

In 1947, members of the "Bulletin of Atomic Scientists" created a metaphoric symbol representing the likelihood of a global human-driven catastrophe. It was called the Doomsday Clock. It shows, in the opinion of the members of the Bulletin, how close we are to armageddon. At the time of creation, it was the opinion of the members that it was seven minutes to midnight. Since then, the mark has moved, forwards and back, twenty-five times to represent geopolitical and climate control change influences. In 1953, they set it at two minutes to midnight when the USA and the USSR started nuclear testing. It fluctuated between seventeen minutes in 1991 to ninety seconds, set January 24, 2023. The current setting reflects tension regarding the war in Ukraine and looming climate control issues.

In October 1962, they set the clock at seven minutes to reflect the events referred to as the Cuban Missile Crisis or the

October Crisis. It is also called the Caribbean Crisis or the Missile Scare in various places worldwide. The confrontation between the USA and the USSR escalated into an international crisis when the American deployment of missiles in Italy and Turkey was matched by a Soviet deployment of similar ballistic missiles in Cuba.

In the course of events, President Kennedy ordered a naval quarantine to prevent further deployment of missiles in Cuba. Saying quarantine, rather than blockade (wording considered to be an act of war by legal definition), prevented a declaration of war. After several days of tense negotiations, an agreement was reached between the USA and the USSR, which allowed the Soviets to dismantle their offensive weapons in Cuba and return them to the Soviet Union (subject to United Nations verification) in exchange for a US agreement not to invade Cuba again and dropped the level of tension to more acceptable levels.

Secretly, the United States agreed with the Soviets that it would dismantle all of the missiles deployed to Turkey against the Soviet Union. While the Soviets dismantled their missiles, some Soviet warplanes remained in Cuba, and the United States kept the naval quarantine in place until November 20, 1962.

During those thirteen days, tension ran high in our neighborhood. The experience for the nine-year-old me was surreal. I was not able to fully understand the reality of the situation. My brothers said, "This could be the end of the world!" Logically, I understood that this was not a good thing, but emotionally, I still functioned, but anxiety was my daily companion. During my brief life experience, mutual nuclear destruction always remained a threat between the US and the

USSR. It was never totally out of mind. There was an ongoing debate about the outcome.

It was inconceivable to me that any such thing could happen. Until Hiroshima and Nagasaki, the use of nuclear warheads was not even possible. The US displayed the will and capacity to use these weapons, and now we considered the possibility of a third world war. It was not inconceivable to my parents or anyone who lived through WW2, but well within their experience from the last war. The whole world hung on the words of newscasters with high anxiety.

In retrospect, Kennedy's handling of the affair could have been disastrous. Kennedy got credit for taking the world off a ledge, but the Russians also exhibited great restraint during the crisis. As things cooled down, there was a global sigh of relief as the situation wound down.

10

Interlude: John F. Kennedy Assassination

In our household, we leaned more toward the theory that Kennedy's presidency was the new Camelot. Mom had her ceramic cup, with Queen Elizabeth's likeness imprinted, a memento of the Queen's Canadian tour including Windsor during her visit in 1951. We also had a coffee table book featuring John F. and Jacqueline Kennedy, celebrating the New Camelot. I don't think these things were indicators of any firmly held political stance regarding the royal family or the American Republic. Mom was just a collector.

In 1963, I was in grade five. On November 22 of that year, President John F. Kennedy was assassinated. The event got indelibly etched upon my mind. We were between classes; I was descending a flight of stairs when a commotion arose. Everyone said, "What's happening," while the reply, "President Kennedy has been shot!" reverberated through the stairwell.

The assassination occurred during a two-day, five-city fund-raising sweep through Texas. As Kennedy's motorcade made its way toward Dealey Plaza, Kennedy took a fatal round from the nearby Texas School Book Depository. Although he was rushed immediately to Parkland Memorial Hospital, President Kennedy died half an hour later. Vice President Lyndon B. Johnson (LBJ) assumed the presidency after Kennedy's death.

The accused gunman, a former US Marine, Lee Harvey Oswald, was arrested seventy minutes after the shooting and charged with murder. Oswald never made it to trial but was killed on November 24, 1963, by Jack Ruby (a Dallas nightclub owner with Mafia connections). The killing of Oswald got caught on a live television transmission.

A ten-month investigation by the Warren Commission concluded that Lee Harvey Oswald acted alone. A 1979 report by the United States House Select Committee on Assassinations ruled that the Kennedy murder was likely the result of a conspiracy. Even today, many theories abound about that day.

On a more personal level, the assassination got widely covered and pre-empted regularly scheduled programming. Although I recognized the importance of the event and sympathized with the widow and her young children, I was annoyed that my favorite shows were bumped and found the media coverage of the event tedious.

My feelings were aroused enough that I marked the world event with this composition:

President John F. Kennedy

Cape Canaveral it used to be,
But now it's called Cape Kennedy.*
It's named in honor of a great man,
Who always lent a helping hand
To all minorities alike
To help them gain their Civil Rights.

But fate had it that he should die,
And in November of '63,
Came the death of Kennedy.

A shot rang out in Dallas skies,
And with it rang fearful cries
As he slumped down in his seat.
But no matter how they tried,
Kennedy laid down and died.

It is a day we shall all remember,
From January through December.
A day of death for a great man,
That famous man named Kennedy.

*Reverted to Canaveral in 1973; The Space Center remains as
the Kennedy Space Center.

The world was shaken by the assassination and the preoccupation with those events still exists to this day. The theories spawned are numerous and multifaceted, including speculation that Jimmy Hoffa got the Mafia to do it, or Fidel Castro retaliated for the Bay of Pigs fiasco, or anti-Castro Cubans were angry at the failed coup, and so on. In 1979, a Congressional Committee even reopened the case, raising the possibility that Kennedy was killed by conspiracy.

Conflicting statements regarding the number and location of actual shooters abound. The official version concludes that Oswald acted alone and fired three shots from the book depository. Another report surmises a fourth shot came from the grassy knoll. There have been three locations proposed for the origin of the shots (the book repository, the grassy knoll and the Dallas County Records building), with some thinking the kill shot came from the grassy knoll. People question the suspicious death of witnesses and the allegations of witness intimidation. The truth is elusive. For me, all the attention spent on the details confused us and didn't change the outcome. The information disclosed underwent intense scrutiny long after the fact, reviewing documentaries and historical records. I stand by my original impression that it messed up my preferred television programming because it was preempted.

Historians further surmise what might have developed had Kennedy finished his term or even been elected to another. There are feelings that LBJ just continued on the path that had been laid down during the Kennedy administration and that the US involvement in Vietnam would have unfolded as it did regardless. There are doubters who suggest that Kennedy was not dug in and might have withdrawn support for the weak and inept South Vietnamese government. This is only contemplation of an alternate reality that never was.

11

Primary School Continued

Misfit

A shell among its own;

Close, but so very far away.

Insoluble.

Impregnable.

Alone.

Grade six started like any other year with a new teacher. Her name was Sister Edmond, a gentle, elderly nun. I continued in my role as observer, obsessed with reading; my classmates judged me as "not that smart." The first term report cards documented a personal best to date. It put me at the top of the class.

Then, shockingly, came the news that Sister Edmond was terminally ill.

Her death followed shortly after, initiating a string of substitute teachers. The fluctuating circumstances led to a drastic academic decline for me and the rest of my class.

Rumor had it that we couldn't get a permanent replacement because the substitutes were warned that our class was a bunch of uncontrollable hooligans. The rumor gained credibility when the next substitute arrived. It was a week from hell. He physically and verbally abused us, calling us names like "rigor mortis." He pulled our hair and stood on feet that projected into the aisle, saying, "Get your feet out from under mine." Additionally, he punched a student who stood up to him. Bobby was about fifteen and was rumored to have a part-time job at the abattoir as a knocker (the person who delivers the stunning blow to the head of an animal before slaughter). The next thing we heard was that "rigor mortis" was fired.

Then an earnest search for our full-time replacement teacher began. The decision finally got made to place Mr. Jessop in charge of our class. He maintained a relationship as my teacher and coach until I moved on to high school. Mr. Jessop encouraged me to get involved with the school sports programs. He even sent a note to my parents, suggesting they support the endeavor. As a result, I received a couple of notably different Christmas gifts that year.

Mom went to the sports store and bought me a basketball and a baseball glove. Although I had told her I wanted a fielder's mitt, Mom got talked into buying a catcher's mitt. The salesperson told her it was a good deal and priced for a quick sale.

On Christmas day, hiding my disappointment regarding the catcher's mitt was difficult. However, I quickly learned to appreciate it. After seeing and using the glove, my classmates were impressed to have something like that available to them. It resembled a circular, well-padded cushion with a deep pocket and closed webbing.

The back catcher could easily handle fast pitches without the stinging impact felt using only a fielder's mitt. The glove had to be there and I was automatically on the roster when impromptu games got set up.

However, I was still the last player chosen to be on a team due to my poor understanding of the rules and my perceived weakness in the batting lineup. I usually got single or double when at bat, but I was no longer hitting them out of the park like I used to; we now played on a regulation-sized field. Also, I needed to learn about leaning off of or stealing bases. Finally, I needed coaching about what to do and why it mattered. Because of that catcher's mitt, I was always invited to play.

Mr. Jessop also urged me to get involved in Intramural basketball. Although I had been playing basketball at the Sinclair's, I had no exposure to anything but Horse or One on One. At school, we played on a court and had an umpire, adding structure to our games. I could take great hook shots and made the occasional "swish" while playing at the Sinclairs, but I was not familiar with what penalties applied and what to do during a foul shot. I had no coaching previously and was the last man picked for impromptu games. I rarely got possession of the ball.

Through his observations, Mr. Jessop determined I had some talent for Track and Field events. In his coaching role, he always scouted for talent. Mr. J. had observed me fooling around in the schoolyard with a shot (for shot-put). I tossed it around aimlessly, but he saw something there. He had also witnessed my sprinting abilities. He asked me to be on the Track and Field Team, and to practise for shot put, sprinting and relay racing. I also tried out long jumping. Our team could have shown better at the athletic meet later that year. I was the only representative on our team to enter the shot-put event. With no previous coaching or preparation except my fooling around, I placed last in that event. With the long jump event, I placed in the midfield of competitors, not in the top echelon.

Regarding the relay race, I was supposed to be the starter for the shortest leg, the hundred-yard dash. However, on race day, the runner for two hundred and twenty-yard leg of the race got sick. I was substituted in that position. Our backup runner replaced me as a starter. The rest of our lineup remained unchanged.

The race started, and I was ready to take the handoff of the baton. Since I had been the starter, I was comfortable with the handoff but lacked familiarity as a receiver. The handoff got flubbed, either because of me or the substitute starter. Our team was now running in last place. I picked up the baton and poured all my effort to make up for lost time. We were still in last place when Mark, our anchorman, took the baton. Mark, with wings of Mercury on his heels, managed to overtake the third-place anchorman. He saved us from the disgrace of last place. Given the circumstances, I felt this was as good as placing first!

****

Around this time, a playground accident added to my reputation as an oddball. We were playing "horseback fights," which entailed paired teams, one riding piggyback on his teammate. Each team tried to knock their opponents over. If you got knocked over, your crew would switch who was piggybacked and re-enter the fray. It was a fun thing to do.

In any case, I had just assumed the horse position, carrying my partner on my back. I was hit from behind and fell face-first onto someone's head just as he stood up. I bet the crack to the back of his head hurt because my face sure did. I arose with a numb and profusely bleeding nose. In the lavatory to clean up, I saw my reflection in the mirror and noticed my sinuous nose.

Despite some discomfort, I remained at school and felt special because of all the attention aroused by my cool S-shaped nose. When I got home, Mom started to wail in a way reminiscent of an old skit. The tale recounts the story of a kid with a laceration to his skull. He arrives home after a meandering walk, bleeding but carefree, until he hears his mother's wails of fear and distress. Then he wails in sympathy with his mother's reaction. Recreating the skit, I began to cry because of my mother's response upon seeing me.

It was late Friday afternoon when we set off for the hospital. Upon our arrival, they informed us that all the city's Ear, Nose and Throat doctors were out of town attending a conference. A Plastic Surgeon would handle my operation in their absence. I got admitted to be prepped for surgery the following day.

Because of my age, I got placed in the children's ward. I had to wear a horseshoe-shaped ice bag over my nose to control the swelling. I got annoyed answering the same litany of questions from every attendant who bustled in. "What happened to you? Over the next four hours, I recounted the tremendous horse-fighting contest a dozen times. Furthermore, I got ticked off about missing my "The Addams Family" that week. Trying to sleep in the ward that night, the noise and ambient light made for a long, sleepless night.

The following day, I found a sign over my bed that read, "Nothing by mouth." I thought that it meant that I had not been sick overnight, but I soon learned that it meant no food or drink before the surgery. Around noon, I was taken to the operating room for the procedure. I was given an injection and asked to count backward from one hundred. I remember getting to ninety-seven, and then my next memory was of the recovery room. Later, when I was back in my room, I viewed the results of the surgery in a mirror. Across the T zone of my face, covering my nose to the nostrils, was a cast in place for the next two months. Mom was unhappy when I asked if I could get my classmates to sign it and replied, "No!" She thought that it would look too odd. I was released before noon the next day with an appointment for a follow-up in three weeks.

That Sunday at services, the first kid who saw my face cast burst out laughing, nudging the guy beside him. This reaction was typical; I got greeted that way wherever I went until the cast got removed. There was nothing to do but ignore them. I was an object of ridicule for the duration.

The next grade came with some new challenges. As we grew, expectations of us rose. I had several favorite subjects: History, English and Science especially.

However, I wasn't exceptionally self-motivated by these subjects. They were easy for me because a good memory was enough to get by. Then a Science project was assigned. We

could make something or care for an animal. I evaluated my
performance to date, considering the project's contribution to my
final mark. I felt I could take the hit, so I didn't submit a project.
It wasn't just laziness but a realistic look at my situation. I had
little to no parental oversight and expected no help from that
quarter. Our financial situation prevented the purchase of
materials, and I had no idea what to do anyway. My actions
hinted at elements of Aristotle's scientific method, expanding
my observer role to include the capacity for supposition and
conclusion.

12

Grad Year Primary School

My final year at primary school occurred during Canada's Centennial Year, with its celebratory pomp and circumstance. Throughout the year, television and radio ads publicized Expo 67.

Our principal honored the event, tasking the grade seven class to perform a play about Canada's Confederation (and as a sendoff to the graduating class). It was a splendid endeavor, full of lively, fact-filled dialogue. Unfortunately, no one in Grade seven was up to the task of the leading role of John A. MacDonald. The only likely candidates had the roles of George Brown and Tupper. For this reason, I got commandeered for the role. My prodigious memory came in handy when learning the lines.

The night of the performance, the principal's introductory remarks promoted my suitability, citing my great memory. However, I flubbed a line and needed prompting. Hopefully, only the cast members noticed. Nonetheless, we got our picture in the Windsor Star and were pretty stoked about it.

The next event on memory lane was a Speech Contest. I produced a self- proclaimed masterpiece about Thomas Alva Edison, the inventor of the incandescent light bulb. I went to the podium, confident that I would win. I did not anticipate the caliber of my competitors. I have a monotonous, lackluster voice. The winner recounted the flooding in Venice that year and its effect on the libraries there. A large number of books were destroyed. She spoke eloquently and enthusiastically about the rescue and refurbishment efforts to save as many water-damaged books as possible.

There was also an excellent and topical speech describing animation, a la Walt Disney; far better than mine. I learned humility that day.

One day, I had brought my lunch to school because Mom was babysitting that day. The routine was to eat your bagged lunch in the classroom and then await the resumption of classes. You could go to the schoolyard after or remain in place. I was the only one bagging it that day, so I thought I was alone in the room. Unfortunately, one of my classmates arrived and entered the room. I can only guess at his motivation, but he came at me with extreme malice. We wrestled for a few minutes, knocking over desks and making a lot of noise. I had just gained the upper hand and prepared to deliver a blow to his face. Mr. Balto, one of the teachers, arrived and yelled, "Stop it right now!" The fight ended, we got separated and Mr. Balto seemed to know who instigated the fight. He said I reminded him of Cassius Clay. He had to explain who that was, though, but I appreciated the compliment.

On grad day, I finally felt accepted by the guys. After the proceedings, I got invited to a pizza party. The following day, at the party, the girls were in charge. To encourage mingling, they suggested snowball dances. At the end of each record, someone said "Snowball" to signal a change of partners. I made sure that I alternated switches between Michelle and Judy, who had short blonde hair and a porcelain complexion. Later, when I got home, my blood ran high, and my mind raced as I sought sleep.

The most consequential event that year occurred in October. Returning home after school, Harry rode toward me on his bike, equipped with a banana seat and monkey handlebars. He said, "Hey, there's a meat wagon outside your house, do you want a ride home?" Clueless, as usual, I asked what he meant.

"An ambulance,

Do you want a ride?"

I got behind him on the banana seat and rode toward uncertainty.

13

Dad's Passing

Call it Hope

Her hair is gray beneath its color,

And her face is wrinkled;

Not with age but from experience.

Lines of worry left their trace

As one by one, her loved ones fell.

She stands alone, stripped of worth,

But she goes on living

Hoping that someday

She will be united

With the ones she lost.

Harry and I arrived just as the paramedics loaded Dad into the ambulance, covered with a coarse, gray, woolen blanket. An extremely agitated Rod was right behind them. On his return from school, some odd noises sparked investigation, which led to Dad, sprawled on the bedroom floor, unable to raise himself. Dad repeatedly looked at his watch, giving the impression that he knew he was late for his night shift. Rod told me to go inside the house to wait for the remainder of the family to arrive. He raced to the car and followed the ambulance to the hospital.

As I sat alone at the kitchen table, cocooned in silence, I contemplated that I was the last one to see Dad well. We had shared lunch that day. As this sunk in, I became overcome with grief and wracking sobs engulfed me. I wept for an hour before anyone else arrived home. I'm unsure who came first or what happened next because I was in a daze.

The next day was Saturday. Some news began to trickle in. Dad had suffered a stroke that left him paralyzed on his left side and robbed him of the ability to speak. All we could do for now was wait and see.

We went to the early Sunday mass the following day, but Mike suggested he stay home to field potential calls from the hospital. Upon our return, Mike ran toward the car in a highly agitated state. He got in and said, "The hospital just called and requested that we get there as soon as possible." Dad took a turn for the worse. Upon arrival at the hospital, we rushed to Dad's room. We were met by a nurse who said that Dad had just passed. Neither Rod nor I entered the room. Rod asked the nurse if he might get a tranquilizer and started pacing the hall. I stood at the entrance of the room staring at the ashen husk that had been my father. I sunk deeper into my daze. On our return home, Mom hugged me tightly and, with tears in her eyes, asked repeatedly, "How will we survive? How will I be able to raise you now?" I went outside for some solitude and fresh air. As I paced in our front yard, Jasmine, our next door neighbor, called out to ask about Dad's condition. "Dead," was my monosyllabic reply.

Over the next few days, there was a flurry of activity in preparation for Dad's funeral and internment. Details dribbled in about Dad's insurance coverage and benefits from Ford, his employer for thirty years. It seemed that the current union contract provided surviving spousal benefits for two years from the date of passing. In retrospect, that feels unfair since the next contract provided survivors' benefits for life. After two years, Mom and I were left to survive on Mother's allowance and whatever else could be scrounged up.

The viewings and funeral were another issue. They spread over three days. We greeted mourners and people I had never met streamed by offering condolences. They assured me that Dad had saved them from the demon drink. I was impressed, but still felt shortchanged somehow.

14

Changes

Although adolescence is normally a time of life changes, such as puberty, adjusting to and gaining a level of comfort about yourself, Dad's passing introduced a multiplier that intensified the period for me.

After Dad's death, I entered the metaphoric crucible. Experiences during this period led me to believe in guardian angels, the concept that it takes a village to raise a child, the idea of six degrees of separation, and that perhaps, like cats, we might have nine lives. These beliefs formed because of people who lent me a hand, close calls that made me feel that someone watched over me, and the feeling that I had, perhaps, just used one of the proverbial nine lives: a mix of random occurrences and coincidences.

From that time until my graduation from university was a difficult period of growth. I experienced many disappointments and made many sacrifices. I got blessed with luck and influential good advice. Some people came through for me. Many people let me down, and there was a lack of consistent follow-through.

I was alone a lot during the next five years. Mom pursued her life. She had to take odd jobs, make contacts for our mutual benefit and carve out a life for herself. My brothers had their own lives to live too. Mike bought the family car, eventually got married and moved on with life and work. Teddy was married, living and working in Detroit. Rod moved to the other side of Windsor to attend university. He completed a B.A. in Psychology by attending classes without a break and using intersession courses to accelerate his progress. He satisfied the degree requirements in two years.

Under the circumstances, I became the man of the house. I had to go to school, do chores and assume the role of designated gopher. I was responsible for gardening, painting, garbage disposal, grocery shopping, and repairs around the house. Although Mom provided the cash, I did the shopping and banking. If I wanted any spending money, I had to get a job. I also had to build a nest egg for my education. The only respite in my life was listening to music.

This arrangement caused a lot of frustration, which only sometimes found productive expression. When I was called upon to do a chore, (like paint the inside of the house), things got thrown around and broken. I eventually stopped these destructive behaviors because I bore the cost of replacement for damaged goods.

Once, Mom told me to go into the backyard to cut up the Christmas tree, placed outside about three weeks previously. The city would not take it away in its current state. I experienced an eruption of burning stomach acid, scorching from my gut to my chest. I had no desire to do the task. As I reluctantly set out, axe in hand, Tim Williams happened to be passing. He began to sing, "I been working on the railroad," in time with my axe blows. That was the last straw! I rushed toward Tim, brandishing the axe and yelling at peak volume. I told him he'd better shut up or I would make him stop. Fearing me in that state, he went quiet.

Another time, Mom went out without leaving me a note detailing her whereabouts or estimated time of return. Since she was adamant about knowing my whereabouts, I always left notes. I was frustrated at this perceived inequity.

As I was silently fuming, I took a phone call from one of Mom's friends. In answer to her query, I said Mom was out. The caller asked when she was expected to return. I replied in agitation, using the words churning in my mind, "I only live here; nobody tells me anything." Of course, this got back to Mom in a follow-up call from her friend, and I was labeled "rude."

There were other disappointments, too. The Big Brothers Program made two attempts to match me with a male role model. One of the guys brought me to his farm and set me loose on chores. First, I had to muck out the horse stalls, then cut his grass on a sitter mower. He also taught me the rudiments of driving his tractor. He only appeared once. This suited me fine; I had chores aplenty at home, I didn't need more.

Another guy, who had a Cessna, brought me to the airfield to show me the plane but was surprised by my lack of excitement. Had I been thinking correctly, I should have shown more enthusiasm. I may have got some flying lessons out of the arrangement. Oh well! It was not to be. He never returned.

The Big Brothers organization eventually told Mom that since I would age out in two years, it might be impossible to match me. Volunteers wanted a longer-term relationship with their Little Brothers.

There were also lots of lost opportunities during this time. I called the YMCA to determine the cost of martial arts lessons. Three hundred dollars was the answer.

Given the state of our finances, that was more than I could handle. I concluded that martial arts lessons were only of use to people who couldn't defend themselves in the first place. This proved to be rather ironic in my case.

When I got a job at Danny's (an altar boy connection) Dad's store delivering groceries on a bike, Danny and I split the hours. I got all the hours when Danny wanted to play football on the school team. It was a suitable outcome with respect to my income, but it destroyed my hopes of playing football at the varsity level. We couldn't both be on the team, and someone had to work. Again, Oh well!

My life now revolved around school, my job and my chores. As such, I only read the paper sporadically, focusing on the comics section, a brief perusal of the front page headlines, and later, the Ann Landers section. The rest of my current events were relayed by radio or television news programs, but predominantly from neighborhood scuttlebutt. I was still relatively sheltered, living in my own world, caught up in the science and historical fiction that was my preferred reading. I always seemed to be behind the curve but used specific observations to make decisions and resolutions.

I observed Mike, who went to a boys-only trade school, making attempts to approach girls with varying degrees of success. He used to write a script before he called a girl on the phone so that he wouldn't appear tongue-tied. Once, I observed him say to a girl who had liked him until this incident, "How many wrinkles are in a monkey's ass? Smile; I'll count them."

That went over like a lead balloon. Whether this was Mike's intention or not, it exemplified the lack of awareness of social graces that was the family affliction.

Rod also went to an all-boys school and was as awkward as Mike. I resolved to be bolder and more confident in my approaches to girls than my brothers. The first step toward accomplishing that was to gain more exposure to girls. I opted to attend a co- ed high school. After a church youth dance during my first year of high school, Mike called me a hero because I asked a girl from my class to dance. He was surprised that his little brother could do that.

Rod had been counting the donations at the church to earn extra cash before he moved to go to university. Realizing the situation I faced at home, or perhaps in the wake of Rod's lobbying, the pastor allowed me to take over the position. After proving myself, I came by even more jobs: tending the concessions stand at church functions, filling out charitable donation receipts at tax time, and the most lucrative, although short- lived, grounds-keeping job. It is my understanding that most of these were volunteer positions, but I got paid for all of these functions, because the pastor sensed a need in my case. The grounds-keeper job was significant. It was a paid position and would last for as long as it took to accomplish the pastor's summer to-do list. I helped the full-time grounds-keeper, pulling out selected overgrown shrubs, cutting the grass, and trimming hedges. The grounds-keeper was strange. He greeted me daily with, "Hi, how are ya? How's your mother?" He also used the term "thusly" when demonstrating a new task.

The intention was for this job to last most of the summer. I attacked the job with gusto, not considering working at a pace intended to ensure job security. I remember breaking at least three spades in my efforts to remove shrubs, due to improper use, and undue haste. Eventually, I learned better techniques, including the use of an axe to severe the roots, before attempting to pull the stumps out. I didn't really mind the effort because wrestling with the stumps was building muscle.

I usually accomplished in a day, tasks that required the groundskeeper much longer to complete. I cut all the grass on the property, which occupied a city block, over two days. As a result, I exhausted the projects so quickly that it only required three weeks of work.

I was well paid for my efforts, though, as the minimum wage at the time was seventy-five cents an hour. I got forty dollars a week for pulling stumps. A schoolmate observed me toiling one day as he made rounds on his bike delivery job. He asked me about the pay, and I told him the truth. My answer caused some jealousy. Shortly after that, he challenged me to a fight. He had his posse with him, and they joined in with their taunts. I refused three times in a row, but he kept pushing until I accepted the challenge.

I was unaware that he was taking boxing lessons. When I finally agreed to the fight, I approached it as a wrestling match and had already trapped his forearms in my grasp. He asked me to let go so that he could take off his shirt to avoid damage. I complied with goodwill. When he refocused, he came back swinging. No one had coached me in boxing, and I was no match for him. I could only keep backing away while he battered my skull. I ended up with severe swelling in my mastoid sinuses after that.

Mom wanted to get the cops involved, but I begged her not to, as that would only escalate the matter. I later achieved closure with the boxer. As we shook hands, I sensed that he felt that he was in the wrong that day. Perhaps I gave him too much credit?

I continued with my delivery job at the market. A couple of incidents stand out in my mind. Once, I had a delivery to 27-- Cadillac. Two streets on my route had names that started with C. The other street was Chandler. One road separated them.

Anyway, on that day, I absentmindedly went to 27-- Chandler. I entered the open back door, announcing that I was from the market, and began unpacking the groceries on the table. The homeowner said they hadn't placed an order and was bewildered by my presence. I asked, "But isn't this 27-- Cadil...?" As soon as the words were half-formed in my mouth, I repacked the groceries and left for the correct destination, giving apologies for my intrusion. Upon hearing this story, Mike teased me unmercifully.

Another influence in my life was the boarders that stayed at our house. The tenants paid weekly for shared accommodation, two to a room, with food included. These men were itinerant tradesmen working on local construction jobs, who usually stayed for from three months to a year at a time.

Around this period, I developed an obsession with the game of pool. My first exposure was at a party hosted by Parents Without Partners. I liked the game and began to frequent the pool hall near home. I read anything that I could get my hands on that pertained to pool and practiced to hone my skills. I eventually convinced Mom to let me buy a table from Sears so that I could practice at home. I bought a six-foot by three-foot wood-based table, set it up in our cramped living room, playing around obstacles and taking care not to jump any balls into the CRT (cathode ray tube) screen of the television.

I also had a school friend with his own table who was more skilled than me. We played for hours at his place. I lost consistently until my skills improved enough to allow me to, finally, win a game. Mark was so upset that he threw one of the balls against his basement wall, cracking it, fueling his anger to greater heights. Mark was a born athlete and he taught me how to improve my basketball skills too.

Other events left a lasting impression on me. As recipients of Mother's allowance, Mom and I had dental, prescription, and optical coverage. The plan provided a monthly benefit card to be surrendered to the provider for services rendered. I attended an appointment with my long-term dentist. I was unaware of the procedure, so I was surprised, when the dentist started to angrily complain that he didn't have my coverage. He had already administered the topical anesthetic but complained that he couldn't proceed now because he wouldn't get paid. He finally decided to go ahead after Mom assured him by phone that she had the card and would deliver it ASAP. The damage was done. I resolved never to go to that dentist again. His tirade was extremely insulting and belittling. I vowed never to treat anyone like that.

Another incident occurred at our customary optical firm. I broke my glasses during volleyball practice and needed a new pair. Since I was replacing them I opted to upgrade to wire-rimmed frames. When retrieving my new glasses, the counter girl sneered at me and said, "Welfare doesn't cover these." I was enraged. I went to the nearest local branch of my bank and had money transferred for withdrawal. This process was not as simple as it is today and took about forty minutes. I returned to the optical outlet and faced the same counter girl. I said, "Get my glasses," slapping the cash on the counter at the same time. She said in a derisive tone, "I never thought I'd see you again." I have never returned there. The emotional turmoil of these events is expressed in the poem the following poem.

The Cockleshell

Tranquility;

Vaguely disturbed by distant rumbling,

Perhaps of impending danger foretelling.

Upon the Sea of Tranquility

Sails a cockleshell;

A lone cockleshell.

Suddenly the full force of the rapids

is upon him.

He struggles, trying to reach the shore,

But, no longer can he see his goal.

He is swamped and tossed

Upon the waves. He is lost.

Oh, where has the Sea of Tranquility gone?

As his strength wanes

A foreboding crevasse before him yawns;

He knows he is done.

With his last burst of energy

He swims blindly from its rim

And finally breaks, once again,

Upon Tranquility.

15

Frosh

At the close of summer 1968, the time to ponder the uncertainty represented by high school ran out; the future had arrived. I was Frosh. Rumors circulated freely about the gauntlet Frosh faced on their first day. I imagined hoards of older students descending on me, demanding I carry their books, hurling verbal abuse and bullying me. I stood tall, ready to face whatever came my way. The first obstacle I encountered was the bus driver asking if I needed a transfer. I was clueless and queried, "What's that?" I discovered that I needed and received one. At the transfer point, I stood with a growing knot of regulars, swelling as other buses dropped their loads. After drop-off from the trip's second leg, traversing the two blocks to the school, none of the feared abuses materialized. I arrived unscathed. We got directed to the gym for our first assembly. Teachers herded us into grade groupings, and we stood in anticipation of announcements. A short time later, I sat in my homeroom, awaiting the start of classes.

As the year progressed, the unfamiliar became routine. I was still introverted and perhaps, shell-shocked, by Dad's death, and the rapid adjustment high school demanded. I did as expected and continued to be a good student.

Some of the kids in my homeroom were repeating the grade and got referred to as "flunkies." One of the flunkies was a lumbering brute who delighted in bullying those he deemed weak. He formed alliances with a few others in the class to create a reign of terror. He was large and used his presence; a sinister tormentor. He used physical and verbal abuse to cow his victims. One of the taunts he directed toward me referred to my facial profile. He said that I had a crooked nose. Having experienced this kind of ridicule before, I was unphased and replied, "It should be, it got broken in three places." Another time, he said that I reminded him of a woman, perhaps implying I was gay. I replied, "If I remind you of a woman, you've got bad taste. I've got the flattest chest I've ever seen." My homeroom teacher witnessed the exchange and smiled at me conspiratorially. Tony was not my only tormentor, nor was I his only victim.

Once on the bus ride home, a different bully approached me saying, "I saw your dad downtown on the weekend…," leading up to some embarrassing comment that might have referred to Dad as a homeless person. Not waiting for the other shoe to drop, I cut him off with, "Good; if you see him again, tell him to come home. He's been dead for over a year now." That shut it down cold.

A couple of times, I found that my pants had stains, probably caused by sitting on the remains of a Werther's caramel ditched when a teacher got suspicious. I didn't know who the culprit was, but it caused a brown mark on my pants, meant to embarrass me. I suspected that the offender was Gordon, who sat behind me. Gordon made a more brutal attack later that year. I suddenly felt a stabbing pain in my buttocks. It was not long-lived, and I wasn't sure what caused it. Then I felt

it again, even sharper. I looked behind me to find Gordon
hunched over, hands beneath his desk, holding a mathematical
compass with the point directed at me. Unconvinced anyone
would do such a hateful, unprovoked thing, I warned, "One more
time, Gordon." Probably he thought that I was a wimp because I
usually stayed quiet and attentive in class, or he took my
warning as a dare. Whatever the reason, he did it again. Making
good on my threat, I swiveled slightly to my right in my seat for
added momentum, then swiveled left, finally connecting with an
open backhanded blow to Gordon's left cheek. We jumped out
of our seats, and as I turned to face him, I noticed how red his
cheek was. He was angry and threatened me, saying, "I'll get
you back!" I growled back, in my fight-or-flight response state,
"Try it and I'll lay you out."

In my Phys-Ed/Health class we had a lecture that piqued my
interest. The teacher brooked the subject of "the talk." He said
we shouldn't be embarrassed about the discussion and indicated
his willingness to tackle any questions. One of the guys at the
back of the room asked about "blue balls" When he posed the
question, I was "clueless" as usual. The teacher explained to the
best of his ability and then encouraged more questions. Shortly
after that class, Mom got a call from Mike, now dating his future
first wife, asking for Mom's advice. He experienced a very
specific severe pain and wanted to know whether to consult his
doctor. Mom didn't know the answer, so she called our
pediatrician for further information. I wasn't eavesdropping, but
could hear one side of the conversations and was able to make
some deductions.

After speaking with the doctor, she reconnected with Mike
and told him what she had learned. After that call, I commented
that he must have "blue balls." Shocked, Mom said, "How do

you know that?" I explained the lesson in Health class, and she confirmed my supposition. It was the first time I had been ahead of the curve with that kind of information, and I felt a sense of satisfaction.

My favorite, my grade nine science teacher, Mr. Gagnon, had a knack for a concise presentation of complex subject matter. He was also funny but would not allow class disruption. In one instance, after repeated warnings not to wear his thin blue nylon jacket indoors, Mr. G approached Tim, demanded his jacket and tied it around Tim's neck like a giant blue bow tie. Tim sat red-faced through the rest of the class and never made that mistake again.

My reference to Mr. G is not just because I liked him but to underscore that teachers have the same problems as everyone else. During that year, Mr. G got diagnosed with adult-onset leukemia. Unfortunately for Mr. G, the disease is aggressive, swiftly progressive, and terminal. Mr. G. was diagnosed mid-year and had passed on by the year's end. It affected me because of the proximity to Dad's death and a diagnosis like my brother Dennis. I mourned his passing.

Because of my teachers, I finished the year in my school's top ten grade nine students and repeated the feat again in grade ten. I maintained an A average until grade twelve, after which responsibilities at home, work, and other interests hindered my continued presence in the academic elite.

16

Home

As previously indicated, I was left as the "man of the house" when my Dad's passed. Any male role around the home now fell to me. Mom also thought that men should be conversant with housekeeping, so I had to vacuum carpets, wash dishes, sweep, and wash floors; all added to my delivery job and school responsibilities.

One of my pet peeves was garbage removal. It wasn't so much the task, but more that Mom met me at the door with bags as soon as I got home. When I complained about it, Mom explained that she thought she was saving me time, preventing me from having to make a special trip after my shoes were off. At the time, it felt more like a directive than help.

In adulthood, I felt the same way about many of my job requirements. I read a book called "The Tyranny of Work," which suggested on the job dissatisfaction derives from the fact that employers makes the decisions about what to do and when to do it. There is much greater employee satisfaction if tasks get assigned with a deadline and the employee is allowed to decide how and when to carry it out. Many disagreements between Mom and I were of that nature. Years later, I came across a plaque showing an orangutan, hair standing on end, saying,

"Why do I gotta take out the garbage?" When I gave it to Mom, we both had a good laugh.

One Friday afternoon, Mom greeted me at the door and told me I had to weed the garden immediately. When I refused, an argument ensued. I left the house in a huff and rode the bus for the next three hours. I knew she had plans to go out that night, so I stayed away until I thought she'd be gone. When I got home, she and her male friend were there. She apologized for the argument and said she couldn't leave the house until I got home safely.

Another incident arose regarding outdoor Christmas lights. I got ordered to get the string of lights working after it's sudden failure. I was raging as I started testing bulb after bulb to find the faulty one. It was after dark, and a passing kid yelled, "That kid's stealing light bulbs." The irony of the situation didn't pass me by. I started to chuckle as I sprang into action, chasing the kid as he hurried away. Laughing inwardly, I pursued him for a block and a half before I returned to finish the chore. The kid ran like the hounds of hell were on his tail and I had dispersed my anger.

One other event stands out in memory. Tasked with painting the outdoor trim, I borrowed the Sinclairs' extendable ladder. I set the ladder improperly and began to climb carrying the full paint can and brushes. Halfway to the top, the ladder slid down the wall with me on it. The paint spilled all over the house. Trying to avoid injury, I jumped off before the ladder hit the ground. I ended up with barked shins from the rebounded on impact. A kid yelled from across the street, "Ha ha, you fell down." It took all my self-control to keep from crossing and smacking him.

17

Work

One day in mid-September, I met my friend Danny on the bus. Thinking that there might be a chance of a job, I asked him if his Dad needed any help at the grocery shop. Danny said he'd ask. The next day, he said that a position for a delivery person had just opened. That was how I came to be a grocery bike delivery person. The shop was a Mom and Pop operation offering canned goods, confections, and a meat department. The butcher's name was Larry, and he used to tease me about being "dumb as a fox." Larry and Danny's Dad served as male role models for me.

Among my duties, I had to restock shelves when needed. I also had to manage the bottle returns. It just required consolidating bottles into their designated crates so that they were ready for exchange when new stock arrived. Most importantly, after closing, I had to clean the butcher block. It required a bit of effort with a wire brush to remove the remnants of the day's work. This was a must to prevent bacteria from colonizing the block and prevent a Health and Safety violation.

Eventually, I was invited to do odd jobs at the family home, helping Danny to paint as the need arose. We were painting the stairway and Danny replayed the song, "In the year 2525," all day long as our brushes spread the white emulsion on the trim of the stairs. I never liked that song after that day.

I had various adventures while working there. Often, I would be drenched to the bone after delivering on a rainy day. On one of those days, I wore a new pair of blue jeans. After the shift, I wanted to warm myself and clean up. As I stripped off in preparation for a relaxing warm bath I laughed to see dye from the jeans had turned my legs indigo. Once, a five-dollar bill escaped my pocket as I returned to the store.

Scrambling, I dropped the bike and ran headlong into traffic to retrieve it. My hasty action initiated a chorus of blaring horns from oncoming traffic. I narrowly regained safety after trapping the scudding bill.

At home, Mom allowed me to have beer as I did my homework. She bought a case every so often. As long as I paid a quarter a bottle, she was okay with me having a cold one. I used to enjoy doing my math homework sipping Molson's lager. When the drinking age got lowered to eighteen, I consumed more than I ever did under Mom's arrangement. Anyway, one hot summer day, as I delivered his order, a customer asked me if I wanted a beer or a root beer. Unassumingly, I replied, "A beer."

I was surprised when he reached into the fridge and handed me an open bottle of beer. I thought nothing of downing it before I returned under the hot summer sun.

Back at the store, Danny's Dad approached me with concern. Apparently, the customer had called and ratted on me. I explained what happened and asked Danny's Dad, "What was I supposed to do? I never expected him to give me a beer!" Danny's Dad said, "Don't ever do that again," and left it at that.

The next time I delivered to that customer, he posed the same question and I made the same reply. He returned with a root beer.

Mom was concerned about our tight budget and, on my behalf, asked her friends if they were aware of any openings. Mom's male friend, Theo, whose son Morty owned a manufacturing plant, told me to apply there for a summer job. He suggested that I lie about my age to circumvent child labor restrictions. I did that and ended up employed there. My wages increased from the minimum wage offered at my delivery job to about five times that. The factory job only lasted for the summer, but it provided enough to support me through the rest of the year. I was expected to contribute a portion of my earnings to the family budget. I jumped at the opportunity and entered the echelon of factory workers.

Factory work was more physically demanding than my delivery job and required some adjustment. For the first week or two, I came home bone tired. I started to work out with weights to bulk up. Eventually, I acclimated.

There is a greater chance of injury in a factory. Preventative safety features of the machines are sometimes disabled to increase production. Low production numbers brought the foreman's wrath and could result in dismissal. Once, I was a little slow getting my hand clear and felt the edge of the press tickle my fingernail on the down stroke. I still have all my digits, but that doesn't mean there weren't close calls. While the foreman moved a load of unsecured steel on the forklift, part of the load hit an obstacle in its path. I saw that it would be swept off and began to run. The falling load partially crushed a barrel that occupied the area I had just vacated.

I learned another lesson when I tried to brute force a jammed steel feeder, delivering a blow to the steel ribbon with the heel of my hand. It caused a laceration that I cleaned and bandaged. I continued working without telling the foreman about the injury. When I got home, I reexamined the wound. It didn't look too good, so I went to the hospital. I made the mistake of saying that it was a workplace injury. It required three stitches, triggering the notification of workman's comp. The next day, I got called into the office and was loudly reprimanded for not reporting the injury. I was unaware that the company got fined by workman's comp in that situation.

Being naive, I failed to consider the consequences of dwindling supplies, repeating the mistake I made as a groundskeeper. I observed the supply of steel decreasing but continued to work at the pace I was accustomed to. The next day, the foreman told me to go outside and cut the grass because they didn't have enough steel to run. I completed that in an hour. When I reported back to the foreman, he looked at me and said, "Why did you work so fast? I haven't got anything else for you to do now. You're on layoff."

The following summer, I returned to the same employer but at a new location, on Walker's Line, a two-lane Highway. Mom was concerned for my safety riding my bike on the highway and asked Theo to see if his son could arrange a ride for me.

Morty's secretary lived about a fifteen-minute walk from my place, so I went there each morning and got a ride. She was married, but I don't remember any kids. She had Eastern European roots and was a curvy blonde. One of her peculiar habits was to drive, aligning her car over the center line unless there was oncoming traffic.

18

High School Revisited

Life skills also get developed at school. It is a practice ground for students to grow into functioning contributors to society and gain recognition for participation in sports and clubs. Skills are developed and values are instilled. School letters are awarded for activities other than academics. I joined clubs and other endeavors as I was able to, but never lettered in anything but academics. My life situation limited participation in other areas, but I enjoyed experiences when I could find time.

I gained exposure to sports in primary school and found that I enjoyed them. I especially wanted to represent my high school at the varsity level, gaining a spot on the football team. I knew I had the speed to succeed because I had been on the track and field team in primary school. I may have even had the bulk to be a lineman. Unfortunately, Danny, my boss's son from the market, made the team, so I had to shoulder the bulk of duties at the store. I couldn't participate in many after-school events, so my usual and customary was to work for a few hours after school and then do my homework after that.

On weekends, Mom attended meetings of her Parents Without Partners Groups or went double dating with friends from the group. I spent my weekend free time at home alone watching old movies or other television programs until my brother, Rod, suggested that it would be better to get more involved with school activities; at least I wouldn't be so lonely. The easiest thing to do was to volunteer for charity events like can drives or service club activities to raise money for the school or community groups.

After a few of those events, I had contacts that led to club participation.

My first outing, we collected nonperishable goods for the local food bank. We went from door to door, asking for donations. We successfully gathered enough to fill a truck with the proceeds. Of course, the benefit for the volunteers was the pride of accomplishment and a chance to mix with their schoolmates. On the can drive, I observed a stunning, self-assured redhead from one of the other canvassing teams. I thought she was older than I was because she seemed to know many other participants and radiated confidence. In reality, she was a year younger. She was petite with a milky complexion and blue eyes. She wore a knitted tam with alternating green and yellow concentric circles. I felt I just had to know her.

Unfortunately, I didn't know her name and only caught glimpses of her now and then throughout that evening and occasionally at school in the following days. I discovered that she had an older sister and started to chat her up, gathering information about my quarry. It was probably unfair to Brenda, but it was the only way I knew to get to Yvette, the focus of my search. I spent so much time on my mission that it engendered comments about Brenda having a boyfriend. When I felt confident enough to take the plunge, I asked Yvette out. I was smitten and continued to pursue Yvette for some time.

I planned an outing to the amusement park on Boblo Island, reachable only by boat. Wanting to look my best, I decided to go without my glasses. I was nearly blind but thought I cut a dashing figure. When I arrived at her place, she introduced me to her mother, saying, "Mom, this is Doug, but he looks better with his glasses on." That blow to my ego was fatal to the relationship. After the outing, I took Yvette home and never asked her out again. I still maintained contact with Brenda in a platonic relationship.

Through contacts made at the can drive I developed a friendship with Jack. We volunteered at a home for troubled girls every Saturday; he was my ride.

Eventually, we dated girls who were best friends and double dated because Jack had a car. I met the girls together through the School Volleyball Team. After I found the factory job, I had more free time, so I got active in other clubs. Volleyball got suggested by my classmate and fellow Drama Clubber Janek, who was the team manager the previous year. He wanted a spot on the team this year and was determined to play on the current squad. I signed up when he asked me to go with him.

I wanted to be accepted so much that my adrenaline levels spiked at the tryout. While practicing proper volley technique, the coach noticed that my hands shook uncontrollably. He asked me if I had a medical problem or if I was taking anything that caused the shakes. I said no. Then, when we practiced our overhand serves, mine constantly hit the net. The coach told me he was cutting me from the team, but the manager position was mine for the asking. I accepted. Although I knew Janek from Biology and History classes, we became close friends after getting parts in the play. Theatre Arts Program students got the lead roles. Smaller parts got awarded to Club members like Janek and me. Other positions were available as backstage hands, makeup staff, stage managers, and in the promotions department. There was some crossover on the Vollyball team and the Drama Club.

Given my past lead role as John A. MacDonald, I felt comfortable auditioning for the drama club. My primary motivation was to gain a part in the prestigious club, a past winner of the Sears Drama Award. Members of the club had even performed in a documentary about drug abuse narrated by Sammy Davis Jr. In their next production, I got a role. Two friends, Diane and Susan, were on the makeup staff.

During Volleyball home games, I noticed the two girls hanging around me while I served as the scorekeeper. They approached me and I liked both of them. I wanted to ask one or the other for a date as the opportunity arose. The first chance came up with Susan, and she accepted my invitation. Soon after, Jack was dating Diane, and that was that; we double dated often.

Jack and I discussed many things during our rides to, and while doing tasks at, the Inn. Once, Jack spoke about our girlfriends. He admired Sue for her tennis skills; Jack and Sue were both in the tennis club. He said he might like to date her one day. I said that I admired Diane and that we should switch dates, like with Snowball dances. He seemed to agree.

Susan and I had a rocky relationship. Sue claimed to be a Manic Depressive, which manifested throughout our time together. Things would be going fine for a while then she'd say

that she thought we should see other people. Since she was my
first steady girl, perhaps I scared her with my intensity. I was
looking for some of the tenderness in short supply at home. I
sometimes tucked my hand into her waistband while she sat on
my lap. Occasionally, I tried to go further, like in the game
Chicken or Go. She was adopted and possibly felt I was
imposing on her because she knew intimately the unintended
consequences that might develop. I was not empathetic with her
point of view because it was not something in my life
experience. Her family was very religious; her Aunt being a nun.
Sue was one of seven girls in the family, all but two being
adopted. I realized, after we started dating that her father was the
school guidance counsellor.

Whenever she suggested seeing other people, I agreed.
There was always someone else that caught my eye among other
members of the Drama Club. I could have been more discrete. If
I asked someone to an event and got refused, I just turned to ask
another (within view of the girl who declined). After a week or
so like that, I called Sue and asked if she wanted to get back
together; she always said yes. She had not been asked out in the
interim and was, perhaps, jealous. That cycle repeated for
months.

Sue's Dad asked me to help with the installation of their
above-ground pool. In the process, because I had kicked off my
shoes to prevent them from filling with sand laid as a foundation
for the bottom of the pool, I gashed my foot near the ball joint on
a sharp piece of metal. Assembly halted to allow a trip to the
hospital for stitches. On the way, Sue sat beside me, holding my
hand. It was one of our rocky times, but I took it as a positive
sign and said, "So you really do love me, don't you?" She
replied, "Only in the sense that one loves her fellow man."

Shortly after that incident, things were still rocky, and she invited me over to play cards. Diane was there, and Sue set out a bowl of chips. One of her younger sisters snuck a chip as she walked by, and Sue slapped her face, saying, "Those are for us." That was the last straw for me. I held hands with Diane under the table for the rest of the evening. When Diane suggested she was going home, I said I would walk with her as it was on the way to the bus stop. When we got outside, I again took her hand, and she gave no resistance. I asked her to go out with me. She said, "Only if Jack says it's okay."

Reminded of Jack's conversation on the way to the Inn, I said I'd ask. I called Jack, referred to our previous conversation, and then asked for his decision. In my defense, Jack could have quashed the whole thing right then and there by refusing. Instead, he waffled and said, "What can I do about it?" leaving me unanswered. I called Diane to let her know what happened, and she still wouldn't commit. The next thing I know is, in the eyes of the trio, my name was Mud.

I learned a lot from Jack during the time we spent volunteering at the Inn. He was a year older than me and had a close relationship with his father. Because of that, he had some skills regarding quick fixes and home repairs that I lacked. As friends, we had shared many exploits. The first time that I went to a hockey game was with Jack. His Dad had some connection at the arena and got us a gig manning the penalty boxes during a Junior league series. It opened my eyes to a whole new aspect of the game. I gained a better understanding of the flow and could see plays develop in real-time. I am not expert enough to coach the game, but I can better enjoy the dynamics. Anyway, it was a blow to lose Jack's friendship over my gaffe.

Jack and I also had some dangerous adventures involving cars driven at excessive highway speed, up to one hundred miles an hour on the 401. Jack's car had no seat belts, not uncommon in old cars then. We pulled out of the lane to pass a truck and encountered another eighteen-wheeler in the passing lane. We barely had time to slow down to avoid a collision. We also drank. At one New Year's Eve party, Jack got so drunk on high-balls, mixed by me, that he was laying on his back on the basement floor, making "Snow Angel" motions and yelling "Happy New Year" while other couples kissed, standing around him. I was as bad as he was, having matched him drink for drink. Brenda drove us both home in Jack's car that night, returning the car the following day.

Jack's Mom had rheumatoid arthritis, and his Dad couldn't deal with the reality of her chronic pain. He had an affair with another woman and decided to leave his wife for the other woman. I'm sure that had negative effects on Jack during his graduation year. He was faced with some hard decisions. He decided to enter the priesthood. I assume it was partly because the church would bear the cost of his education. In any case, my gaffe coincided with Diane learning about Jack's choice and their subsequent breakup. I still had hopes that Diane would date me, but she had soured on Jack and me, if not on all men, and refused to speak to either of us.

Sue was bitter about our breakup. At the wrap party for our current play, she signed my program, saying something about plenty of fish in the sea. I was confused because she had implied that I meant no more to her than any guy on the street. How could she feel such upset about my exit from the on-again, off-again, merry-go-round that typified our relationship?

Around that time, a gray book appeared in our house. One day, I noticed it on a high shelf in the closet and asked Mom what it was. She told me that I was forbidden to read it. Well, banning me from reading something was just a dare. It took me a while to find it again because she hid it after her proclamation. The title of the book was "Health, Sex and Birth Control, by Percy E. Ryberg, M. D. This was "the talk" on steroids. It gave me a sound foundation to understand and engage in sex as a responsible adult. I don't know if that was Mom's intention, but the book wasn't well hidden and no one mentioned it again. I read it when Mom was on dates.

Mom didn't seem surprised when I started bringing home Playboy magazines and even took it in stride when she barged into my room without knocking and caught me masturbating. Mom was embarrassed but apologized for her invasion of my privacy. She said it was normal. I was grateful for her understanding and direct manner and I didn't develop any sexual hangups during this stage of maturation.

Buses ran every half hour at peak times and every hour otherwise. Sometimes, it was faster to walk than to wait for a bus. Alternatively, while walking, you could snag a ride by thumbing it. I often reached my destination, walking before getting a ride or seeing a bus.

Hitchhiking could have been a more reliable means of transport. I was always jealous of Kolaff, one of my fellow Drama Clubbers, because his thumb seemed golden. He usually got a ride any time he tried, and usually, the driver was female. He was tall, with shoulder length, raven hair, a mustache and an erect posture that made him look like a Russian Cossack. My luck was never that prodigious. I put that down to my fine, chestnut hair that haloed my head like a dandelion gone to seed.

There was one instance that did put my instincts on high alert. Two guys in a Camero stopped for me and let me into the back seat. The Camero was a coupe, so once in the back, I could not exit unless they allowed it. I don't know whether these guys were stoned or goofing, but they seemed out of it. The one in the passenger seat said in a voice sounding like Tommy Chong from That 70's Show, "Hey man, have you got twenty bucks you can lend me?" As it happened, I had fifty dollars with me, but I replied, "If I had any money, do you think I'd be hiking?" He said okay, but within two minutes, he asked the same question. I imagined them driving me to a remote place, beating and robbing or even killing me. I said I had reached my destination, and they let me out, to my great relief. To this day, I wonder if they were goofing on the random hitchhiker.

Another risky behavior that I engaged in was smoking. I had been exposed to secondhand smoke at home when my Dad and Mike were smoking, but that wasn't why I picked up the habit. It was more because of members of the Drama Club smoking during rehearsals that I started. There were so many smoking members that the rehearsal hall was always thick with smoke, which made non-smokers nauseated. When I began to smoke, I no longer felt sick. I smoked for eight years before quitting but never really enjoyed it. At one point, I was smoking two packs a day, sometimes lighting one cigarette from the stub of my last. Eventually, I was able to kick the habit.

In my final year of high school, the provincial government lowered the drinking age to eighteen. Their motivation was to garner new untapped voters in the next election. There was also pressure coming from the States, where protesters said that if they asked young people to fight and die in Vietnam, eighteen-year-olds should be able to drink. Shortly after the age lowered, students started to take lunch at the nearby bar to have a cold one with lunch. Once, while Janek and I were doing just that, we got sent a pitcher of beer from another table. When the barmaid pointed out our benefactor, our principal raised his hand and smiled. After I turned nineteen, the drinking age got raised to nineteen. Too many students were taking liquid lunches, creating problems for high schools across the province.

Early during my high school years, I became a regular moviegoer. I had not seen films until then because most of what I wanted to see was "restricted," meaning that you had to be at least sixteen to gain admittance. One of my classmates told me he had seen one of these films (we were in grade nine then), and I asked how he got in. He said no one asked for I.D., so you could get in if you paid the price. I tried that and found it true, so I became a regular moviegoer. The problem was that most of the time, I went alone. I was alone at home, in the theatre, on my treks to and from stores and other destinations. When I started going to parties tied to the Drama Club, I found that I could feel alone even amid a crowd. Even at sports events, I was alone unless I was successful in asking a girl to go with me or accompanied by Jack, Janeck, or another friend. This feeling of isolation was prevalent through most of my high school years.

In my last year of high school, Mom went to Britain with Theo for two weeks, leaving me to fend for myself. During that time, I ate bread and peanut butter for most meals. When she returned, she remarked that I had lost weight. I was eleven pounds lighter by then.

It was summertime, I was working in the factory and Janek and I were volunteer ushers at the University of Windsor through a program hosted by the Drama department. Local high school students could view the complete season of the performances by acting as volunteers. After seeing the first performance of any play, your time was your own until intermission or the finale, when you herded people in or out. Janek and I played a lot of Foosball in the adjoining student lounge. Once, we went to a student pub and split a pitcher of beer. That time, we got warned that we would get ejected if we ever drank again while in the program. We gained a lot of friends and acquaintances among that crowd. One of the guys was the manager of the ticket office.

He looked like Bob Crane (the actor), and we became chummy with him. While Mom was in Britain, I threw a party for this group of friends, and we drank all the alcohol in the house. I felt that this was my coming-of-age party.

About six months after the breakup with Susan, I started dating Mona. She was in a church choir, and to get more time with her, I joined too. I had no great desire to spend more time in churches, but I did want to see more of her. I became friends with the guitarist for the group, Randy (of the Detroit River incident), who went to my school.

We double-dated every weekend. I'm not sure who benefited most from the arrangement. As he drove, his girlfriend up front with him, Mona and I were fogging up the back window with our lip exercises.

Randy and I got involved in our school coffee houses. These were just gatherings where students could perform or recite their poetry while having coffee with like-minded people. I wrote some poetry then but was useless as a musician. Randy tried to teach me to no avail. He handled the music, and I performed Alice's Restaurant, doing a near-perfect imitation of Arlo Guthrie. Sometimes, we rehearsed in the school chapel, which was usually empty. He told me about a time he had been rehearsing there for the choir, and someone entered the chapel. Randy had hidden beneath the altar and had been unobserved. As a prank, while the other person contemplated in silence, Randy said in a loud, deep voice, "You." The contemplative replied in a quavering voice, "Who, art thou?....where art thou?" then fled the "supernatural" revelation.

19

Furthermore...

I continued as the Volleyball team manager. To provide more experience for playing away games, the Coach set up a practice at my brother Mike's school. When finished, we moved to the shower room to clean up.

One of the guys noticed that the dressing room opened into the pool area. No one was in that area, so we moved en masse, in our birthday suits, into the pool. We were splashing and horsing about when the female lifeguard, who had been occupied locking doors after the open swim night, returned and ordered us out. No one moved. Exasperated, she repeated the order with more authority and volume. Still, no one moved. I don't know when or how she became aware that we were all nude, but she blushed and said, "Oh!" and then left while we scampered out like rats fleeing a sinking ship.

The Drama Club threw some wild parties. As a member, I got invited. Most times, alcohol was available. I was in the club but not the Theater Arts Program, so I existed on the fringes. I assumed my observer role; watching from the fringes I noticed a drunk girl crying because a certain boy wouldn't even look her way. I felt a pervasive loneliness even among the crowd. At another party, I was present and observant. A large bowl on the fireplace's mantle provided a cornucopia of recreational drugs.

Tablets and capsules of all colors of the rainbow were available. I stuck with my drug of choice, alcohol, but there were blues, reds, yellow uppers, downers and who knows what else.

After this party, I wrote a poem about a fictional bad acid trip.

The Drunks Grin On

Young experimenters flying high,

Give the child a tab to try,

And watch him as his trip begins.

Their faces lift in drunken grins

As he soars to heights they never knew;

Seeing, smelling, tasting blue.

And in the grandeur of his flight,

He hurls his soul with all his might

And sees a heap of lifeless child

While about his body, with eyes wild,

The drunks grin on.

Another party springs to mind. At the last performance of
The Queen and the Rebels, an event was planned at the house of
the female lead. On the last day of our run, her parents vetoed
the party. Without hesitation, asking permission, or even
considering whether our home could host a group that size, I
announced, "We *gotta* have a party! Impromptu party at my
house after the play!"

I hadn't even arrived to greet my guests, as a proper host
should have, being delayed removing my grease paint and
getting a ride home. Mom, Teddy and his wife, Sherry, stood
open-mouthed as the crowd arrived and quickly grew. Mom was
super gracious, considering she had no prior knowledge of the
event. Struck speechless, Mom noted a growing pile of removed
shoes at our doorway. She asked what was happening when I
arrived but rolled with it. Our director brought some
refreshments and a cake and thanked Mom profusely for
providing the venue. We sat around, smoked, drank and ate cake
until the buzz wound down. It was a party to remember, but it
was probably much less luxurious than expected. Mom took it in
stride.

Shortly after that party, the newspaper advice columnist
Ann Landers published a short questionnaire for teens to rate
their behavior. The ratings ranged between Pure as the driven
snow to Irredeemable. I was shocked that my answers regarding
smoking, alcohol consumption and whether I had made a
member of the opposite sex cry labeled me Irredeemable. I had
no criminal history, didn't engage in illegal drug use and had not
been involved with any sexual scandals. How could that rating
apply to me?

The following year, we performed the farce See How They Run. By then, I had been typecast as an old man. My life experience must have made me seem old. In the farce there were no senior male roles, so I took on the responsibilities of House and Promotions Manager (shared with Janek). During preparations for the performance, the female lead applied her makeup, wearing only her bra and panties. I ensured that my duties as House Manager provided ample trips through the green room. During one of those trips, I observed Angie making a pass at the producer's husband. He was helping with scenery but vacated the room without comment after her solicitation. It may be hard to believe that such activities happened at high school, but the previous year, the senior student lounge, a perk to acknowledge the senior students as the adults they were becoming, got removed because a couple got caught copulating in the closet.

Some sensational events occurred in the world in general during those years. Several Rock Operas got released. Hair, Godspell, Jesus Christ Superstar, and Tommy were all big hits. Another phenomenal event was the Woodstock rock concert on Max Yasgur's dairy farm. It was declared a disaster area due to wet, stormy weather before it ended. And let us not forget the Vietnam War and the FLQ crisis.

While exposed to many protest songs and thought-provoking debates about the issues, I mostly observed. I was a few years too young to take an active part. I did, however, consider what actions I'd take if confronted. I became anti-war and a proponent of people's rights.

My existence, concentrating on introspection and reading, isolated me. World events, like the Moon Landing or the war in

Vietnam, got registered but were not closely followed. I didn't go out of my way to watch coverage of the Moon Walk or consider casualties and body counts from the war. It was just data.

Along with my interest in pool, I continued to enjoy basketball. After getting some coaching from Mark, my success rate improved drastically. I became a Gym Rat, practicing daily for half of my lunch break and the following study period. I was putting in my ten thousand hours. I got a basket ninety percent of the time; most swishes from around the key. I would play two-on-one possession against two other Gym Rats and overheard one say, "He's too good; we can't beat him." I was terrible in an organized game because I could only dribble with my right hand, but I felt good about myself anyway.

I spied a girl with long, dark, wavy hair at a football game, standing in the row before me in the bleachers. We struck up a conversation. She was full of joi de vivre as she waved her hand, notable for the clunky purple costume jewelry, in my face for emphasis. She seemed to go out of her way to run into me daily, trailed by her taller, cuter friend. I discovered she was in grade ten. I was in grade thirteen.

One day, Geek and Mouse, their self-styled nicknames, approached me in full view of the glass-walled guidance office. Mouse said, "Say Hello to me." I said Hello, then she stood on her toes, twined her arms around my neck, and kissed me full on the mouth. I thought, "Well, I can't let her get away with that!" so I held her waist, bent her back, and performed a "Rhett Butler" kiss, as from Gone with the Wind. Janek, my constant cohort, started laughing and said, "Doug, a nun is watching you." With my back to the guidance office, I broke off the kiss, looked to my left and right, saw no nun and returned to my exploration of Mouse's lips. Notably, they started to warm, and I enjoyed the sensation. Finally breaking off, I turned to find my grade nine French teacher and guidance counselor, mouth agape, who was the nun that Janek had referred to. As I fled the scene, Mouse called after me, voice full of longing, "You've got my number!"

20

Bad Teachers

There were a great many teachers who helped me through the maze of high school:

Mr. B., my grade twelve chemistry teacher, whose demonstration of the chemical process of nylon production failed, reminded me of the Mr. Wizard show. Assistant Billy would quip, "What next, Mr. Wizard?" before each new demonstration. I repeated that line aloud in class. Frustrated, Mr. B. threatened punishment, but never followed through.

Mr. L. passed me in the hall one day, reached out his finger and smudged my glasses saying, "Your glasses are dirty." I took the end of his tie, wiped the smudge away with it and replied, "No, they're not." He gracefully accepted this, saying, "I guess that's fair." The list is too extensive to continue. These people spring to mind when I say, "It takes a village to raise a child."

Conversely, I encountered some bad teachers. The problem in both cases was that each of them acted in their self-interest. The first was another newly minted teacher. He customarily taught for half a period, assigned a problem set and then left the room to enjoy coffee in the teacher's lounge across the hall. I noticed this pattern early in the year but said nothing.

Once, I had trouble with a homework problem, struggling with it for forty minutes before approaching him for guidance. He started to demonstrate the answer on the board, repeating all the steps I had tried and coming to the same dead end. Instead of apologizing, admitting that he wasn't sure, or offering to get back to me the next day with an answer, he glanced at his watch and said, "I don't have time for this right now." He felt his demonstration sufficed. Feeling frustrated and betrayed, I too departed, no closer to a solution.

A short time after that, Mr. F. did his usual and customary. He taught for half the period, assigned a problem set, and drifted off to coffee nirvana. During his absence from the room, I did three of the four assigned questions. I intended to complete the remaining questions at home, being distracted by the misbehavior of my peers. They told jokes, drew doodles on the board, and created general mayhem. Mr. F. returned from the teacher's lounge. He glared at me and bellowed," Landgraff, are you finished with the assignment?

I said, "No, but I've done all I'm going to do right now!" He came back with, "Put it on the board."

I refused, and he asked if I was challenging him. "No, you're challenging me."

At this, he growled, "Vice Principal's office after school." "I'll be there!"

He wanted revenge. He intended to force me to write his exam. By his reasoning, if I didn't pass it, I wouldn't have enough credits to graduate. He was unaware that I had taken an extra credit Physics course the previous year and would graduate no matter what happened.

When I faced the Vice Principal, I emphasized my past performance and the extra credit evidence. I pointed out that I could complete my year without sitting the exam. I had gained some knowledge during Mr. F.'s course regardless, a fact that remained no matter how we moved forward. The VP asked me what mark I thought I deserved in the course. I told him at least seventy percent. He said it would be shameful if that weren't on the official record and cajoled me into writing the final, even though I wanted to refuse on principle.

The exam Mr. F. set may have been challenging because I was the only person sitting that exam. There was a question I couldn't answer. My final mark on the official transcript was seventy percent. Coincidence? In my graduation yearbook, he signed something like I'm pleased to see you graduate with such high marks, except algebra 552, maybe. Years later, I saw Mr. F. in a Chapters store. He was pushing his kid in a stroller. When I tried to approach him to apologize for my part in the fiasco, he fled without facing me.

The second example of a lousy teacher was similar. Todd Test Tube was the Math and Science Department Head and my grade thirteen chemistry teacher. He was also a city councilor. He could affect my future significantly, given my desire to become a pharmacist. Chemistry marks are assessed heavily during the admission process. I perceived a potential problem regarding him in grade twelve during my extra credit Physics class. The Physics lab abutted the Chemistry lab. One afternoon, our physics class was disturbed by a loud boom from the next room, followed by the sound of frenzied activity. Our instructor investigated to see if we should evacuate. He returned with disturbing news. Todd Test Tube, a mocking nickname for him coined after this event, had done his usual and customary:

teaching for half the period, then assigning a problem set while he slipped into the adjacent supply room. Are the similarities to the Mr. F. situation now apparent? Mr. Tube had allowed a free period for his students to experiment with concepts of interest to themselves. Unlike Mr. F, Mr. Tube was not in the teacher's lounge but nestled in the supply room, working on his interests but close at hand.

One group of students wondered what would happen if you added water to a strong acid. Mixture in the wrong order results in rapid, violent boiling, a reaction referred to as the heat of hydration. The safe procedure is to add acids, especially strong acids, to water. The students compounded the problem by placing a watch glass atop the beaker after adding the water. That produced a restricted opening for the release of pent-up energy. The rapid reaction caused a directed spray of hot acid solution to explode through that opening, covering one of the students with hot caustic liquid.

The following frenzied activity resulted from the efforts of Todd and his students dragging the drenched victim to the gym shower room for decontamination. Once there, he was stripped and sprayed down. A portion of the boy's outfit had burned off on the way to the shower, but skin contact was minimal. At least Mr. Tube's proximity and fast action prevented severe disfigurement. Statements from Mr. Tube's students led me to believe that he was not a good teacher.

I attended Todd Test Tube's class the next year. In the first semester, my mark was disappointing. It was four points below the class average. Concerning because I had exceeded the class average by at least twenty-four points the previous year. I had some issues understanding the material, but when I asked for help, Mr.Tube just turned to a paragraph in the text, pointed to it and said that provided the answer. I explained that I had read that section on my own, and it didn't help me. He just waved it off. With my aspirations to enter pharmacy school, I was concerned.

In the designated smoking area, called the corral, where smoking was allowed on school premises, I discussed the situation with Mick, who found the same issue with the Chemistry class. I found out later that Mick was also seeking entrance into U of T for pharmacy. We both felt that Mr. Tube was not giving his best effort to help his students. I convinced Mick to accompany me to plead with Mr. Tube, asking for more help. Mick took the lead, explaining our issue and asked Mr. Tube to make a greater effort. Here, I made the mistake of adding the inappropriate phrase "Like teaching." We both needed to do well in Chemistry, but I had just thrown a wrench in that with my tactless addition to Mick's initial approach. After that, our marks suffered from Mr. Tube's bias.

I resolved to try a political solution to my problem. Mr. Tube was running for City Council, so I volunteered to help with his campaign. I delivered his propaganda and knocked on doors to speak to voters on his behalf. Additionally, I stopped my participation in the Drama Club, abandoning my part as a crowd extra in our production of *Jesus Christ Superstar* to devote more time to my studies. I typed and illustrated every assignment, trying to impress him with my diligence. My approach may have worked because Mick later complained that he had gotten higher marks than me on every test, but we both ended with the same final mark. I endured years of bad feelings emanating from Mick because of this. As graduation approached, Mr. Test Tube asked me what my plans for the future were. I said I was going to be a Pharmacist. He replied, "You'll never make it."

About eight years later, I attended the grand opening of one of my corporation's stores. Todd Test Tube was there as a representative of the City Council. I approached him to ask if he remembered me. He claimed that he didn't. I reminded him that I had helped in his campaign for City Council. He still denied knowing me. He did ask what I was doing now, to which I replied, "I'm a Pharmacist-Manager for this company. He moved on to mingle after that. I blame these two teachers for costing me an Ontario Scholarship. No matter how *you* view it, I fell short of the criteria by one and a half percentage point.

21

Kelsey Hayes

The Factory

The day is young; It's seven o'clock.

A few, with sleeping eyes,

File past to punch the clock.

One has laughed, some others talk.

The whistle blows,

The shift begins.

The machine is cold,

And gray and dead.

One pulls a switch; it springs

To life, and Bam, Bam, Bam

The beat begins;

The music of our life's delight.

In the sombre shop

A song breaks out.

It helps to pass the time.

It helps a man forget about

The pain that climbs his spine

While standing fixed

For hours at a time.

The whistle blows;

Machines all stop,

And it sounds like death

In the cold, gray shop.

One man eats ham, another lox,

Each hunched atop

His black lunch box.

Conversation seems quite hushed,

But that's not really so.

It's that the silence rings in ears

Making voices seem low.

To end the lunch,

The whistle blows.

The dark machines

Take life again.

The afternoon is long.

And each man will, within

His thoughts ponder the beyond,

And wonder at

The life he's drawn.

Before each stands

A cold machine,

But each can see, instead,

The visage of his steadfast wife

Within her boxlike bed;

Sure to succor lend

At daylight's end.

The summer of my high school graduation marked another transition. Although I had previous experience working in a factory, I moved up a notch when I found employment at Kelsey Hayes, a union shop that manufactured car wheels. This job came with union wages, a significant bump up.

The old saw, "It's not what you know, it's who you know," loomed large in this. Morty's dad, Theo, was still dating Mom. He knew the Kelsey Hayes plant manager and put in a good word for me. Mike's father-in-law was a union steward there and put my name forward. I had "pull" from both sides of the employment equation. In early June, I got called in for an afternoon interview and was hired on the spot to start at the three o'clock shift change.

I started in the shipping department. My job was to pack wheels into racks.

The rims rolled onto a collection track, getting pushed forward automatically, then transferred using a hand-controlled pneumatic device. Each rack held about a hundred and fifty rims. When the foreman switched it on, lifted a load, moved it to the rack, dropped the load, then returned the lift to its original position and turned it off. No one mentioned that the lift didn't need to be turned off after each unloading. I maintained the demonstrated sequence, switching off between loads. It was hard to coordinate with the advancing line; each time the lift got deactivated, pressure had to build in the lines on reactivation before moving the next load. I struggled with this for a week before anyone realized why I had difficulty keeping up. I worked twice as hard as needed. Thankfully, one of the other operators noticed the problem and showed me the proper technique.

At the end of my first day, I was bone tired. I had expected to get a bus home, but they went out of service an hour before my shift ended. I had no money to take a taxi, so I walked the six miles home. After that, I took my bike to work.

There were other packing methods besides the racks. Four-man teams palletized the rims for shipping. The packaged pallets were stacked six high (equivalent to a three-story building) for storage. The men rotated every hour through four tasks: inspection and labeling, stacking, layering and banding. Being the new guy, no one told me about the rota and I got taken advantage of. The inspection and banding jobs were less taxing, so the full-time guys claimed these for the first two weeks, leaving me to alternate between stacking and layering. Stacking involved moving and placing wheels on the pallet. A sheet of corrugated cardboard was set between each layer to guarantee stability. Because I was gullible, I did as directed, enduring the initiation ritual. Another prank sent new hires to the tool crib to ask for a left-handed monkey wrench (as a way to teach them to think before acting). At the crib, you'd be turned away empty-handed and told that the guys were pulling your leg. Eventually, you were accepted and treated as an equal.

Besides the pay bump, the most notable difference between work at non-union and union shops was that here union AND management monitored your work. If you made another guy look like a slacker, you got approached and questioned, "Have you got any smokes?" If you did, you got told to smoke three cigarettes before you did any more work. A union steward shuts your machine down if you try to work through a break. He'd remind you that the union won the privilege of breaks through complex negotiation, so you must take the time, in solidarity with your union brothers. It wasn't an issue in most cases because the production numbers got set high as stretch targets (barely achievable). For the most part, no one reached their number before the shift ended.

I've addressed the possibility of injury before, but I restate it because a moment's inattention can have devastating consequences. There were living reminders among our long-term employees. They had legacy jobs, sweeping up around the shop. They were past victims of accidents of varying severity, some with lost fingers, hands, or whole limbs. I heard stories about how so and so lost his arm while he tried to clear a jammed machine. It was still powered up and somehow activated, crushing whatever limbs were in the way. Another story was about how the overhead crane had dropped a load of steel sheets that severed or crushed anything in their downward path. I heard of the death of a schoolmate's father (a Ford employee). As he was leaving the foundry department from his last pre-retirement shift, he died when the molten contents of a ladle spilled on him and killed him. These might seem like fables used as warnings, but I was witness to one near fatality.

Palletized rims got stacked by forklift until shipped. Some lifts had roll bar cages to protect the operator, and some didn't. Once, an operator placed a pallet on top of a stack. While backing away, his fork knocked the pallet so that it came crashing down upon him. Luckily, he was in a caged lift. The bars surrounding him got bent, being displaced by about a foot, but saved his life. Anyone near the accident in progress, scattered to get clear. The shaking, ashen operator got helped from the lift truck and was sent home to calm down.

We got warned not to run in the factory. During my second summer there, I got delayed, speaking to the foreman after a lunch break. I ran toward my machine to make up for the slight delay. As I passed an obstructing wall, I moved into the path of a forklift loaded with a ton of steel. I couldn't stop until I was right in the path of the oncoming load. The operator hit the brakes, but that didn't mean the load momentum was arrested. I thought, "Jesus Christ, this is it," imagining the load sliding forward, crushing me beneath it. Luckily, that did not happen. I got thoroughly cussed out by the driver but was thankful to be around to endure his tirade. My guardian angel earned his keep that day.

At one post, I worked between two lines of wheels running counter to each other. My job was to transfer rims from one line to the other. The foreman told me that my transfer rate should ensure a rim placed every third or fourth hook on the receding line. I used momentum guiding the rims from one line to the other, without taking the full weight of a wheel; throwing them from line to line in a fluid motion. At the break, a coworker told me he owned a dojo and was impressed by his observation of me throwing the wheels. He said I would do well in martial arts. He invited me to his gym. I never took him up on the offer, but I was pleased with his comments.

After the break, I noticed significant gaps on the approaching line, which affected results down-line from me. Suddenly, the foreman was there, yelling at me, saying, "WTF are you doing?" I was confused because I couldn't understand his complaint. I couldn't move rims that weren't there. The foreman told me that workers further down the line were blaming me for reduced productivity. I dutifully ensured that a wheel was on every third hook of the receding line, even though I had to run down the approaching line, removing rims and rolling them to the opposing line to accommodate. About forty minutes later, the foreman was back yelling, "WTF are you doing? The guys down the line can't keep up!" Thoroughly frustrated, I lost it and replied, "WTF do you want? I'm just doing what I'm told!" He wasn't pleased, but I heard no more from him.

Commonly, at lunch and other breaks, we would play Euchre or poker if we had time. Two guys bet their pay on a poker hand. The guy who lost made an accusation of cheating. At the end of the shift, as we walked to our vehicles, the loser drove into his opponent, throwing him about ten feet forward. I didn't stick around, but I learned not to gamble with ridiculous stakes to avoid unpleasant consequences.

On the job, I met a wide selection of characters. One of the guys had a degree in English Literature. He always carried a paperback novel in his back pocket to read during downtime. He avoided interactions with coworkers by burying his nose in a book. Another guy experienced Detroit during the riots of sixty-seven and was in country during the Vietnamese war. He never faced the enemy there, being one of the support personnel in logistics. He said that he felt more threatened during the Detroit riots. He told the story of driving after curfew one night and having the cops shoot out his rear window. He also said that, in Vietnam, he just got clear of his truck when he got thrown to the ground by the force of the explosion that destroyed his vehicle. I guess the danger is relative to experience and expectation.

I met the most mysterious person I encountered there only once. He wore glasses and was about my height, in his late forties, with graying hair and wearing a gray jumpsuit. I didn't know who he was or why he approached me, but he offered me an all-expenses paid vacation to Rome. He pointed out that if anything unexpected happened, it would only result in the authorities saying I was young and made a foolish mistake. I would get away with a warning. I thought, "Why would I want to go to Rome? I don't speak Italian and have no relatives there." I politely declined, saying, "No, thank you."

The man disappeared like a wisp of smoke, never to be seen again. I only realized my close call after seeing the movie Midnight Express. I had been approached to be a drug mule, only narrowly escaping a dangerous proposition. My spirit guide put the right words into my mouth at the right time.

Before my last summer at Kelsey Hayes, Mom took a call asking about my availability for work. I was still in Toronto writing exams. I took this as a sign of their high regard for me and followed up as soon as I got into town. I got rehired and started at the beginning of that week.

This session, I worked in the shear department. A shear is a machine about the size of a Ford Econoline van. Perpendicular to that sits an electromagnet that lifts sheets of steel to be run through the machine in the first step of processing. The resultant strips are about nine feet long and nine to ten inches wide.

The machine has a left and right operator station, meaning that two men work in unison. When the steel is perfect, things work very well, but with warped sheets, the electromagnet malfunctions often, dropping the load before it is in the proper position. Then, you have to wrestle it into place and your shift becomes a waking nightmare. I got told by some of the guys that men twice my size refused to work on these machines because of the physical demands. We were the elite workers of the factory.

The shear department was the exception to the rule that production numbers weren't attainable (although we had to break company rules to do so). The last cut of every sheet had to be flipped and pushed through manually We learned that vital seconds got saved if we didn't push that strip through, but bumped it through with the next sheet. The final cut also required coordinated, manual activation of the machine. I figured that things would go faster if I held my activator ready so the machine would be activated by my partner when ready, saving seconds with each of these cuts. The stroke counter, on my partner's side, could be surreptitiously advanced by a flick of his finger. I knew that this might be happening but never actually encouraged the deception. Every team in the department did it. Anyway, bumping the last cut through and my practice with the last cut wasn't sanctioned by the company. If the advancing sheet slid under the final cut instead of bumping it through, the doubled thickness risked breaking the blade. My innovation with the activation button was a potential health and safety violation. We risked getting fired for breaking the rules. My partner and I developed into the second-fastest team in the department. We usually hit the target with twenty to thirty minutes to spare at the end of each shift. Eventually, we discovered a couple of showers on the premises. Since we had half an hour of free time each shift, we started to shower there so we'd feel fresh on the way home.

Once, I was out of the shower and fully dressed, but my teammate was still in the stall. A guy urgently rushed into the area and yelled, " Get out, get out, the transformer's about to blow. The transformer was on the roof, adjacent to the showers. I yelled to Bob to get out of there now! He ran out in his birthday suit, grabbed his clothes, and we scampered down the stairs. Bob, still dripping, waited till we cleared the danger zone before attempting to cover up. Luckily, disaster was averted by the electricians that day, or half of the building would have been destroyed. Fond memories!

On another occasion, a tour group passed us. This was a novelty and a break in the routine. We all stood tall to impress the tour like a well-trained team of horses pulling proudly together. A stress reliever that I resorted to was singing, emulating members of a chain gang or other work crews; I would trance myself into rhythm with the machine by cycling through my repertoire. The noise level in the factory was over ninety decibels, so no one noticed my voice over the din.

As time wound down and my next year of education approached, I began to evaluate the wisdom of pursuing higher education. I knew that factory work was tedious, but as the foreman pointed out, it paid well, seemed secure with many benefits, and could offer a decent lifestyle.

The first year in pursuit of my degree had been challenging. Mona wanted to get married and I had done a poor job during the year of keeping in touch. I needed to improve communication during the long-distance relationship or risk losing it. In my heart, I was committed to marrying Mona after graduation. Still, classes and labs translated to more than forty hours a week when accounting for additional assignments, essays and reports. When I tried to write letters, my mind went blank. A five-minute phone call cost me twenty dollars. Train tickets were similarly expensive. I was on a budget of four thousand dollars a year, so finances were tight. I was almost convinced to drop out. Mom said, "Go back, do it for me." I thought, if I go back, it won't be to please you. I decided to go back and resolved to do better.

22

Toronto; Residence

Looking back on it, I was haphazard and unprepared for the University of Toronto. My decision to become a pharmacist was more of a fluke than a calling. I got urged by Bill, the boarder, to study engineering based on my math marks. A job fair I attended allowed students to approach professionals, gathered in one convenient location, to ask about careers in their field. I asked at the engineering booth, "If I become an engineer, what will I be doing?" The representative gave me a typical engineer's answer: technically correct but totally useless. He said, "I don't know." I left the booth thinking, "Here's a guy who doesn't know what he does for a living." I was unimpressed. In hindsight, an explanation that engineering encompasses many specialties, such as civil, mechanical, geological and chemical engineering, would have been more helpful. His answer was technically correct; he didn't know what specialty I might take, but it was uninspiring and totally useless to me. In my years in Toronto, I hung out primarily with engineers, feeling more comfortable with them than members of my class. When asked about what engineering field I was studying, I'd answer, "Pharmaceutical." I still maintain ties to a core group of engineer friends that I met in residence fifty years ago.

The next professional I approached was a pharmacist. He was enthusiastic and represented his profession well, saying he loved his job and outlined all the pluses of a rewarding pursuit. I checked the literature to see if I had the skills needed and what the income and working conditions were like. My background prepared me to follow a discipline of the scientific method. From a very early age I had skills as an observer. I later developed the capacity to form theories and methods to test them out. I could draw conclusions from my testing and observations. My education gave me the tools to pursue a science-based career. I decided that pharmacy suited me.

Because of funding issues, I never visited Toronto to tour the campus or check out the housing situation. There was only one school of pharmacy in Ontario then. It was in Toronto. I spoke to Mick and Robert, who had gone to evaluate residences there. They both said New College was the best. I never requested information directly from the residence, so I missed out on some information about recommended vaccinations. To get a placement at New College, duplicate applications were required. I filled out spare application forms, one each from Mick and Robert, and got accepted.

Now, I was sure I had a place to live, but that Labor Day, boarding the train to Toronto, I didn't have a clue of the exact location of the place. I said goodbye to Mona and boarded the train. Her flirtatious comment regarding how it was unfair to leave her alone on her labor day, echoed in my mind.

Luckily, I sat with Nick Plotter on the train, who knew where New College was. We disembarked in Toronto and went to the Pizza Pizza Restaurant for supper. After that, we proceeded to his residence (Tartu College, on Bloor Street, just across from the infamous Rochedale College) to retrieve his car. He delivered me to my front door at New College.

The policy of the residence was that first-year students shared a room.

Sharing allowed time to adjust to the new city and prevented total isolation during the year. Our room was relatively spacious and overlooked the quad, facing the women's wing. My early arrival on a holiday weekend meant that I spent the next few days in relative isolation. Only a handful of students had taken residence. I got my first choice of accommodation and began to establish myself in place. I realized that I lacked a face cloth, soap and a few other toiletries. Thus went my initiation to independence and institutional living.

I felt a bit of homesickness the following day, breakfasting in the cafeteria. I was one of three or four people there. I ventured out to remedy my forgotten toiletries and to familiarize myself with the neighborhood. Many pedestrians populated the streets. I was a city boy, but still experienced culture shock at the greater population density.

Shortly, students began to show up as the resumption of classes loomed. My roommate, Pete, arrived, and we introduced ourselves. He was a country boy from the London area. Initially, we got along well, but Pete's commitment to the course waned as time passed. Undoubtedly, my habit of binge drinking to the point of illness every Friday night wasn't endearing, contributing to his disillusionment. In addition, I had more healthy finances that allowed me a wider range of entertainment opportunities. At first, though, we were both excited to embark on a new path.

In preparation for initiation, we received a list of things needed for the actual activity and other ice-breaking assignments. On the actual initiation night, we were led to various locations on campus and chanted under windows, asking to get wet. Our requests brought buckets of water raining down on us.

Many remarkable things occurred in residence (two years at New College and one at Tartu College). Gerald had a motorcycle and transported it to our floor, using the elevator, and cleaned it in the shower room. I have a photo showing a group of guys gathered around him and the bike.

Some of the guys grew their own marijuana. You could always tell when they were harvesting because they tied their produce in pillowcases and dried the plants in the laundry room dryers. The tell-tale scent permeated the whole wing. Often, the halls were full of students sitting on the floor playing cards or board games, while one end of the hallway, a brick wall, served as a perfect goal net for ball hockey. I was a pretty good goaltender. It made studying in your room difficult, however, because of the many distractions. Around exam times, many of us chose to study in the libraries.

One night, while I was out, Pete, with the rest of Bolton House, decided to rearrange my side of the room. They stapled my class notes together, put staples in my shower towel, removed the base of my bed (leaving just the metal frame), and short-sheeted the mattress. They put a condom filled with shaving cream into my closet. Most of their jokes failed because I had previous experience with initiation in the factory and knew something was up.

Bolton House ordered custom-made navy and gold hockey jerseys as a sign of solidarity. I bought one. The front was emblazoned with Bolton in navy blue block letters. On the back, it had your chosen number and a smaller Bolton across the shoulders. I took the number 00. Joe also wanted 00, but I claimed it first. Because of that, Joe nicknamed me the Big Zip. In view of the fact that he had wanted 00 also, you can figure out his motive.

Joe and his roommate, Gerald, were responsible for another of my nicknames. Joe and I were in the same Math tutorial and sat together when Debbie arrived. She was wearing calf-high leather boots and a mini-skirt. When I saw her, I said, "I gotta get a date with those legs." For whatever reason, whether in harmless fun or ridicule, Joe and Gerald started calling me "Stud" after that.

Joe and Gerald ensured that the Stud nickname got widely disseminated. I was often hailed with it, from blocks away or in pubs as I entered by people I didn't even know. Even now, some fellow graduates refer to me as "Stud."

At a work gathering a couple of years after graduation, a rowdy group started stomping, clapping their hands and chanting, "Stud! Stud! Stud!" to get me to acknowledge the moniker. Debbie, now my wife, sat with a Mona Lisa smile at the bar and was asked if she knew who the mystery man was. She just said yes but didn't reveal my identity. When I appeared, the crowd cheered, and the woman beside Debbie asked, disappointed, "It's not him, is it?"

We often amused ourselves playing ball hockey on the front plaza of the Lash Miller Chemical building across from New College. More often, we practiced shots against the brick wall on our floor in the res. One night, we went to Nathan Phillips Square to play on the ice. The guys convinced me to play goalie against my protestations about not skating. As I said, with ball hockey on paved surfaces, I was pretty good in goal. I was doing fine until the last play of the game. The score was even, but I faced a breakaway. I moved out to cut the angle. My opponent took a weak, bouncing shot. I swiped at it and missed. Scrambling to try to knock it aside, I swiped again and missed.

Some of our pranks would have resulted in charges anywhere else but on campus. One Christmas season, a rogue group dragged the hundred-foot Christmas tree from Queen's Park back to the residence. Once outside the residence, they cut the top six feet off and brought it in to decorate. The authorities had no trouble following the drag marks back to New College, but I never heard about any charges being filed. Perhaps there wasn't a floor-to-floor search?

I learned things in university outside of the classroom. When meeting people for the first time, it is customary to want to make a good impression. I wanted to present myself as I wished it had been, not as it was. Although I played pickup football in high school I implied that I played at the varsity level to match my fantasy. I forgot that there were two witnesses at New College who might refute my story. The lies I told came back to bite me when a Bolton House resident, who had been quarterback on his high school varsity team, threw a bullet pass directly into my hands. The ball rebounded off my stinging hands as he turned away smugly.

I also discovered that sometimes our game was not what it appeared to be. During a pickup football game, with members of each gender interspersed among the teams, I kept breaking up passing plays. The intended receiver was a girl named Darcy. After my fourth successful block, one of the larger guys on *my* team (who outweighed me by about thirty pounds) grabbed me by the collar and snarled, "Let Darcy catch the ball. The game we were playing wasn't football as much as it was an opportunity to grab girls. All subsequent plays with Darcy as the intended receiver got completed.

One of the first things to adjust to is acceptance of being average. In university, exams are set to test student's general knowledge and the ability to apply it. I remember a chemistry exam where I could only answer half of the questions. The class average for that exam was forty percent, but my final mark was reported as a higher passing grade after adjustment to fit the normal curve. I wondered how this was useful. It seemed wrong to make such adjustments. My engineer friends were going through the same thing, so I altered my thinking.

Another thing I learned about was confirmation bias. I declared my candidacy during the election for class president. My friends encouraged me and told me I'd win.

Unfortunately, I went down in defeat. I learned to poll a broader sample of opinions and realized I was still misreading cues.

I learned that people misrepresented themselves. I met Sarge with a group of friends, who presented him as someone who had the inside track. After the meeting, I had the impression that Sarge was an agent provocateur, planted to ferret out would-be troublemakers. I was not an agitator, so I never went there again. Another time, as I made my way to early morning classes, I was approached by a stranger carrying a sizable paper grocery bag. He asked me if I wanted to buy some "grass?" I wondered if I could look at it, so he opened the bag, and the contents appeared to be sweepings from someone's newly mowed lawn. Upon seeing that, I politely thanked him and moved on. Perhaps the long, flyaway hair, haloing my head like a gone-to-seed dandelion, convinced him I might fall into his net. I felt like I had avoided an undercover sting operation.

Group outings introduced me to a wide variety of pubs and other drinking holes on or near campus, such as the Legion Hall, where the beer was a dollar a glass. The Brunswick Hotel, within walking distance of the residence, offered a choice; the upstairs bar featured jazz groups, such as the Downchild Blues Band and the Climax Jazz Band. You could opt for the lower environs, where watered-down, cheap jugs of beer were served and it was always open mike night. Local talent performed renditions of "Oklahoma" alongside "I've got a Lovely Bunch of Coconuts."

I attended my share of fraternity parties and other gatherings. Although this example was not the only time words got exchanged, it was notable as it came to blows. It was a gathering of classmates. One of the guys there habitually called me an asshole for reasons still unclear to me. I had stepped onto the balcony for a bit of air, and on return to the interior, my glasses fogged up. I took them off I've got to wipe the fog off my glasses."

" Don said, "You fog off, Landgraff."

"You fog off, too, Donny."

At that point, Duke grabbed the front of my sweater and the shirt beneath it, twisted them in his fist and jerked down, stretching the threads of my favorite sweater. I responded in kind. Shoving his face closer to mine, he threatened,

"Apologize."

"Why?"

"Tell Donny you're a f--king a--hole."

I was not going to be forced to tell anyone that without objection, and I realized that the only thing a guy like Duke would understand was my fist. Following my brother Mike's mantra to "Strike first and hard," I punched him in the face; he responded in kind. Donny jumped between us to push us apart. I stopped immediately. I usually prided myself on avoiding violence. Duke was determined to have the last word. Striking over Donny's shoulder, he hit me in the left eye, driving my glasses into my cheek. Only then was Donny successful in tearing us apart. I swung my arm over Duke's shoulder and proclaimed to everyone, "Look what my good friend did to me!" Donny and Duke left the party shortly after that.

A few days later, Donny revisited the altercation, saying that I had ripped Duke's favorite shirt. Thinking about my inability to avoid the violence, I said,

"I'd rather not talk about this. I'm not too proud of my performance." "Yeah, Duke would have killed you. He's the goon on our hockey team." "No. I mean to say, I should have been able to stop the violence."

Donny never understood that I wasn't concerned about appearing weak because Duke gave me a black eye. I was upset about being backed into a corner where the only solution was violence. I later learned the reason for Donny's attitude leading to his dislike for me. Donny was gay. I had repeated some anti-gay jokes that were acceptable in general then.

Another thing I learned in the labs was that, just as in the factory, accidents happen. During one experiment in the Chem lab, we were using a weak acid solution. You took the solution from a large glass container, about the size of a beer keg, near the front of the lab. While I was getting my allotment, the glass spigot, which was secured in place by some rusty-looking wire, came away in my hand, dousing me. What to do? The stuff was spilling all over. I shoved the spigot into place, then ran to the closest sink and rinsed my hands for a while. After I assured myself that I had successfully cleared away the solution, I got the lab instructor and told him what had happened. He said that I had acted appropriately and went to deal with the faulty equipment.

In third year, I encountered some bad teaching assistants (TAs). One of the Biochemistry TAs that I approached by phone for help said to come over to his lab. When I got there and explained my issue, he got angry saying, "This is basic math! You're interrupting my lab time for this?" It reawakened memories of a certain former math teacher. He showed me the solution to my problem, but I felt that his flash of attitude marked a failure on his part. He was paid to help students, not to make them feel small.

About a month later, I arrived a half hour late for a pharmacology exam. The Biochemistry TA was invigilating. When I arrived, just before entrance would be denied, he gave me a toothy, Big Bad Wolf smile and let me in. My mind was in overdrive. Late for the three-hour exam, I flew through the questions, answering them without hesitation. I left before the three-hour time limit, along with the majority of my classmates. After the exam, the TA/invigilator approached again with a big smile on his face, asking, "How do you think you did?" I replied that I'd get either an A or a B. His smile disappeared and my prediction proved true.

In our graduation year, the Faculty of Pharmacy held an open house. I volunteered to be a test subject in a demonstration of how much drugs and alcohol affect an impaired driver. One hour before testing, subjects were administered a five-milligram dose of Valium and a shot of Canadian Club rye whiskey. Under simulated driving conditions, the subject's reaction times after seeing a red traffic light were measured. We first tested the subjects before and after drug and alcohol administration. Every other subject showed an impaired reaction time. My reflexes improved. My anomalous result indicated that I was so uptight under normal circumstances that I performed better after a depressant.

I had a habit of weekend binge drinking to relieve pressure kept me on an even keel. I recalled one particularly trying week when I headed out thinking, "I'll show them, I'll get drunk." Immediately the contrasting thought, "Who would that show anything, and who would it hurt?" came into my mind. It felt like a message sent from outside myself. I took note and drank moderately that night. The possibility of a guardian angel or guiding presence is presented for serious consideration.

23

Toronto Continued

In my second year in Toronto, I continued to reside at New College. I returned with mixed feelings. I was excited to renew acquaintances formed in the first year, especially with Joe. I returned ahead of the crowd the same as in the previous year and felt the same sense of relative isolation. Anticipatory stirrings enveloped me as I waited for friends to arrive. I placed a high value on the ties with Joe, but when he arrived, he was distant and ghosted me, obviously not valuing our friendship in the same manner.

The first year had been challenging, but I resolved to do better. It meant buckling down and learning to be more time-efficient. It also meant that my long-distance relationship with Mona continued to suffer. At Thanksgiving, she followed the adage of "Dump the Turkey" and told me that she was leaving me for greener pastures. I was devastated. Over that Thanksgiving weekend, I begged her not to leave me, buying her flowers and gifts to prove my devotion. She maintained a hard line, refusing to waver.

I stayed with Mom for the weekend in the apartment she shared with Theo, her second husband. They had a small Bonair trailer in the parking lot, where I disappeared for privacy. I spent three hours there weeping inconsolably. It was the most heartrending experience I've ever endured. Usually, I ended the relationship, so this was a new experience for me. I was committed to marrying Mona after graduation. She didn't want to wait that long.

I composed the following song after she duped me.

Rock My Soul

Rock my soul to the depths of hell,
Don't know for sure, but it could be my death knell.
Hit me hard what you said last night.
Told me you wanted me out of your life.

Oh, I feel like I'm dying,
I'm feeling so cold.
The heat of our love's gone,
And I'm so alone.
Thought we had a love so true.
But that hope is gone now, all cause of you.
Wanted to ask you to be my wife.
Thought I could give you a perfect life.

How could you do it?
You cut me so deep.

I'm hurtin' so badly,
I can't even sleep.

Who's that guy you've seen on the sly?
While I was at work so we could get by.
Couldn't you wait 'till I had things set?
You don't even know if we'd make it yet.

Oh, I feel like I'm dying,
I'm feeling so cold.
The heat of our love's gone,
And I'm so alone.

Told you I loved you, and I've been so true,
Too bad I can't say the same about you.
Had it been diff'rent, I'd have none of this strife.
Guess I'd just better get on with my life.

How could you do it?
You cut me so deep.
I'm hurtin' so badly,
I can't even eat.

Rock my soul to the depths of hell,
Don't know for sure, but it could be my death knell.
Hit me hard what you said last night.
Told me you wanted me out of your life.

Oh, I feel like I'm dying,
I'm feeling so cold.
The heat of our love's gone,
And I'm so alone.

Things'll be diff'rent now that I'm free.
I don't need you, if you don't need me.
I'll find me another, and happy we'll be
Find me a woman who'll appreciate me.

How could you do it?
You cut me so deep.
I'm hurtin' so badly,
I can't even weep.

I wanted our relationship to continue, so I went a little too
far to demonstrate my desire for and commitment to Mona. We
had sex using the pull-out method. Until then, we had limited
ourselves to deep kisses and mutual, manual and oral
stimulation.

Mona called me a month later to tell me she thought she was pregnant. I had an anxiety attack. I was short of money then and hadn't planned to return home until Christmas. I needed to *do* something. I called every adviser known to me. They were all unavailable. I went to the Don of our house and asked to borrow money for a train ticket, but he was as broke as I was. Finally, in full panic mode, I went to the Newman Centre, the Catholic church on campus, and asked to see an adviser. He lent me the money to travel, and I took the train to Windsor.

When I arrived at Mona's door, we embraced, and she hung tightly around my neck. She said, "I got my period today." The weight lifted from my shoulders.

Possibly, the close call raised Mona's expectation of a proposal, but I couldn't see a way to make it work. I didn't have the money to support a family yet. After that, Mona continued with her resolve to cut me out of her life.

****

In my first year, I accompanied Debbie to several social outings: an event at Ontario Place, a couple of pub functions and to see the movie Nicholas and Alexandra. It was a three-hour movie, and we had to leave before it ended to abide by the curfew set by Debbie's mother. Debbie had skipped a grade and was only seventeen. As we left the movie, I held her hand and briefly thought, "I could leave Mona for her." I told her about my arrangement with Mona for the sake of full disclosure. She felt I was a player who wanted a girl in every port, so she kept her distance.

At the entrance to one lecture, she spoke to a guy she had known in primary school. Possessively, I asked, "Are you coming in?" She replied, "I'm talking to Albert!" I went in alone, fuming and thinking, "She's talking to ALLLLbert!" Another time, with the other couple in tow, I asked if Debbie would complete a bowling foursome. Debbie accepted but later told me she felt pressured into it. She only went so I wouldn't be embarrassed in front of my friends." After that, we parted ways.

After my relationship with Mona ended, I started seeing Veronica, one of Mona's friends, whenever I was in Windsor. I accompanied her on babysitting jobs, where we necked and "dry humped" after the kids got put to bed. I enjoyed the heat we generated. She was pretty, but her habit of frequently changing the color of her hair put me off. I never knew what she would look like from one date to the next. She wasn't Miss Right, only Miss Right For Now.

Mona kept sending me confusing signals, leading me to believe we still had a chance. After Christmas break, she called around midnight from the Royal York Hotel. She and Veronica were in Toronto. She invited me to come over with a friend for drinks.

I went down the hall to Jack's room and knocked. Jack was already in bed; I may have awakened him. I said, "Get dressed, we're going out." He wanted to know more before committing to the venture.

He accompanied me to the Royal York and we spent the night with the girls: me with Mona, Jack with Veronica. No one slept or shed clothes, but we spent the night necking. At six a.m., Jack and I left the hotel to return to New College. Jack exclaimed that he had never had a stranger floss his tonsils with her tongue like that before. He enthused, "I'm gonna write a book about you one day."

****

An allocated portion of our fees was paid for access to the gym facilities at Hart House. I regularly worked out with weights and circuit training. Access to other events was provided in the same way. I attended three of four lessons in alpine skiing at Horseshoe Valley Ski Resort in Barrie. I was informed about them by John, a classmate and resident at New College. He said the second week's lesson was approaching and asked if I wanted to go with him. I wondered about being behind, having missed the first lesson. He said it would be okay. When we got there and were kitted up (all equipment provided), I ventured out to the tow ropes.

It was my first time on skis. I followed John's example, and we finally got to the top of the bunny trail to await the start of the lesson. As we gathered around the instructor, I accidentally slid backward down the hill. Calling on instincts honed by gymnastics, I leaned forward, planting my right ski pole in line with my center of gravity and pushed off. Simultaneously, I flipped around on my skis. After shuffling back to the group, I set my skis perpendicular to the slope to prevent another unintended slide. I asked the instructor if missing the first lesson would hinder me in the following three classes. She said, "If you can do what you just did, without previous training, you'll do fine." I received a certificate of completion with all of the other skiers, the same as those who had taken the full course.

John got me involved with Judo lessons, too. John thought we would be partnered for the lesson, but I was bigger and heavier, so I got paired with a bruiser. He outweighed me by twenty pounds. We were the two bulkiest guys attending and the group's best match for weight. His first statement was that he studied Aikido and knew six different methods to kill me. That, plus the cost of the required judo gi, put me off. I never went again.

Before the end of the second year, John asked me to share an apartment with him in the third year. In early August, John called me and alerted me that we needed to go apartment hunting in Toronto. I assumed we had lots of time for that, but John made me realize how foolish that was. I took a weekend to an apartment hunt with him, and we found a place on Spadina. When we moved in, I could see Casa Loma from my bedroom window. I ignored the landmark, only blocks away, until I revisited Toronto as a tourist. John got into his first year of med school under an early admission program. I progressed to my third year in pharmacy.

During that year, I visited Windsor twice. On the return trip, after Thanksgiving weekend, the train stopped in London to pick up more Toronto-bound passengers. I took the opportunity to visit the lavatory during the stopover. Upon my return, my former spot was occupied, there being no fixed seating arrangement. I looked around for another spot. There were two available. Either choice placed me beside female passengers. I thought it was either there or there and chose a seat.

During the trip, I noticed that the woman beside me was an attractive blond with an incredible figure, wearing a scarlet clingy sweater. She had a rosy complexion, green eyes and freckles across her nose and cheeks. We talked, and she told me she was returning from visiting her boyfriend at Western. She fell asleep, and I took the risky chance of adjusting my position, just on the verge of crowding her. When she awoke, she asked me if she was crowding me. I answered negatively, thinking my gambit was discovered and I'd be accused of invading her private space. I wondered aloud whether I was crowding her. She said no, so I didn't move. Later, we were holding hands. As we disembarked in Toronto, I got her contact number, and we parted ways. Unsure of the advisability of further contact, I waited three weeks before calling her. When she answered the call, she said, "I never thought I'd hear from you again, but she agreed to meet. That was how Lena and I started our year-and-a-half-long romance.

Her parents liked me because I called her Dad sir upon our first meeting. I often visited and took meals with them. Once, Lena's Mom served dessert asking her husband, "What do you want Dumbo?" He replied, "Apple pie with ice cream". She then turned to me, asking, "What's your pleasure, sir?" I replied, "I'll have what Dumbo's having." We all laughed, and I felt accepted as part of the family.

When Lena acquired an inner ear infection, causing her to lose her balance, I carried her to her downstairs bedroom. She encircled my neck with her arms and placed her head against my chest, closing her eyes as we descended. She later told me that this romantic gesture made her fall in love with me.

At the end of my third year, John told me he couldn't stay in the apartment and set his departure date. We had to find someone to take the sublet on the apartment soon because I couldn't handle the rent alone. I wanted to stay in Toronto because of my relationship with Lena. I had yet to get an apprenticeship placement, but funds were depleting rapidly. As an apprentice, I would no longer enjoy the union wages of factory employment. I wasn't sure that my earnings would be sufficient for me to remain in Toronto.

Luckily, we found someone to take over our lease, just as a vacancy at Tartu College opened in the suite where Jack, Randall and a couple of other guys I knew from New College lived. I found an apprenticeship placement in Etobicoke, an hour away by bus and subway. I almost lost that position with demands for a dollar more an hour than was offered, needed to afford rent in Toronto. A classmate knew the owner and vouched for me, and I was hired. Finally, I had long-term accommodation, an apprenticeship position, and the semblance of a life for the foreseeable future.

Lena occasionally had access to a car, which made things somewhat bearable.

She lived in Scarborough, so our dates got arranged around bus and subway schedules when the car was unavailable. We saw each other regularly, and she picked me up from work several times. We presented as a young married couple, a misconception I didn't correct because it was in line with my fantasy. When I moved out of the apartment on Spadina, the building manager assumed the move was triggered by a marital breakup and told Lena to "Take him for all he's worth!"

Lena and I enjoyed an active life and spent as much time together as possible.

She was a gymnast, planning to attend Queen's to get a Human Kinetics degree. She picked up occasional jobs, refereeing basketball games, and I accompanied her. We also spent time with her family. Her family rented a cottage for the weekend, and I was invited along. Another time, her family was away, but Lena had to work. I spent that week at her house. We were careless, and her mother found telltale evidence. She kept our secret because Lena's Dad wouldn't be as forgiving. She issued the usual warnings about avoiding pregnancy, citing her sister's past unplanned pregnancy. I became comfortable with hopes of a long-term future with Lena.

There were indications that we might be heading for trouble. Lena stubbornly held opinions in variance from mine. Regardless of the evidence presented, she doggedly maintained her views, causing more than one argument. At the end of that summer in Toronto, John invited me to go camping in Algonquin Park with him. He had been there with the Scouts before and had utterly enjoyed it. We were going to canoe through Rock Lake to a portage, then carry on to Penn Lake. Assumptions about skills occurred on the part of both parties. John assumed that I could swim and drive and had experience with orienteering since he had acquired those skills when he was in high school. I took it for granted that he was an accomplished woodsman.

I had only been camping and canoeing once. My camp-out had been in a flat landlocked field for one weekend. My canoeing experience was limited to one outing in a rented canoe. My paddling expertise was rudimentary. I had no experience with the J stroke, had never portaged and didn't drive because Mom and I lacked a car.

John and I got a late start. We arrived on the shores of Rock Lake around seven in the evening. I thought John would camp in the tourist campground, as it was getting dusky, but he wanted to push on. I had yet to learn our destination or how far away it was. The lake was serene, and there was a full moon. These were beautiful conditions for our purposes.

Neither of us wore flotation devices. We set off like the Courier de Bois of old. I took the canoe's bow, and John was aft because he knew how to do the J stroke. I watched for submerged rocks and logs or deadheads, as John referred to them. I kept a steady rhythm, dipping deeply with each stroke. At about midnight, we reached the portage site. We were lucky to make it there without incident. John suggested we continue to the quarter-mile portage. I insisted on camping and would go no further until morning. John reluctantly agreed. We pitched a tent on the rocky ground and slept fitfully.

We covered the portage quickly the following day and arrived at our insertion point into Lake Penn. Looking around, I saw many deadheads and submerged rocks. I was thankful that my guardian angel put the right words into my mouth the previous night. After another couple of hours of paddling, we arrived at our destination. We pitched camp and enjoyed the outdoor playground we would inhabit over the next few days. John jumped into the frigid waters of Lake Penn, and I followed him, doggy paddling around near the shore. It was only then that John realized I was a non-swimmer. He continued to request my company on further outings, so it mustn't have weighed heavily on his mind.

Over the next few days, I got more familiar with "all things camping in the wild." Having missed the scouting experience, I lacked skills that may be assumed for a guy of a certain age. The concept that food must be stored off the ground hoisted over a tree limb, to avoid drawing wildlife into the area made sense. Suspending food stashes in the trees made it harder for animals, especially bears, to reach the supplies. John vetoed insect repellent because he claimed that the fish smelled it and wouldn't bite. Instead, we went without and were swarmed by black flies. A deer fly bit John behind the ear, drawing blood. Our catch consisted of one out-of-season large-mouth bass, which we released.

After three days in the wild, we prepared to return to civilization. During that trip, I fantasized as I paddled, imagining a dramatic drum beat in time with each stroke. When we reached the car, I had a three-day stubble and salt-encrusted sweaty armpits. I felt grungy and wished for nothing more than a warm shower.

On return to the city, after satisfying my need for refreshment, I went to visit Gianni and his wife. Once there, I borrowed Gianni's ten-speed to run an errand. Windsor has a flat prairie terrain, which limited my proficiency with handbrakes. As I rode Gianni's bike, I placed my hands in ready position on the front and rear brakes; I hit a lump of asphalt left from construction. By reflex, I tightened both brakes on impact, locking the front tire and throwing me over the handlebars. I dove face-first into the pavement. I remember trying to prevent the accident by adjusting my weight, but sadly, it was too late. I heard a kid yell, "What a wipeout!" as I became airborne. I protected my head with my hands and arms.

When I contacted the pavement, the force got transmitted through my right forearm, causing a fractured elbow. I also sustained a patch of road rash, about the size of a quarter, on my right inner wrist. I rose and remounted the bike, not realizing that my elbow was fractured. When I tried to lift the bike to carry it up the steps at Tartu College, the immediate stabbing pain caused me to drop the bike. Not understanding why, I tried again to lift the bike with the same result. I headed to the hospital for damage assessment. I was advised to keep my arm in a sling for about three weeks. The area of road rash healed without incident but remained a bright pink for a long time.

Lena and I continued our relationship, and I began to think more about our future. She started at Queen's and would enter her second year as I graduated. After that, only a four-month apprenticeship and the Board Exams stood between me and my license. It was said that if you got to the fourth year, you had it made, but that was not a given.

With a view to our future, I began to fantasize about married life with Lena while she worked through her HumKin degree. I'd get an internship, and we'd live in the married students' housing. As the saying goes, man plans; God laughs. I was totally into this imagined future, but it didn't come to pass.

Lena slapped my face in a mall, in the presence of friends, imitating her female companion who had just hit her boyfriend. I was not impressed and hit Lena back, misunderstanding that perhaps the action was meant to be a love tap. I didn't give it much thought beyond that, but Lena must have.

When Lena took residence at Queen's, she began to change. Queen's and U of T have a longstanding rivalry on the football field. At the Homecoming game, which traditionally pitted Queens against U of T, I assumed that we would sit in the U of T section for the game. Lena wanted to sit in the Queen's section to share her school spirit. I complied.

I tried to call her early on a Saturday morning close to Thanksgiving. Her roommate said she was out. I called again about two hours later, and Lena still wasn't in. On the third call, several hours later, her roommate expressed annoyance with my "constant badgering." When Lena returned my call about four hours later, she angrily asked what was so urgent. I was stunned by this reaction because I thought she would know I was thinking of her and missed her. She continued, "And don't expect to be invited to Thanksgiving dinner."

Once again, I was the victim of "Dump the Turkey." This time, I reacted differently than I had with Mona. Perhaps the memory of that heartbreak was still fresh, I don't know. I got off the phone thinking, "I might as well go visit Mom and Theo then. I packed and caught the train to Windsor that night. The next day, when Lena called to reverse her decision about Thanksgiving dinner, Randall took the call and said, "He's gone home to Windsor." After that, I had no contact with Lena. Alone again.

Anguish

Crucify me now,
For what I did a couple of years ago.
I ain't nobody's saint,
I didn't know how to go.

I never took a vow
To be true to you, alone.
And that picture that you paint
Just doesn't say it all.

24

Debbie and other Driving Issues

After our dalliance in the first year, Debbie faded in importance. We dated at least once in each subsequent year before graduation, and I interacted with her like any other classmate. She had a steady boyfriend for a while, and I developed other fledgling romances that fizzled out.

There was a beautiful redhead that I pursued through the closing months of grad year. The logistics of graduation, relocation, studying for Board exams and doing internship reports caused me to "ghost her" unintentionally. With all that was happening, I failed to call her until three weeks after I moved for my internship placement. Her father had been a long-distance trucker who left her mother, so she feared I was just like him and dumped me. Yet another romance died in its tracks.

My internship placement was about an hour's drive from Windsor. I accepted the position, planning to purchase the business upon my licensure. I misinterpreted the situation, assuming that the offer to purchase had only been extended to me. I subsequently found the store was already on the market and might get sold before I got licensed. I felt betrayed and left as soon as I was certified. That was shortsighted. Nothing had prevented my making an offer to purchase, and no betrayal had occurred.

The distance from Windsor was an issue for several reasons. I didn't have a car, so I was limited to public transportation. In the past, the lack of a family vehicle held me back. Now, with a steady income, I could change that. I arranged for three driving lessons and set about becoming mobile. After completing the lessons, my instructor deemed me ready to take the test. Graduated licensing had not been introduced then, so trying after this short interval was conceivable. Because the test center was in Leamington, a relatively small town with less traffic than Windsor, my chances of passing were maximized. I passed on my first attempt. The next hurdle was to buy a car.

I shopped, with Mike advising me by phone. I was leaning toward purchasing a Chevy Nova when Mike drove out to chauffeur me to dealerships. He made advance inquiries and had found a good deal for a Mercury Monarch in Leamington. Initially, I was not too fond of that option, but Mike pointed out that Dad had worked at Ford Motor Company for thirty years before his death. With that, we set off to test drive some cars. I was still leaning toward the Chevy, but Mike finally convinced me to get the Mercury.

As a novice, I let Mike be my spokesman at the dealership. The deal made, I was the proud owner of a new 1976 Mercury Monarch with a V8 engine, automatic transmission, AM radio, and aftermarket-installed AC. The package, priced at just over five thousand dollars, was available for pick up in a week. The next task was to arrange insurance before the delivery date. Mike said something about requiring PLPD in the policy. I said,

"What is that?" I was uneducated about auto ownership and its complexities.

I made arrangements for my drop-off to pick up my new car. It was the first time I drove alone. The dealership, on Highway Three, a two-lane throughway, required merging into fast-moving traffic on departure. As I waited for an opening with the brake engaged, my foot shook like I had palsy. My first solo trip to Windsor was also harrowing. The reality of a driver's responsibility hung heavily on my shoulders. Although I had no accidents in the first year and a half, I drove aggressively and pulled many risky maneuvers.

After my internship, I found employment in Windsor. I continued with fumbled attempts to form a romantic connection. I was interested in a technician there who egged me on, using me to create jealousy in her actual quarry. I liked another technician in our bowling league, but she had a boyfriend. I drove her home after bowling, and she invited me over for dinner, giving me hope of success in the long run. It might also be a gambit to keep me interested in case her other relationship fell through.

To add a further layer of complexity, Mona reappeared. I had thought that possibility was a dead issue long cold, but she knocked on my apartment door one afternoon. I didn't think Mona even knew where I lived. I was shocked when I answered the door and encountered her, framed at the door, in a tube top and short shorts that she knew I would appreciate. I immediately responded to the sight of her well-shaped legs and invited her in. She claimed that she just intended to show me her new car. It was a Ford, probably provided by her fiance, since he was an engineer employed there. I test-drove it. Then we parted after she invited me to drop by her place anytime. When I did show up at her home unexpectedly, she said, "Are you trying to break up my engagement?" Not sure of her intent, I replied, "I know I could if I wanted to, but I don't want to," and left, never to see her again.

Still single, I made plans to visit Steve in Stroud since I would be in the area. I also arranged to meet Debbie for dinner in Toronto, where she was doing a residency at Women's College Hospital. In a discussion about the current state of our lives, Steve and I spoke of the difficulty of making connections after formal education ended. I mentioned the upcoming date with Debbie, and Steve suggested that I might reignite that relationship. I said, "Are you kidding? She's frigid. She keeps telling me to get lost." Six months later, we were engaged.

Leading up to the engagement, Debbie and I burned up the telephone lines. Our combined monthly phone expenses were about three hundred dollars. We engaged in long conversations. When she came to Windsor to visit, I took her to dinners, indulging in lavish meals, including Caesar salad, made at the table side with fresh eggs, pressed garlic, and tossed in front of you before being served. For dessert, we had Cherries Jubilee, also prepared at the table side, and specialty coffees afterward. Once, I bought her a dress to wear on one of these outings. She remembers warmly the dinner at Sir William's, where I said she had a beautiful smile. When she went back to Toronto, I slipped into a feeling of loss.

Being practical, I asked Debbie, "If I get you an engagement ring for Christmas, will you accept it?" She breathlessly answered, "Yesss." Now knowing that my offer wouldn't be rejected, I prepared to make it official during the Christmas season. I debated whether to purchase the ring ahead of the proposal or whether to wait and involve Debbie in the selection. I thought that she would be more pleased to select the ring together, so I got her a token Christmas gift to put under the tree, thinking we'd buy the ring after that. She couldn't keep quiet and told all her colleagues at work that I was getting her an engagement ring for Christmas. She was not impressed by the framed Impressionist print I gave her as a token at Christmas, feeling that I had reneged on my promise. The day after New Year's, I said, "So do you want to shop for rings today?" Off we went to make it official.

My first accident occurred in January 1978, after a ski vacation. Debbie and I had just pledged our troth. Unexpected events extended my homeward-bound trip as my holiday wrapped up. With Jack taking his turn behind the wheel and the vehicle full of passengers and their luggage, he hit a concealed deep pothole. We were going through Marmora, Ontario, and it was raining heavily. Rainwater filled and hid the crater. Hitting it caused a blowout and bent the wheel rim. We emptied the trunk at the roadside to access the spare, changed the tire and repacked. Then, we located a restaurant to fill our growling stomachs. The meal was so filling that I declared we were "pigging out in Marmora," eliciting general agreement and laughter.

We continued to Toronto after that, and I couch-surfed at Debbie's overnight. Because I no longer had a viable spare, I arranged a one-day extension to my vacation. I made an appointment to purchase a new tire rim and get a front-end alignment at Canadian Tire for the following Monday, planning to return to Windsor on Tuesday.

Tuesday morning, I awoke to a blizzard. I was concerned about the weather and tried to check road conditions with the CAA. After multiple unsuccessful attempts to connect, I should have concluded that the volume of calls indicated hazardous roads. Still, I was concerned about the reaction if I called work to request a further extension. I decided to set out and brave the storm.

It was my first time driving in whiteout conditions, which I call white- knuckle driving. The crosswinds whipped snow into a white screen, limiting visibility to a meter. I was tense when, suddenly, visibility improved immensely. My relief was tangible. My limited winter driving experience made me overconfident, and I made no weather-appropriate adjustments. I imagined the snowflakes crossing my windshield represented tracer bullets. I was flying a critical mission over enemy territory (in keeping with my childhood wish to be a fighter pilot). Traffic proceeded slowly. I accelerated, passing others, determined to exploit the improved visibility. The trip home took four hours in good condition. I was approaching Kitchener on the westbound 401. The road was clear, and visibility was good as I mounted a rise. Posts and cables lined the side of the highway to prevent rollovers to the surrounding lowland.

Suddenly, I hit a patch of black ice. As I skidded toward the median, time slowed, and the following sequence unfolded in what seemed to take five minutes. I turned into the skid as taught but kept skidding toward the median. Assuming I overcompensated and hoping to prevent more severe outcomes, I executed a hard right. The car went into a slide perpendicularly across the two westbound lanes.

Next, I made a hard left to correct that move, propelling me into the roadside barrier. The front left quarter panel crumpled on impact, and the car swung one hundred and eighty degrees. My momentum spent, I sat uninjured, thanks to seat belts.

I listened to the engine, which wheezed like an asthmatic. It didn't sound good, so I turned the car off. I restarted the vehicle, hoping for better results. The engine sputtered but did not regain life. I got out to assess the damage. At the front of the car, I saw that the radiator had been displaced and moved about a foot back into the engine compartment. Most of the grille got ripped off at impact. The road was strewn with fractured car parts and one headlight, ripped from its socket, lying about twenty feet away. Circling the car, I noticed the smashed left brake light. I lamented my stricken vehicle, less than a year and a half old.

I now thought about getting to a phone. I flagged down the first car that approached and asked for a ride to the service station at the next exit. The guy who stopped for me was one whom I'd passed earlier. Given the weather, he felt compelled to comment on my recklessness. I bit my tongue, remaining silent. I was well aware of cause and effect. Thank you!

Anyway, I called the police from the service station, connected with Rod to come and get me, and put me up until I could arrange a way home. I called work to arrange a further extension to my vacation, got lectured by the police (who tracked my car down), alerted the insurance company and got a bus ticket home. I felt the presence of my guardian angel, who had come through for me again.

The accident yielded further lessons. The insurance company and the police told me I should have remained with the car rather than trying to access a phone. The snowplow operator, hindered from his task by my abandoned vehicle, alerted a towing company for removal. No one knew the vehicle's location yet, and I got billed for the towing costs.

Shortly after the return of my car, a kid threw a snowball that landed right at the center of my vision on the windshield, startling me. I immediately gave chase; the culprit remained close by. Shifting into reverse, wheels churning, I caught up to him and jumped from the car. Grabbing his lapels, I prepared to tell him he could have caused an accident with that stunt. He struggled to free himself and almost succeeded. He slipped from my left hand, sliding and almost falling in the attempt. My right hand held firm; a fall prevented.

Before I could vent verbal abuse upon the kid, a police car, siren wailing, arrived on the scene. The officer detained me and released the kid. During the subsequent discussion, the cop warned me that the kid's parents could sue me for laying my hands on him. He also accused me of throwing the kid to the ground. After I explained everything to his satisfaction, the cop let me go; again, he stressed that I should not repeat that scenario.

I was upset with myself for the rest of the day. It was my first experience with road rage. It wouldn't be the last. To say that I was immune to the effects of people's stupidity, never experiencing an angry response, would be to deny my essential being. Two weeks later, while driving Debbie to an appointment, another kid threw a snowball at my windshield, startling Debbie. She said, "Someone should teach that kid a lesson!" I sagely explained how that could be a bad idea and drove on.

25

Mom Revisited

Mom was a middle-aged widow with a dependent child at Dad's death. The family history and financial burden left her in doubt about the future. There had been little time to build a significant cushion between the last payment of medical expenses and Dad's passing. There was only a small life insurance policy and a ticking clock on survivor benefits from Ford Motor Company. I do not know how much debt remained on the house mortgage or other obligations, nor how much of Dad's pension plan benefits got passed on. I can only say that we ended up on Mother's allowance and continued to reside on Central Avenue. Mom used the house as an income-generating asset by taking in boarders. She took babysitting jobs and eventually found employment as a Personal Support Worker. We did not live a life of luxury.

Mom did all she could to pursue community and government support through the programs available. She approached the Big Brothers Association to procure a male role model for me, which yielded poor outcomes. She joined Parents Without Partners to get social support from others in the same situation. Through Mother's allowance, we had a drug and dental plan. She got as much support from her sons as possible, but most of the weight was borne by me. I felt somewhat abandoned by my siblings and left to fend for myself as best I could.

The third time Mom wanted me to paint the house's interior, I was working at Kelsey Hayes. I said I would pay to have it done, but there was no way I would be saddled with that job again. She grudgingly agreed and hired my cousin, Dennis, and his girlfriend, Chicky, to do the job. During a meal break from painting, Mom, Dennis, Chicky, and I were around the table talking. Mom, speaking about her date the previous night, blurted out enthusiastically, "We had a ball last night." Chicky looked wide-eyed at Dennis, who turned to me, and then we all broke out in giggles. It was the seventies, and in slang terms, balling implied sexual congress. Mom was baffled by this reaction and wanted to know what was going on. I said, "Tell ya later." After Dennis and Chicky left, I explained our amusement and, horrified, Mom exclaimed, "I hope they didn't think that's what I meant." I assured her it wasn't.

After a while, Mom and Theo started to be exclusive. Theo's son Morty hired me for two summers in his factory. Eventually, when I was in my second year at U of T, Mom married Theo. I gained two stepbrothers and a step-sister, but a problem arose when OSAP wanted to know all of Theo's financial information. It might impact my eligibility. He supplied the information for my third year but refused to do so for my fourth year. I understood his viewpoint on the matter. He did not all of a sudden become my Dad. I was of legal age and independent, so why was the government nosing around? In my fourth year, I got cut off from OSAP. I appealed that decision, saying, "If you cut me off, I will starve to death." They reinstated my support.

Once, when Lena and I were visiting Mom and Theo at their new residence in Stoney Creek, my stepbrother, Lenny, and his wife, Krista, happened to drop in. Lenny asked Mom, "Is that Doug's girlfriend?" When Mom replied in the affirmative, Lenny asked, "How long are they staying?" I found out later that Lenny and Krista had a big fight that night after Lenny suggested they revisit Theo the next day (while Lena and I would still be in residence.)

Mom was Theo's third wife. His first wife, the mother of my step-siblings, passed away, but his second wife left him. The second wife tried to warn Mom about Theo, but Mom refused to listen, thinking that wife two was expressing sour grapes. In the long run, Mom should have paid heed. Theo was a closet alcoholic, abusive under the influence. Mom told me about the problem after they moved to Stoney Point. She said she knew trouble was coming whenever she heard the cupboard door open, followed by the scrape of the forty-ounce bottle of whiskey. After two years of verbal abuse, coupled with the isolation of their remote dwelling, Mom gave up. She called Teddy to come and get her. Theo verbally harangued her as she sat for a half hour awaiting her ride. At her departure, he would only allow her to take a suitcase of clothes, and he kept everything else, even common property purchased together. Shortly after she left, he posted a personal classified ad to the effect that he would no longer be responsible for his spouse's debt. Before Mom remarried, she had no trouble getting credit, but after her name change, she could not get credit under either last name. He also cut her off of his drug plan without warning. It caused an outstanding bill for her medications (about six hundred dollars) at the store where I was employed.

Mom moved into a one-bedroom apartment on Brock Street near her sister. In the early portion of her residency there, she seemed to fall back into her comfort zone, exhibiting fierce pride. Once, after a period of absence necessitated by my hectic schedule, She greeted me at her door with, "Oh, it's you; I thought you were dead." I pointed out that her greeting was not welcoming and contrasted it by suggesting she say, "Oh Doug, I'm so glad to see you. It's been a while. Please come in." She seemed to respond to that well and altered her greetings after that.

She remained in her apartment on Brock until she got so ill we thought she was dying. That triggered the drastic action of her moving in with Debbie and me. We joined the ranks of the sandwich generation. There wasn't much consultation with my siblings; it was just assumed I would resume the role as I had when Dad passed on.

Debbie felt unduly pressured and demanded a family meeting. Mike did not get involved, and Teddy was in no position to help, so it fell to Rod and me to work it out. Debbie suggested some changes, like shared custody, but the only thing that changed was that Rod's family and mine took Mom out to Swiss Chalet once a month. Debbie wasn't happy, but I felt it was the best we could hope for.

Eventually, Mom recovered enough to move into another apartment. She was fine for several years, but she developed a fear of living alone and passing away unnoticed. Mom developed panic attacks, accompanied by symptoms of a heart attack, and went to the hospital by ambulance twice weekly. Debbie, disabled by then, spearheaded the search for a nursing home. We found a suitable place in Waterdown. Mom resided there until her death.

Mom was hospitalized about a month before her death with numerous non- diagnostic symptoms. The doctors tried to nail down a diagnosis, but nothing seemed forthcoming. Rod presented himself as the family liaison to the hospital, so information only passed through him. My attempts to get information, advancing questions that would give meaningful data to a medical professional, were stonewalled and referred back to Rod. Rod had done his usual and customary presentation to the doctors, pumping up his image as a self-employed CEO and owner of a company.

Eventually, Rod convinced the doctors that Mom's condition would be the same at the nursing home as in the hospital and had her released.

A week before her death, Mom complained that everything hurt. Even the weight of her covering sheet caused her pain. I looked into her eyes and said, It's okay, Mom, you've done enough; you can let go now." Immediately, her eyes and face transformed from a mask of pain to a beautiful, peaceful glow.

A few days later, a message was left on my answering machine, to call the nursing home ASAP. I thought there might be a problem with the monthly rent check. I called immediately upon receipt of the message but was told that Rod had preempted me again. I had to call him for details. Rod informed me of Mom's passing. Even knowing that she was near the end didn't reduce the shock of the event. In all circumstances, you die alone because no one can accompany you on the final step. It must be taken solo. Mom passed at age eighty-three.

26

Adulting

Song

My song.

A song of my soul.

From deep within my mind it comes

When the world is filled with sun

And brisk air fills my lungs.

Simple song,

When nature, my song, and I

Are one.

After we got engaged, Debbie relocated to Windsor and took a position in my company. We cohabited in a two-bedroom apartment in the Riverside area. We were breaking with tradition, living together before all the legalities were in place, but it was the seventies, and we weren't alone in that. It was a matter of practicality. We married in Toronto at Our Lady of Perpetual Help Church on St. Clair Avenue on September 9, 1978. We would have scheduled it earlier, but Debbie's sister had gotten engaged before her and had planned a June wedding. It got canceled some months before June.

Some people commented about us living in sin, but we ignored them, thinking we were trendsetters and that our mutual commitment was solid. One of our work colleagues, who lived in the apartment block adjacent to ours, unexpectedly knocked on our door to welcome us to the neighborhood. We invited him in. In conversation, he referenced a couple from the surrounding apartment blocks being very loud in the past, the expressions of their passion echoing between the buildings. He said that they were called" Bumper and Thumper." I wasn't sure if this was a subtle reference to us, but there had been instances when our downstairs neighbor banged on their ceiling to induce a decrease in noise from our apartment. One never knows. In any case, Debbie and I started house hunting to ensure more privacy and moved into our first home in Kingsville in January 1979.

The first years of our marriage were the happiest in my life. We were relatively free of responsibility, the only debt being our mortgage. We were both earning well. We had friends in the area. I got a promotion to manager at a store my company had just acquired. We became shareholders in our privately owned company. Things were looking up.

My toxic mother-in-law, Ma-zilla, made her first appearance during the Christmas Season the year after we bought our house in Kingsville. We had invited our neighbors to meet Debbie's parents and share a New Year's toast with us and the in-laws. During that visit, I voiced dissatisfaction with my job. Ma-zilla said, "You have no right to be dissatisfied. You chose your profession. Debbie's father had to take anything he could get." I said that Debbie felt the same way about the job as I did. Ma-zilla asked how I knew that. I replied, "Because she's my wife."

"Your wife! That's just a piece of paper. It can be torn up!"

Words flew back and forth in our neighbor's presence, ending with Ma-zilla's final indictment, "You're nothing but a bum." From that day forward, my neighbor, Bob, greeted me with, "How ya doin', ya bum."

Debbie and I were significantly affected by this development. We threatened to cut ties entirely with the In-laws, ending any possibility of a close relationship with their grandchildren. They returned to Toronto with that scene hanging before them. Later, the phone rang. I took the call, and it was Debbie's father, requesting to speak to Debbie. I said, "I'll see if she wants to speak to you." He growled, "Just get my daughter on the phone." Debbie took the call and spoke to her dad. Eventually, they reconciled, but the scene was not forgotten.

Ma-zilla displayed her personal quirk liberally. On one visit to their home, after Debbie's father retired for the night, Ma-zilla cornered me and said, "I'm going to argue with you today, so I never have to speak to you again." She added, " I argued with my brother forty years ago and haven't spoken to him since." Debbie overheard this and later told me it made her stomach tighten in concern for the uncertain outcome. Ma-zilla, a non-smoker, took one of her husband's cigarettes, lit it, and blew smoke into my face. I did the same to her and said, " Okay, choose your topic." The argument never took place, the threat lingered and Debbie had a sleepless night.

Some challenges arose with my position as manager. We acquired the business from an aging couple who had seen better days. The husband was an alcoholic who hid bottles throughout the store. He drank at work, and when I entered the picture, I found at least seven bottles in various states of consumption, from completely full to nearly empty.

It was apparent that the husband had not entered the deal wholeheartedly because he did everything to divert me from the tasks required for a smooth changeover. I realized that while attempting the mutually conducted pre-conversion narcotic inventory. The past owner and the incoming manager must conduct this together and simultaneously sign the report to indicate that it reflected the accurate level of stock as witnessed by both signatories. I attempted to facilitate this but got nowhere because the past owner kept talking to and distracted me rather than sticking to the business at hand.

Because I was spending seventy hours a week in the store, Debbie saw very little of me. To allow us some extra time together and to accomplish the required narcotics inventory, I encouraged Debbie to accompany me to the next attempted narcotic count. I kept the previous owner busy while Debbie handled the count, and we all signed off on the official report.

After about three weeks, we relocated to our new location across the street. To aid with the move, many pharmacist shareholders moved inventory from one location to the other; Debbie, the past owner and I, and several other pharmacists were present to facilitate the after-hours move. All of the dispensary stock, including the narcotics and a portion of the front shop inventory, got moved that night. We opened at the new location the following morning, while other temporary staff moved the remaining stock over several days.

At the fiscal year-end, profit exceeded projections, our loss being fifty thousand dollars less than projections. After the second year in operation, we achieved annual sales three times those of the previous owner (about one and a half million dollars).

A problem persisted. The previous owner continued to drink on the job. I reported this repeatedly to my area director, who always replied, "We have to honor his contract, and we can't get rid of him. At the pharmacists summer party, the Vice President of Advertising, one of the founders of our company, approached our table. Debbie and I, as well as several new pharmacist employees, were present. One of the new hires asked the Big Wig about contracts. He replied that no one in the company had a contract. Debbie exclaimed, "Then why can't Doug get rid of his staff pharmacist, who drinks on the job? We've been told it's because he has a contract." I tried to cut her off, but the cat was out of the bag. Our alcoholic pharmacist was terminated a week later. After the termination, he entered the store and asked for permission to retrieve a forgotten item. Thinking it might be a favorite pen or another possession with sentimental value, I allowed his entry. He quickly emerged, holding a partially consumed bottle of alcohol aloft, smiling as he left.

As we approached the third fiscal year, projections came up for discussion. I knew that roadwork would affect accessibility for the next six to eight months and presented my projection, which reflected the fact. Head office disagreed and set our sales target about one-third higher than mine. When the year-end figures came in, they matched my numbers. My yearly bonus, tied to meeting Head Office's projections, was lower than in previous years. Unsatisfied, I wrote a long letter with supporting graphs to ask what more I could have done, sending it to the company's president and waiting for an answer. After three months without a reply, I cornered the president at my store during a district tour and asked, point blank, for his response. He said, "What can I say? You've said it all." That was the only explanation I ever got, but I didn't clue into the subtle message being sent.

Meanwhile, Debbie began to hint that she wanted a baby. By then, we had been married for several years, and I got on board with the idea. I bragged that it wouldn't take long because I was "Stud." Contrary to my boast, it took several months but came to fruition. Once, I came home with a mini stuffed elephant toy and held it aloft, saying, "This is about the size of our little one now." Debbie laughed at the thought.

The moment arrived at three in the morning when Debbie woke me, saying that her contractions were coming strong and regular and suggested that we go to the hospital. I asked her about how often her contractions were coming and she indicated that there was still ample time. We learned in prenatal classes that she should eat something before we left to maintain her strength. I boiled some eggs for her, which she consumed before setting out. The trip to Windsor, where we had booked the delivery, typically took about forty minutes. Traffic was non-existent at three in the morning, and I may have put my pedal to the metal a bit, but we got to the hospital in twenty minutes. Debbie's water remained intact, and we hustled to a birthing suite.

Debbie endured back labor. She demanded constant massage and couldn't move without pain. After a while, she asked the nurse for a drink of water, but the nurse brought in ice chips instead and told Debbie to suck on them. I was gowned, masked and had a bit of a cold developing. With Debbie in back labor, I couldn't leave to relieve myself, let alone get a glass of water, so I sucked on the ice chips too. I continued rubbing Debbie's back, sucking ice chips, and being a concerned father-to-be. After a while, Debbie asked the nurse for more ice chips. Concerned about Debbie's intake, the nurse said Debbie had consumed her limit. Debbie was reduced to tears, saying, "He ate them all," indicting me with her tears.

The nurse relented and brought more. After about five hours of labor, the nurse assessed Debbie's progression; the cervical dilation was about four centimeters. Debbie's water still had not broken, so the nurse induced that. I continued my ministrations with Debbie's back.

I knew I was getting tired, so I could only imagine Debbie's fatigue and discomfort. I thought that going through something like this would surely curtail future maternal yearnings, but it hadn't in past human history, so I could be wrong. After another hour, the nurse returned to measure the cervical opening. It was still about four centimeters. The nurse attached a fetal monitor to the baby's scalp. After another short time, the nurse returned to inform us that the Doctor would be in shortly to administer an epidural. Probably, Debbie had requested pain relief, I don't remember. The original intention had been for a natural birth, but I was on board if Debbie was okay with it. After the epidural, Debbie fell asleep, and I got a break from massaging her back. I left the suite and called Mom to inform her of the events. Mom wanted to be there when the baby arrived, so she said she'd get a cab and be right over. I returned to the birthing suite and dozed in a chair beside Debbie.

When Mom arrived, the nurse informed me, and I asked Debbie if it was okay to leave and sit with Mom. Debbie said okay. Mom was animated and joyful about the new arrival. As we sat there, I brought her up to date with events. Another expectant father overheard our conversation and said, "Don't be surprised if she has to have a C-section. They're just prepping my wife to bring her to the operating room." I ignored the warning, saying, "I doubt that will happen with us. She's dilated to four centimeters. How naive I was.

For the next several hours, nothing seemed to be going on. Nurses came and went, and I shuttled between Debbie and Mom in the waiting room. Suddenly, there appeared to be a flurry of activity. The nurse rushed into the suite and told me that the baby had gone into fetal distress and Debbie was prepped for an emergency C-section. She asked if I would like to attend. I said yes.

I went out and told Mom the news. Her eyes filled with tears. I returned to Debbie's side. Shortly after that, we were on the move to the operating room. Mom met us in the hallway on the way down and told Debbie she was sorry about the development and would stay and pray in the waiting room until there was further news. I went into the operating room with Debbie. I noticed my glasses fogged up with each exhalation through my mask. I had the cover on wrong, or my emerging cold was responsible. I watched the proceedings, and the first sight of blood made my stomach churn. As the operation progressed, I saw them throw blood-soaked gauze into the corner and thought, " You can't faint if you're lying down.

Maybe I should lie on the floor? They might get mad if I lay on the floor, though." At that point, the nurse asked me if I was okay.

"I'm thinking about it."

"Pardon me, what did you say?"

"I'm thinking about it."

"Do you need to get some air?"

"I think it might be a good idea."

"Do you need any help?"

"No, I'm okay."

After that exchange, the nurse guided me from the room, holding my elbow. I felt well enough to return shortly, but I kept my attention on Debbie's face with my back to the ongoing surgery. Soon, the baby emerged. There was a lot of activity as they removed the baby by incubator and took Debbie to recovery. I was hustled away and went to give Mom the news. After that, I went to see my son in the nursery. I looked through the window and saw a child with a shaved cone- shaped head and a couple of IVs attached to the scalp. The child was kicking and crying in the incubator. There was a bowl-like device covering the child's face and head. As he kicked the bottom end of the incubator, he bumped his head against the top. I watched him open his hand, and upon seeing the length of his fingers, I thought, "He's got orangutan fingers! How do you love something like that?" Amazingly, after a night's rest, the next day, my paternal love blossomed.

I tried to ask a nurse about the IVs and the bowl-shaped device. She said that my son had a fever, so they administered preventative antibiotics in case of infection. He was getting oxygen because he developed fetal distress. I asked about his oxygen saturation levels and APGAR score, but the nurse would give me no further information, saying that I'd have to speak to the Doctor about that.

My son had greeted the world at nine-thirty p.m. on November twenty- fifth, 1981. He was just over twenty-one inches tall and weighed nine pounds and one ounce after a sixteen-hour labor following a C-section delivery. I was bone tired. I wasn't allowed to see Debbie because she was asleep. I returned to the waiting room to update Mom and drove her to her apartment, where I fell asleep on her couch.

Refreshed by my deep sleep at Mom's, I returned to the hospital the following day. Debbie said she had a fever and couldn't see the baby until the fever broke. She was still tired, sore and disappointed that she had to resort to an epidural and a C-section delivery. She felt that she had failed in her role as a woman and mother and started to cry, insisting that everything went wrong. I assured her nothing had gone wrong, but it only went differently than expected. She dried her tears, feeling better. I went to the nursery to check in on our unnamed son. As I said, rest or a hormonal outpouring overnight awakened my paternal response, and I felt a bond with my child.

I returned to Debbie, and we discussed the previous day's events; Mom's delight at having another grandchild, laughing over my near loss of consciousness and my hogging all the ice chips. We explored names for our son. A few choices got bandied about previously, but nothing crystallized. We both agreed on Brandan James Landgraff.

Tributes and flowers flooded Debbie's room over the next few days. She entertained many visitors, some from unexpected quarters, like our neighbor, a drug sales rep known to us. Eventually, Debbie's fever broke, and she was allowed to hold and feed the baby. She wanted to breastfeed to give the baby all the benefits that nature intended, like colostrum, provided in the first feedings from the mother. To allow time for healing after the section, Debbie stayed in the hospital for the better part of a week before her release. That also gave her time to bond with Brandan and become familiar with the routine bathing of the baby and advice from the La Leche League. I gladly supported Debbie's resolve to breastfeed. It was good for the baby. I hid my ulterior motive, thinking that I would get a whole night's sleep being exempt from feeding duties. I also considered the savings realized on infant formula.

After three days, Debbie was allowed to come home with Brandan. I went in to tell Debbie that I would pick her up at a prearranged exit, leaving her to sign off the final paperwork. Simple, no?

We thought of ourselves as trendsetters. After seeing the faults with traditional marriage arrangements and all the problems my mother endured with her divorce, I was sympathetic to a woman's plight and supportive of Debbie in her attempts, as a female professional, to reach full autonomy. With that as a goal, I encouraged her to maintain her maiden name for professional purposes. I told her that by not changing her name upon marriage, she'd keep the credit rating she'd already established before marriage, independent of needing a husband's approval. I insisted that she learned to drive and we bought a second car, jointly owned, to ensure that, if ever the need arose, she could leave on her own, taking a car without depending on a third party to rescue her. I believed that, as a couple, all property would be jointly owned, and we switched all documents and banking to reflect that. Of course, that didn't prevent Debbie from having an account in her own name. All bills got paid from the joint account regardless of who contributed what amount (I was earning more than she was). That avoided the monthly messy accounting to split things equally as bills arrived. It worked for us.

As I waited outside for Debbie and Brandan to appear, considerable time elapsed. I went in to investigate the delay. The accounting department would not allow Debbie to sign the billing, as our health care policy was under my name. They would only accept my signature on the form. The clerk held a dim view of our "Common-law" relationship and took great pains to let it be known, even though we reassured them that we were married, with a certificate to prove it. She also implied such a relationship was less than one sealed under the sanctity of marriage. I was annoyed, as was Debbie. The ignorance and prejudice displayed by the desk clerk were insulting. After clearing up the paperwork, we were on our way home. Our neat little family would be home together for the first time.

Ominous dark clouds formed on the horizon, predicting hard times to come.

27

Brothers Revisited; Mike

As I reexamine memories of Mike, I realize that he always had a hair-trigger temper. He was a five foot four inch powder keg with short-man syndrome; always alert for any perceived slight. He had brown hair, hazel eyes and a prominent aquiline nose.

He once heard Prue Grates' brother yell, "Hey, eagle beak," while cruising on his bike. Immediately incensed, Mike began to pedal after the guy, who was on foot. Mike was gaining on him as he peddled furiously toward his adversary. To avoid confrontation, his tormentor ran through a field overgrown with weeds and filled with potholes. When Mike hit one of the potholes, the front wheel of his bike folded inward toward the axle, throwing him to the ground and ending the chase.

As I recall, the Grates brothers and Mike were always in conflict. I recently saw an obituary picture for Al Grates and thought to myself, this guy should not have been casting aspersions about anyone's "beak." The tormentor mentioned above was Al's brother.

Suppose the two boys were out and about, but one lagged the other by some distance. If it was customary for one to address the other by a nickname, like "eagle beak," perhaps the greeting Mike heard was never directed at him at all. I only bring this up because of the picture I saw in the paper introduced the possibility. I could be totally wrong.

After Dad's passing and Mike's taking ownership of the car, Rod borrowed it. While in Rod's possession, he got a flat tire. Rod had never faced this situation before. He felt his inadequacy and entered the house seeking advice, laughing at his failing. Unfortunately, he approached the subject by saying, "Guess what, Mike, you've got a flat." Before Rod could explain further, Mike lunged at him, pinned him to the kitchen table, and punched Rod's chin. Now, Rod's beard will not grow at that spot.

I was surprised when Mike told me, in my middle age, that Dad had given him career advice (which got followed). I thought that Mike had no respect for Dad and often ridiculed him. I never expected that he would accept any advice from Dad.

None of my siblings were expert swimmers. In my case, an incident at the beach where I got caught in the undertow and got pulled under for the third time resulted in an exaggerated fear of water. Dad's stout arms rescued me from the churning waves just as I was dragged down for the third time. I've been wary of pools and lakes since then.

Even though we all attended swimming lessons, we needed to become more relaxed in the water. I remained uncomfortable even into adulthood. I still can't float on my back, an energy-saving resort during extended periods of immersion. I panic when my ears begin to fill with water during attempts to float, so

I always sink. I became less fearful after owning a house with a pool. I began to relax and could tread water, but I could never completely abandon my fear.

I don't know what triggered it for Mike, but he couldn't swim either. One incident in my pool demonstrated this. We were in the shallow end, and I showed Mike the dog paddle. In the shallow end, he performed pretty well. He said, "I should be able to do this anywhere, right?" Logically, that was so. My agreement with the statement prompted Mike to move to the deep end to try this out; as soon as he couldn't touch the bottom, he panicked and sank like a stone.

I was no help saving him, but my wife, Debbie, was able to get close to him and kick him closer to me so I could grab him and pull him to safety. She was almost pulled under by his thrashing but surfaced, sputtering and readjusting the top of her swimsuit. In acknowledgment of his fearlessness, I will point out that he continued to enjoy the benefit of the pool for the rest of his stay (although he remained in the shallow end).

****

As an adult, Mike refused to help Mom around her apartment. He would only grudgingly give in but complained about unfair manipulations reliving past incidents. It surprised me that he cared enough to ask Mom to phone him with daily wellness checks. It surprised me even more that, although he did not attend her funeral, he expressed sorrow at her passing, which seemed odd in contrast to his actions. Mike's actions often contradicted his claims, leading to misconceptions about him.

The summer I stayed with him and his wife during my first apprenticeship session, he told me he worried about me. I hadn't had his visit or phone call for a few years. I doubted the genuineness of his claim. He did not attend my wedding, claiming that he "Didn't go to Rod's, so he couldn't very well attend mine." On the other hand, I had been one of the groomsmen at his wedding, even catching the garter.

Mike was very competitive. He had all of his own bowling gear. When bowling together, I rented shoes and used alley-supplied balls. He was upset, considering the cost of his gear, that I beat him using alley-supplied out-fittings. He was like that when we played Euchre, too. When I won, Mike thought he would improve the odds in his favor by getting me drunk, but that made me play better because I was less tense. Based on our similar sense of humor, I always thought my relationship with Mike was closer than what I had with Rod; I was surprised that Mike was insulted by the birthday cards I had carefully selected over the years (which always had a twist of humor). He claimed I belittled and treated him as a child by choosing those cards.

After Mike divorced his first wife, he expressed regret that he had not attended university. I suggested that it was still possible in this transition period of his life. He was a skilled tradesman, achieved top marks at school, and held management positions. He foresaw that the tool and die trade was being supplanted by computer-generated technology. He could have translated his skills into an engineering career had he wanted, but he felt too old to transition, or maybe the cost was too high. Instead, he became a bus driver.

In his youth, Mike said that he loved the smell of gasoline. It might have been a warning of addictive tendencies. I knew he drank, but not that he drank until he blacked out. He lost days at a time this way. He also mixed alcohol with other recreational drugs. He only revealed that when he became a sober alcoholic and rehabilitated drug abuser. He stopped using but still had to deal with his OCD and Type A personality. He succeeded in the mold of A.A. Sometimes, he was preachy. I guess that's part of the alcoholic personality too.

Mike's disposition made him fiercely proud (similar to Mom's). When he had his first heart attack while shoveling snow, he felt it necessary to bathe before going to the hospital. He lost consciousness for about half an hour when he got into the house. Upon regaining consciousness, he did not call an ambulance but proceeded to bathe and then drove to the hospital.

After his heart attack, which caused significant loss of heart function, Mike's OCD led him to develop a vigorous exercise routine. He felt compelled to adhere to every detail and it never got postponed or modified to account for random events. If we visited during his routine, he apologized but continued what he was doing, expecting our acceptance. His physician told him that this routine probably added years to his life. Mike passed away at the age of sixty-six. His third wife, stricken with lung cancer, predeceased him by about a year. This left him rattling about in his tidy bungalow. His final abode was an assisted living apartment where he passed the last months of his life. He reunited with his estranged daughter years before he passed. He was conflicted but intelligent. His knowledge of technology and military history was staggering.

Near the end of his life, he became closemouthed, maintaining secrets from me and Rod. During my phone calls, he masked the severity of his condition. Sometimes, his answers to direct questions were evasive or misleading. He only informed me of the state of his health after extremely blunt, direct questioning. By the time I understood the full extent of his situation, I had lost precious years of our relationship. At his funeral, his friends spoke fondly in remembrance; his Bible, liberally marked in hi-lighter, was displayed. Rod and I attended with our wives. His step-family, his reunited daughter and her aunt and uncle were also in attendance.

28

Brothers Revisited; Teddy

Epitaph

Strip a man of his possessions
And what is he?
He is himself.
And if he pretends to be
More than this
He is a hypocrite.
And if he thinks
He is more than this
He is a fool.

Teddy shared my bedroom and my birthday. He treated our shared birthday as a special bond, expecting me to feel some tie of eternal obligation. Maybe it should be so, but he presumed the benefit to flow only to him. Anyway, our relationship did not turn out that way.

Teddy began to show symptoms of his psychological issues in his late teens to early twenties. First, he suffered from OCD. He would inspect every utensil at mealtime and invariably reject something, demanding a replacement. He washed and dried his hands over and over ritualistically. This excessive behavior reached the point of self-harm. His hands were raw from constant rubbing. It was distressing to observe. He also exhibited symptoms of paranoid schizophrenia. The combination of his conditions created tension for those around him.

He exhibited his other peculiarities too. First, he fell asleep wherever he was, seated at the kitchen table or in a bathtub full of water. If he did make it to his bed, he set his alarm but ignored it, paying me a quarter a week to be his "snooze alarm."

He had a signature style of dress, preferring to buy his shirts from a formal ware shop in Detroit. His shirts were chosen for their eye-popping colors and frills, like worn with a tuxedo. His attention to his hair style, the odd taste in clothes and other habits made people question his sexual orientation.

He wanted success but presumed it as his due rather than to exert himself. He had paid other people to take exams in his place and confided that it was the only way he got through school. This was a major point of contention between Teddy and Dad, resulting in donnybrooks on our kitchen floor. His lack of respect for Mom emerged as abuse. He had already exhibited his tendency to use force to get his way with Mike and Rod.

Teddy also had an appetite for erotica. He got a subscription to Playboy magazine. I overheard Mom arguing with him about the appropriateness of this publication and the possibility that I might inadvertently see it. Neither Mom nor Teddy were aware that I overheard the discussion, but I made it my goal to find the magazine and see what the controversy was. When I found and viewed my first centerfold, I thought, "Oh, so that's what they look like!"

Teddy's first car was a pre-owned 1958 Impala with two-toned paint (pink and cream), a V8 engine, and white wall tires. In my opinion, it was a beauty.Teddy's driving record was poor. I remember a slew of accidents for which he was at fault.

While visiting Dad's friends in Maidstone (a half-hour drive) with Teddy again acting as chauffeur, Teddy asked Sherry, one of the friend's three daughters, to go cruising in his car. Off they went together. They hadn't returned six hours later, and the families were getting worried. After the seventh hour, the couple nonchalantly returned. They said they had decided to see a movie and lost track of time. That was their first date, and they married (against the wishes of the bride's parents) a couple of years later.

After completion of high school, Teddy entered the job market. His OCD and poor sleep hygiene combined to ensure habitual tardiness. He played a dangerous game in view of this. He threatened to quit if his employers didn't like his work ethic. Eventually, the employers tired of this behavior and let him go. Teddy pushed this gambit until he got fired from every shop in Windsor. He even got dismissed from a shop where Mike was his direct superior. Because of brotherly loyalty, Mike covered for Teddy until Mike's own job was on the line. After that, Teddy was virtually unemployable in Windsor and his relationship with Mike suffered serious damage. Teddy found employment in Detroit and relocated with his wife.

Time passed and I grew older, my brother seemed to regress. He had been a bystander for most of my high school years but became needier, displaying a level of learned helplessness that grew while I was in university. For instance, Teddy and Sherry returned from Detroit and bought a variety store. I visited Mom during reading week, and Teddy said he needed help painting the store. Mom suggested I help, to earn a bit of extra money for school. I estimated the time to completion and felt I could do the job in the remainder of my break. I did not factor in allowances for Teddy's added demands that I help Sherry in the store while he fuddled with his OCD regimen and late rising. To save time by eliminating travel delays, Teddy decided that I should sleep at his place. The plan also accommodated an earlier start to each day. After five days, the job was only partially complete and I was exhausted. Mom stepped in and told Teddy I had done enough and the agreed-upon fee was due in full.

The novelty of the Variety store wore thin and Teddy was ready with a new scheme. His justification for flipping the store was that ownership was a trap, an unacceptable burden, a fool's game. He and Sherry got an apartment in the same building as Mom and lived upstairs from Mom.

At the same time, Teddy attempted to start his own tool and die shop. The start-up coincided with a downturn in the economy. Teddy needed to gain experience quoting prices for jobs, and there was a steel shortage. He under-quoted jobs, argued with the steel suppliers until they refused to deal with him, and supplied his client with only excuses and the sad lament, "But you don't know what I'm up against!"

Teddy's expectation was that after he started the shop and hired tradespeople to do the work, he could live high. His delusional sense of entitlement seduced him into thinking that ownership came with no responsibility except raking in the dough.

After this failure, Teddy intensified his ongoing abuse of Sherry. I previously saw him slap her in the face. With Mom's support, Sherry freed herself from Teddy's grasp, although it was never a complete break.

Teddy and Sherry got separate apartments, a block apart, on Ouellette Avenue. On one occasion, I was visiting Teddy and he called Sherry, telling her to " Bring your frying pan and some bread,get over here and make me breakfast." When I criticized him for this continued abuse of his wife (they never formally divorced), he replied, "If she keeps doing it, I'll keep taking advantage of it."

Teddy discovered another avenue to pursue in his quest for the good life. The government had responded to the economic downturn with retraining grants under the oversight of the Employment Insurance program. It provided EI benefits if you enrolled in an approved course and maintained a passing grade. He relocated to Toronto and took a chef's course at George Brown College.

Because I was already situated in Toronto, Teddy latched on to me and suggested that we split the grocery expenses. He just assumed that I would accept his plan while, at the same time, he expected me to do all the shopping and cooking. It went along fine for a time; after all, ya gotta eat; however, one specific week, I was under immense pressure during exams. I said, "If you want to eat, you'll have to do the shopping and cooking this week." He replied, "all I gotta do is die and pay taxes." I responded, "If you can't exert yourself enough to help, don't come back."

Teddy didn't bend and stopped coming for meals for about a week and a half. Then he called me, full of apologies and pleaded to come back. I had recovered from the pressure of the exam period and agreed, under the condition that he accept some responsibility. It would no longer be a one-way street. Teddy said okay and returned that night, bringing a take-home test and requesting my help. Teddy had completed about a third of the test and said he couldn't figure out the rest. Then he *left*. I thought, "I don't know how he expects me to know any of this stuff when I haven't attended any of his classes," but I looked it over.

Surprisingly, due to my own lessons about nutrition and vitamins, I was able to provide a significant number of answers. A week later, he thanked me for the help, claiming I'd gotten him an A on the assignment.

Continuing with his sense of entitlement, Teddy asked me to trim his ear hairs. It was an intimate request, which made me uncomfortable, so I refused. I suggested he get his barber to do that. He eventually talked me around to compliance. After clearing all the hairs I could see, Teddy claimed that I had missed some, insisting that I continue with the task. I got caught by my neighbor, Randall, in an embarrassingly intimate pose, closely examining Teddy's ear.

Upon completion of the course, Teddy returned to Windsor. He made some halfhearted attempts to use his chef skills, but that soon fizzled out. He continued to make a steady income though, through E.I. benefits set up for career retraining.

As time rolled on, I eventually graduated and entered the job market. I made the mistake of revealing, in Teddy's presence, that with my degree, I could probably get a start-up loan to start in business. At the mention of ready money, Teddy declared that he needed the money more than I did and asked me to get the loan on his behalf. I asked him what he intended to do with the money, but he claimed it was a secret. Still probing, I questioned his business plan and how the venture could hit profitability. Again, he claimed secrecy. I put him off, saying that even if I approached the bank providing that information, they would laugh me out of their offices. Teddy continued his subsistence existence, burning through multiple government programs and grants until they finally directed him to welfare. That was okay with me, but my concerns centered around his continued denial of reason and the enduring defense of his version of reality.

He continued to present the story that his landlord was entering his apartment without permission and making holes in his socks, or removing one of a pair, screwing with Teddy. It spawned the request that I cut a key to his apartment in half to allow him to jam the front part of the key into the lock. Then, his door would only open using the remaining stub key. In that way, he intended to prevent unauthorized entries.

I refused because I didn't have the appropriate tools to do the deed. I also forgot to return the key. A few weeks later, I got a letter demanding I return the key. Any non-compliance on my part would result in slashed tires. I kept the letter and replied, "I'm glad you wrote it. The police have a copy of your letter, and if anything happens to my tires, yours will be the first door they approach." I also sent back his key with my letter.

Another of his delusions involved one of my colleagues. Teddy insisted that Nola, the manager of the store he frequented, was in love with him because she always smiled at him and took pains to explain things to him. I knew Nola was engaged to a local journalist and assured Teddy that her behavior indicated professionalism toward him rather than infatuation. Teddy clung to his delusion. Given the optics of the situation, I was concerned that colleagues would assume I was just like my brother and make presumptions about me.

My life progressed and cycled in a recognizable pattern (engagement, marriage, first house, children) while Teddy continued in his world of delusion. Once, he wrote a book he kept in his constant possession, carrying it everywhere in a black attache. Upon completing the book, he requested Rod's help finding an editor for his masterpiece. Rod had some ties to people with editing experience, so he connected Teddy with a nun of his acquaintance. About a week later, the nun returned to Rod and withdrew her offer because Teddy's book was nothing but pornography. Now Teddy's taint had spread over all of his brothers.

Rod cut ties with Teddy after the embarrassment of the book. Although he had ample reason to cut and run, Mike continued to make an effort. He hosted a regular Thursday get-together with a meal and door-to-door chauffeuring service. Upon pick-up, Teddy told Mike one Thursday, "I hope this week will be better than the usual burgers and fries." Mike was shocked by Teddy's ingratitude, and an argument ensued. It continued until they reached Mike's driveway. Teddy said, "If this is going to be the same old thing, I'm not eating it." Without hesitation or any further comment, Mike reversed the car and returned to Teddy's apartment. Mike said, "Get out and don't expect to hear from me again." Now Teddy had achieved a complete estrangement from two of his three surviving brothers.

Still, I hung on, hoping to be the conduit to a family reunion. After we got married, Debbie relocated and got hired by the same company as me. We purchased our first house, a three-bedroom, four-level back split, in the suburbs (about a forty-minute drive from work). Before Teddy and Sherry separated, Debbie, Mom and I would share a Sunday roast beef dinner at Teddy's place for a while. It was pleasant, but it still caused some discomfort because of the exposure to Teddy's OCD. It also reinforced the obligation expected by Teddy.

Time inched forward, and demands kept coming. One night, during a winter storm and after my completing a twelve-hour shift, Teddy called, demanding that I go to his place to help him figure out how to use a film projector. He planned to buy it from one of his coworkers. He claimed he'd had it for a few days (to try it out), and it had to be returned the next day.

I experienced back spasms over the past few days in addition to the previously mentioned situation and initially refused. Teddy pressed, claiming his need to evaluate it before he had to return it. Against my better judgment, I drove the forty minutes to help my elder brother. When I arrived, he showed me the projector. It took seconds to determine that it was a self-loader. The film he provided to evaluate the machine was pornographic. With that revelation, Teddy admitted that he only wanted to share the movie experience with me and that the rest had been a cover story. Given the circumstances (the storm, aching back, the long shift I had endured, and the schedule for the following day shift), I felt abused and let him know it. He treated my displeasure as water off a duck's back. I left without sharing the film with him.

A year later, I sold one of our cars privately for a decent amount. One day, upon our return from work (Debbie and I were able to arrange similar hours to allow a shared commute), Teddy was at our place, waiting in his car for our return. He said he had heard about our car sale and figured he would get more money for his car if I acted as his agent. He expected the same outcome as my sale. His vehicle was older and manufactured by a different manufacturer. I also notified him that he would have to sign over ownership to me for me to act as his agent. He agreed to everything, claiming that he needed the sale proceeds to purchase a tool required for a new job that he was starting. I decided to help because of the story he spun. He also implied the need for a quick turnaround because of the new position.

Dutifully, I drove him back to his place, keeping his car at mine and agreed to proceed in haste with the sale of his vehicle. A week later, the deal was complete; I called with the good news. He insisted that I drive out that day with the money. With his story in mind, I did as requested. A month later, I asked Teddy how the new job was going. At first, he seemed unsure of my meaning, but then he clued in. He said, "Oh that, that was all bullshit. I blew that money at the track." I had been taken advantage of again.

On another occasion, Teddy told me he had to move and needed my help. He had already secured another apartment, so all I had to do was show up and help him move his stuff. He told me to be there at eight in the morning, but I had other obligations that morning and deferred our start-up to noon.

For some reason, I expected Teddy to have rented a van and packed his belongings in readiness for the transfer. When I arrived at noon, I found this differed from how Teddy operated.

He had nothing boxed and had not even obtained boxes to pack nor a van procured. It floored me. I immediately jumped into action, first getting a van rented, then getting boxes. We packed everything, transferred it to the panel truck and drove everything to his new place. We unpacked the van and then returned the van. It was midnight, and I took Teddy to his new digs to drop him off. I had no intention of going in to help with the unpacking and let him know. He said, "Sure, abandon me now, just when I need you the most!" I thought about what I had accomplished for him in the last twelve hours, told him to get out, and from that moment on, took a ten-year hiatus from the Teddy Show.

Shortly after that, Mom got extremely ill. She was so sick that we thought she would no longer be safe living alone. We thought she would pass before the end of the year. Mike and Rod asked me if Debbie and I would take her in. We hesitantly obliged. The arrangement was that Mike would start preparations at Mom's place (Mike lived within five minutes of her apartment) and that Debbie and I would come to get Mom and her possessions. Debbie and I took our two kids with us in our two vehicles (one of which was an SUV) and headed toward Windsor.

Arrangements were already in place for a moving truck to come on Monday for anything we couldn't fit into our two vehicles. Mike said that would be our responsibility since he had already lost enough time at work. He refused to be there to meet them. Debbie was upset by this. I suggested she stay with the kids while I returned home to install Mom at our place. I had to be home to work on Monday morning. Debbie argued that she would also lose time off work and could do the return with Mom and her possessions as well as I could. We also argued that we both should have been able to make the return trip simultaneously and that it wouldn't be that much to ask that Mike meet the truck. We settled that issue (not to Debbie's satisfaction) and then spent the afternoon packing my SUV. We discarded things that we deemed to be excess to the transfer. We half-filled the dump bin behind Mom's apartment with discards, candles, lace and other material, and many of Mom's mementos. We thought that this was prudent preparation for her looming end.

Debbie and I felt this was the same kind of abandonment by my brothers as when Dad died, but I couldn't see a remedy and accepted that it would be so. About a year later, contrary to our gloomy predictions, Mom recovered and could live independently again in an apartment close to my home. Unfortunately, she lamented the loss of all her candles, lace and material.

During Mom's convalescence with Debbie and me, Teddy began to demand recognition of his rights to contact and even visit Mom. Rod had the technology available to host conference calls because this was necessary for his job. He offered to make this available to allow Teddy and Mom to converse. I agreed to this arrangement for Mom's sake, but in reality, I considered the efforts on the part of my brothers to be only for show. Each week, Rod would call me and ask if I was ready for our conference call. I would agree, and then Teddy was looped in. At this point in the call, Rod would drift away, and the bulk of the conversation got left to Teddy and me. Rod could have participated with more than the occasional comment, but I wondered if he was even there for most of the time.

When I would offer to get Mom on the line so that Teddy could talk to her, he would decline, saying, "I don't wanna talk to her."

Teddy continued to press for his right to visit Mom in person. Again, I caved and allowed this for Mom's sake. We accommodated his stay during his visits, offering room and board and entertainment. These visits became like a biannual vacation trip for Teddy. That was fine for as long as Mom lived with us, but it became a stress for us when she recovered and moved out on her own again. When he visited, I would offer to take him to visit Mom at her apartment; he would say, "I don't wanna see her." Given this, I told Teddy that he would have to stay at a motel for these visits in the future. He surprised me by agreeing to this arrangement. He still expected to visit our house but refused to see Mom.

Sometime over the interval, Teddy finally chose to get psychological help. He moved into the home and got regular attention and medication. He was still annoying but was much improved while under medication. He abandoned his meticulous attention to his hair at my suggestion. Instead, he wore a hat constantly. I was annoyed by his claim that his visits were about seeing Mom. If so, why did he refuse to see her? I stopped his visits because they were more demanding than I could take.

When he was sixty-two, he told me that with the right woman, he wouldn't mind having a child with her. I discouraged this by saying, "Most guys your age want kids to have grown, not be a new Dad." I thought he couldn't care for himself; how would he care for a wife and child?

Teddy was seventy-two when they were diagnosed with lung cancer. When I heard about this, I went to Windsor to visit him in the hospital. When I walked into his room, the first thing he asked me to do was to shave him. Although annoyed, I complied. The nurses were glad of my help. That was the last time I saw him alive. I phoned weekly to speak to him when he went to palliative care, but he was always asleep. More than likely, he was being kept comfortable with painkillers until the end.

His funeral arrangements fell to Rod. I had no experience with that because, in the past, this got handled by others. Mike was not interested in any of the paperwork either. Rod did not want to be responsible for any funeral costs, so he presented a case of poverty to authorities so that none of us would have any economic consequences. It meant Teddy would get buried in a pauper's grave without a headstone. Mike objected to the lack of a monument and paid for one out of his pocket. The celebrant at the funeral was Mike's pastor. The funeral had three attendants, Rod, Mike and I. When the minister asked about our remembrances of Teddy, Mike said, "D'ya remember that time he was hitting us?" to Rod. Mike's pastor got surprised that that would be our last remembrance of our brother. Sadly, this is not the thing I remember most about my eldest brother. After a short time with the minister, we went to Teddys's grave site for final internment. The hole was the size of a cookie tin since Teddy got cremated. The hole was half full of water, which the cemetery representative assured us was unavoidable for the time of year. My last remembrance of Teddy was his urn bobbing around in the water-filled hole. I said to Debbie, "Well, he finally got to go on a sea cruise."

29

Brothers Revisited; Rod

My relationship with Rod got established later than with Mike or Teddy. I knew him more as a caricature than as a person. On one occasion, we had brown bagged it for lunch and followed the usual protocol in our separate home rooms. I finished eating and waited for classes to resume when I heard banging noises coming from the room down the hall. Driven by curiosity, I timidly ventured out to investigate. As I approached Rod's homeroom, I heard the noises again. I stepped into the room to find Rod squatting on the floor. He placed his boots at his knees, giving the appearance of short booted legs, and he had his thumb in his mouth. It was so unexpected that I burst out laughing. Rod had never struck me as having a sense of humor before. Until then, my image of him was as a bumbling scammer who was primarily Mike's foil and sibling rival. We began to get to know each other that day.

Memories of his early driving escapades add to Rod's image as a bumbler. One Sunday, Rod was allowed to drive to Pipi's. Things were going fine until our route required a left turn. Rod misjudged oncoming traffic and turned without having allowed enough time for the maneuver. Judging traffic flow to be menacing, he hit the gas. Rod avoided a crash but took the corner so fast that he lost control of the car mounting the curb. I guess he had also hit the horn while turning because it was now blaring interminably until manually disengaged. Something broke behind the steering wheel, requiring a trip to the mechanic.

While that was occupying our attention, a police cruiser pulled in behind us. The officer investigated to rule out a potential drunk driving infraction. Rod's learner's permit was produced, explanations and warnings were made, and the officer let us go, emphasizing, "Be careful." Rod was so unnerved he couldn't continue and Dad took the wheel.

As mentioned, my brothers moved away from home after Dad died. One Friday evening, Rod visited while Mom was on a date. He found me watching television alone. He suggested I leave the house to attend a dance or sporting event. My usual and customary practice, due to lack of funds, was to watch old movies on television. I had an income now because of my delivery job; a change of pace couldn't hurt. Before that, I thought buying a ticket to a football game cost too much. The purchase of a pass carried the benefit of early dismissal from school. I had been staying behind and found that I got dismissed anyway. I had not considered what I might be missing. In any case, after Rod's suggestion, I became more active in school events. I volunteered for food drives, attended sporting events, dances, or school plays, made friends, and was no longer housebound.

Another of my habits was listening to my records. I started my collection slowly, buying forty-fives because they were cheaper. The first LP I purchased was Simon and Garfunkel's Sounds of Silence. Music became a shared interest with Rod. He was a DJ at the university radio station. Because of that, we discussed music and mutually admired performers. He sometimes borrowed my records to play on air until he stopped DJ'ing. We shared a common bond with our appreciation of musicians like Gordon Lightfoot and Leonard Cohen. He gave me a selection of his old LPs; my introduction to those performers. As I began expanding my preferences, I noticed that Rod became judgmental, disapproving of my choices. I mentioned buying a Best of Bob Dylan LP, and he said, "You won't like Dylan." On the contrary, I liked it very much.

Rod had aspirations to the priesthood. He volunteered at the rectory to gain experience and filled several roles. He counted the Sunday collection and prepared yearly tax receipts for charitable donations. I inherited these duties when Rod moved. Eventually, Rod realized that he didn't have the proper disposition to become a priest, but he still maintained a close association with the church.

Later, as he entered the job market, Rod was variously employed but eventually settled into insurance sales. He knew of my aspiration to become a pharmacist and claimed that one of his clients, who was on the selection committee at the Faculty of Pharmacy, could push my application to acceptance. Over time, I began to doubt the importance of Rod's influence. I learned that there was a quota system that took into consideration an applicant's home base. While marks counted, applicants' origins also factored in. Without that consideration, there were enough applicants from Toronto to fill all the spots. Three applicants from my school, me and two classmates, gained admission that year. There were six applicants from our county chosen.

In the following years, I visited Rod wherever his current job took him. Once, I went to Toronto for a stay, and once, it was in Barrie. Rod had an apartment on Davisville near Avenue Road during his time in Toronto. I phoned to alert him of my estimated time of arrival. He asked that I take an early bus.

Previously, I had only been to Toronto on a school trip to the Royal Ontario Museum. That trip hadn't seemed to take long, so I left Windsor at seven in the evening, expecting to arrive around nine. Once underway, there was no way to communicate my ETA, so I hoped Rod would figure it out and be at the other end to collect me. At midnight, Rod was at the terminal to greet me. He asked why I made such a late start. I told him that I thought the trip would only take two hours. Nothing more got said.

The next morning, I discovered that the Canadian National Exhibition had just opened for the season. Rod, unfortunately, was not on vacation while I was there. I wanted to occupy myself while he worked and went to the CNE. I asked Rod which bus to take and followed his advice. I was apprehensive but thought that if I got lost, I could ask for directions. I spent the day wandering the midway and exhibits, feeling lonely and needing to share the experience.

The next day, I planned to go bowling. I needed to find the nearest bowling alley, so I walked along Avenue Road. A few hours later, still walking, I hoped to eventually come across an alley. When I found one, I spent the next hour bowling by my lonesome. On the trip back to Rod's, I was getting tired and looked longingly at the entrance to the subway. I was too timid to take that chance, so I kept walking.

The following day, I ventured to the Ontario Science Centre. As I wandered, I noticed a girl sitting on a bench. I joined her and started a conversation. She was Barb Crocker, no relation to the Betty Crocker of baking fame. Before long, we walked hand in hand. At the in-house cafe we had drinks and a shared dessert, talking about plans for the future. She entranced me. When she said she had to meet up with her parents soon, I was disappointed but rolled with it. I accepted her offer of a lift. I assumed her parents wouldn't be pleased by my shoulder length, flyaway hair, and style of clothes. I wore hip-hugging indigo, bell-bottomed, wide-wale corduroy pants and platform shoes. Her parents were too polite to object, and my destination was not out of their way, so I got dropped at the corner of Avenue Road and Davisville. I would have liked to prolong our encounter, but that was unrealistic. I hadn't even asked for Barb's phone number.

It was Friday night, and Rod was ready to go out when he got home. He called his married friend, Randy and invited the couple to join us in Yorkville. The Mynah Bird, with its naked chef, was a possible destination but that got vetoed. Rod suggested we see Gordon Lightfoot at the Riverboat. That got quashed because I was underage and might be barred from entry. I have no recollection of our final destination, but by the end of the evening, Randy's wife was a bit drunk and telling off-color jokes. Rod and I returned to his apartment and discussed my scheduled departure for the following day. On Saturday evening, I was sitting on a bus bench in Windsor when Mrs. Roberson stopped and asked how I was doing. I had ducked an appointment for her Saturday morning yard work, telling her I'd be out of town. Now here I was, in Windsor, on Saturday night. I think she doubted my honesty. When she raised the question, I replied, "I've been there and back." She didn't look convinced.

The next time I visited Rod, he lived in Barrie, where he held the position of branch manager at his insurance company. As I approached his ground-floor office across the street from the bus terminal, he saw me through his window and beckoned me over. I made my way there and he flung the window wide, indicating that I should enter. I suggested that I should go through the front door for propriety's sake, but he insisted, so I complied. Once inside, he introduced me to the subordinate whose meeting he put on hold to let me in. If Rod hadn't interrupted that meeting, I doubt that there would have been any issue. Unfortunately, circumstances aroused attention and Rod got reprimanded.

The way my life unfolded seems like predestination. My final twelve years of employment transpired within a ten-mile radius of Rod's Barrie office. I currently reside within the same proximity. Coincidentally, two guys I knew from my pharmacy class grew up close to Barrie: Steve, in Stroud, and John, who became a doctor in Alliston. John, now based in Kitchener-Waterloo, lives close to where Rod finally settled. I was a groomsman at Steve's wedding and was one of the pallbearers at his funeral. I was also John's best man. Years after Steve's death I had a chance meeting, at a conference, with a nurse who had known him. She said he was the best pharmacist she ever met. These connections may have been coincidental, but they engendered my acceptance of the concept of the six degrees of separation I previously mentioned.

While I was still in university, Rod made periodic visits. I shared an apartment on Spadina with John. Rod procured a bed for me. It eased a severely strained budget. Once, his meddling upset me, though. He went through the contents of my dresser. I was annoyed with this violation of my privacy, which he revealed by asking why were there condoms there?

At Mike's wedding, I was not only at Mike's wedding, I was an usher and part of Mike's wedding party. Because of that, I had closer contact with the bridal party than Rod did. I even caught the garter during the reception. I was surprised when the maid of honor started hanging around me after I snagged my prize, snapping the thing I now wore around my left bicep. She was older than me and arrived in the company of a footballer, who I took as her boyfriend. I was even more surprised when she asked me to give her a ride home. Unfortunately, I was unlicensed and didn't have a car, so I asked Rod if he would drive us both to our respective homes.

After we dropped her off, I said I wanted to get a date with her. Rod's sibling rivalry then reared its head. He said, "She won't go out with you. She's older than you!" As it turned out, I asked her out and she consented. Our date was not very memorable. The next week, Rod asked her out. When he leaned in for a goodnight kiss, she pushed her wad of chewing gum into his mouth with her tongue. Things didn't pan out for either of us, but sibling rivalry was now out in the open.

On a different note, we both picked Mom up from her job as a personal support worker. Mom invited us to meet her employer. I had just graduated and Mrs. T's grandson was the manager of a local pharmacy. She said that I could get a job with her grandson. I respectfully declined, indicating that I was otherwise employed. although Rod and I both received an introduction, she ignored Rod while clucking about me, saying,

"He's so clever!" I was aware of that slight and even felt sympathy for Rod. When he later expressed that my only talent was choosing the right profession, I replied, "I guess that was good enough then," affronted by his lack of recognition of the work done and my class standing.

Rod acted as a sounding board for financial planning and was named executor in my will. I trusted him because he had all the qualifications to fulfill the role. I did not follow every bit of his advice, though. Early in my career, I was offered the option to purchase shares in the private company for which I worked. I exercised my option without asking Rod's advice. Debbie also got employment with my company and received a similar option. We took advantage of that too. Rod seemed too curious about our net worth, claiming he needed to know as my executor.

Once, Debbie complained about our tight finances. She felt that I was placing too much emphasis on savings for the future. My objective was to provide security for retirement; there was no company pension plan. Rod supported Debbie's point of view, encouraging us to sell some or all of our shares to ease the burden. I kept that advice in abeyance. Debbie questioned Rod's need to know our financial details, thinking he was too eager to know. I trusted Rod had my best interests at heart and I ignored Debbie's concern.

In finance, there is a concept referred to as agency costs. It means that finance and trust fund managers have a self-interest in their dealings with clients. They must make a living too. There is a chance that they will place their interests ahead of yours and only consider *their* gain in a transaction. You have to be vigilant of the possibility and guard against being taken in by men like Bernie Maidoff.

Time passed, and Rod assumed the role of adviser and facilitator for the family. He handled all of the final arrangements for Mom and Teddy's funerals, burials, and tidied final loose ends. Rod had a friend in Kitchener, an undertaker, who arranged everything in Mom's case. Rod claimed that this was best. I didn't investigate because I didn't want the job. I agreed with Debbie, however, that most of Mom's friends couldn't pay their last respects due to the change in venue. Only twenty people attended Mom's funeral; Rod and I and our immediate families represented eight. Mike did not come, nor did anyone else from Windsor. Many of the remaining mourners were my, or Debbie's, friends. None were Mom's contemporaries. After the funeral, Mom got transported to and laid to rest in Windsor, beside Dad, in a pre-paid plot. Sadly, attendance at the internment was limited to immediate family only.

When Debbie became disabled, Rod offered to negotiate with Debbie's disability insurance provider. He assured us that his experience with the industry would be an advantage. The company offered four thousand dollars in settlement. Rod said that was the best we could get under the circumstances. He urged us not to engage a lawyer, saying that the lawyer would be the only beneficiary from that. Debbie continued to search for a lawyer and found one who specialized in these cases but worked on contingency. That lawyer negotiated a significantly better settlement than Rod urged us to accept.

While Rod was involved in the negotiation with the insurance company, he kept using a lot of industry-specific jargon. Debbie got the impression that he was "mansplaining" to her. Rod kept insisting that Debbie didn't understand what he was saying. Eventually, Debbie convinced me that her viewpoint was correct.

I urged Rod to "speak English" when he got into technical issues. He continued using jargon, perhaps to avoid peer judgment for not spewing "buzz" words, or it was simply beyond him. In any case, Debbie was particularly annoyed with the jargon and mansplaining.

In character with family traits, Rod exhibits OCD (and maybe hyperactivity disorder) tendencies. During visits, he doesn't settle but busies himself with chores, it reminds me of Mike's habits concerning his exercise regime.

30

Brandan and Amber

Brandan's birthday was a month before Christmas. We did all the new parent activities, gushing over the child and imposing our hormonally induced euphoria on all and sundry. Neighbors were invited to viewings of our child and to endure anecdotes and photographic documentaries of the addition to our growing family. Bob, our neighbor, presented the practiced, hardened appearance of a tough factory employee but displayed some contradictory behaviors. He loved portraying Santa Claus. He donned his suit in early December and facilitated a private photo shoot. I was behind the shutter and took the shot entitled "Santa and Son." I entered a copy of it into a photo contest hosted by the Canadian Pharmaceutical Journal, and it placed second among the entries, being published on the inside front cover.

As I said, the paternal hormones had kicked in, and I was deeply affected. I appropriated Teddy's "nibbles" and lavished them on my son. Occasionally, he seemed to throw a fit of temper and indicate his annoyance at this practice, pushing me firmly away with his head. I didn't think about it much then, but it might have been a clue to future revelations.

Debbie stayed home with Brandan until the end of her maternity leave. She had to deal with on-demand feedings, recovery from the C-section and all the other adjustments required by novice mothers. I supported her totally in this resolve to breastfeed. I cheered her on, restating all the benefits for the child and mother, leaving unspoken my ulterior motive of uninterrupted sleep. I had to be rested and alert on the job. I agreed with Debbie's requests to outsource some of the childcare demands. We hired a cloth diapers service so Brandan wouldn't suffer the irritation that sometimes arose from disposables. It also relieved the burden of diaper sterilization so that Debbie could benefit from the increased bonding time with Brandan.

All too quickly, maternity leave was over, and Debbie returned for her first post-partum shift, working a Sunday at the local outlet of our employer. It was only six hours long, and I could exercise my parental responsibility on my own for the duration. Things were progressing nicely in the early hours of my first solo run. Nap time, the first agenda item, was handled efficiently. I put Brandan into his car seat, drove around the block, and he was asleep for the next little while. He was an excellent sleeper, so the transfer from car to crib went without a hitch.

After his nap, Brandan needed feeding. I followed all of Debbie's precautions perfectly. Feeding and burping accomplished, the air started to fill with the unmistakable alert that a diaper change was next. No problem. I then remembered something about Brandan's iron requirement. I got out his Fer-in-sol, laid him on the hallway floor, and measured the dose. When I gave him the iron, he started to spew like a geyser. Probably, the iron curdled his feeding, upsetting his digestion. I panicked. Grabbing him by the feet, I rushed into the bathroom, holding him headfirst over the toilet so that his puke would not get all over the place. Brandan, finding himself suspended upside down after such rough handling, wailed like a banshee. Shaken but not defeated, I regained my composure and cleaned and calmed Brandan. After that episode, I became uncertain of any action performed until Debbie returned. I greeted her at the door, presenting Brandan, held at arm's length, saying, "He's all yours. What's for supper?"

We needed a babysitter before Debbie resumed work full-time. We had good luck in the search. We found a woman who had about seven kids and loved children. She treated Brandan as one of her own. This arrangement was perfect, but all good things must end. That babysitter relocated, so we were searching for daycare again. We found fortune again with Louise. She also had a large brood and treated Brandan as if he were family. We settled into a comfortable pattern.

Time passed. I needed to find an outlet for weekly work pressures and forge a semblance of work-life balance. Something that had worked for me since high school was the use of alcohol as a pressure release. I was binge drinking on weekends, habitually consuming a liter and a half of wine each Saturday and Sunday evening. I usually drank less on Sunday, so I would be fresh and alert on Monday. I never felt out of control, I never blacked out, and I always knew where I was and what I was doing. I thought I had it under control, but regular binge drinking may indicate a high-functioning alcoholic. Parenting articles recommended pregnancy be undertaken before the age of thirty, as the odds of success dropped drastically in older mothers. There were significantly higher risk factors for mother and child beyond that age. Debbie was approaching thirty. Brandan was over a year old, and we were committed to having two or three children. I felt the time was right, so we began trying for our second child, hoping for a girl. When the second pregnancy attempt succeeded, the doctors implied that a C-section was optimal based on the results of the first pregnancy. The risks of uterine rupture were too high. We heeded that advice. A due date of November tenth was calculated, the procedure scheduled, and we looked forward to a second coming.

As Debbie's birthday approached, Audra, Debbie's best friend from high school and Randall's wife visited before the blessed event. Debbie began to experience contractions, and I was concerned about the risks of delaying the hospitalization because of the previous C-section. Audra agreed to stay with Brandan while we went to the hospital. After Debbie was admitted, the doctor said that the birth was not imminent. The procedure was scheduled for October twenty- ninth, the day after Debbie's birthday. Our second child would arrive as a birthday present. I was tired and told Debbie I would be at Mom's sleeping, much to Debbie's dismay.

Amber arrived on October twenty-ninth, 1983, weighing seven pounds and three ounces. She was twenty inches tall. Her head and face were much prettier than Brandan's since Amber had not suffered fetal distress. We now had the Millionaire's family, a boy and a girl. Unfortunately, when I got home, after an absence of a day and a half, Brandan greeted me with, "I hate you Dad." Sensing his insecurity with his new role as big brother, I assured him that that was okay because I loved him.

In-laws, neighbors, and friends arrived to see our new addition. They crowded around Debbie and Amber, clucking and cooing and making comments."She's so cute."

From behind the scrum of adults, at about knee level, a tiny voice said, "I'm cute, too!"

I realized that Brandan was feeling ignored and unappreciated. After almost two years of being the center of attention, he now had to share the spotlight. I thought this was normal sibling rivalry that would soon pass as he adjusted to the current situation. Shortly after that, Brandan began to claim that he wasn't Brandan but was now "Eileen." Falling back on my knowledge of pop psychology, I assumed this was just another approach to regain attention, thinking that Brandan associated the loss of the spotlight with Amber's gender being more desirable. This, too, shall pass, I thought. Time marched on, and Brandan seemed to adjust but still insisted on being called "Eileen. We continued to assure Brandan that we missed and loved our Brandan and wished for his return. Perhaps there was no more to this than my initial impressions, but it stayed in my mind.

Over time, on days that I exercised my parental responsibility, a term that Debbie insisted upon using, instead of babysitting, I found that, while Brandan continued to be lulled to sleep by the round-the-block car ride, Amber remained alert in her car seat rubbernecking. She stayed awake for more than an hour. Different child, different personality.

Often, I would combine the act of parental responsibility with other chores. While Amber and Brandan were in view, I would perform tasks like raking leaves in the yard. I would let Amber cry to encourage self-calming rather than constantly hold and cuddle her. Once, Bob, my neighbor, was returning from his walk and asked me what I was doing to the kid, as he had heard her wails from over a block away. I told him I was letting her exercise her lungs and that it was good for her. Eventually, I bought a Snugly and did my chores carrying her that way. It had been good enough for hunter-gatherer societies, so it was good enough for me and Amber. One of Debbie's cherished memories is the sight of me and Amber working before my first computer with Amber in her Snugly.

31

The Wrong Foot Forward

I still believed that the only requirement to get ahead was hard work and demonstrations of intelligence. I was misguided in that belief. Once, I had not affixed an auxiliary label to an inhaler while being observed by an influencer from our board. The inhaler in question was an anti-inflammatory used for the lungs. Abe Kinder saw me preparing it for a patient and noticed that I didn't affix the warning label, "Do not exceed the prescribed dosage." At that time, only six inhalers required that label attached under the law. They were of a different drug classification than what I had been handling and were specified in pharmacy jurisprudence. I told Abe, "I didn't affix the label because it's not required by law, but it wouldn't hurt, and I complied with his suggestion. I then found the passage in the Pharmacy Jurisprudence reference source kept on the premises at all times. I showed it to Abe. It clearly stated and listed the six inhalers requiring such labeling. During Abe Kinder's term as president of the Ontario College of Pharmacists, I observed that this law was amended to reflect Abe's viewpoint.

I had already taken some wrong steps with the letter to the President of the company, but a more damning incident arose during grooming for future advancement. To date, I thought I was in good standing with my employers. I got invited to focus groups for input into future decision-making. At one such group, I held a strongly opposing viewpoint to that of the Vice President of Operations, Garth Vinder. I swayed support to vote against his proposal with a passionate outpouring of my opinion. I still had not learned to read the signals and, thus, marked myself for negative attention.

32

Pressure Rising

Clouds were gathering over me. Garth Vinder had me in his crosshairs and locked in his sights. Acting through my area director, Vinder, brought pressure to bear. Jim rode me hard about a complaint about me. When I tried to defend myself, I emphatically said, "She's lying." The force of my denial prompted Jim to say, "That just proves her point, you're being rude right now." I don't recall all the details related to the complaint, but it might have been raised by the previous owner's past customer-employee after his termination for drinking on the job. My staff assured me the complaint was an attempt to malign me for the circumstances of the termination and I took them at their word. A short time later, Jim indicated that he wished Garth Vinder would quit riding him so hard, perhaps as a hint to warn me. If so, I missed the sign and held Jim responsible.

Hoping a change in venue would help the situation, I remembered the relationship I had with the previous area director, John Giroux, who had recently relocated to Burlington. He was now the area director of the Hamilton district. I thought that might alter my circumstances, so I relocated to Burlington. I was not yet aware of the depth of feeling I had engendered in Garth Vinder, nor that Vinder would continue his designs by redirecting the pressure from Jim to John and thus to me.

The relocation to Burlington came with some readjustments. The first, most noticeable, thing was the sticker shock of housing costs. Our first house had cost under sixty thousand dollars. Because of the economic climate, we sold that house for enough to pay off the mortgage. We started over from the position of renters because our first purchase was equivalent to having rented for five years, maybe even worse than that because renters would have been saving a down payment. We suffered due to the recession and loss on the house sale.

The prices of houses in Burlington were near the hundred thousand dollar mark, a significant increase from the marketplace we were vacating. We house-hunted over several weekends but faced the pressure of a looming closing date in Kingsville. I wanted to rent until we were more familiar with the area, but Debbie insisted that she didn't want two quick moves and insisted on purchasing. Debbie chose a bungalow on a quiet street in a good neighborhood. Although I preferred other homes more, I told the real estate agent to do whatever it took to get that house. We now had a residence to move into.

I was required to continue in place for a month until my replacement arrived. I took a room in a local motel and visited the family every weekend. Debbie had the kids with her and handled the move. We met with John Giroux beforehand and were guaranteed continued employment within our company after relocation. Things were falling into place. Eventually, everything cleared, and I could join the family again.

Eventually, work sorted itself and I was assigned a store in Hamilton, with the lowest square footage, that boasted one of the district's highest sales per square foot.

I had been reading a book about getting and using power. It suggested ways to make your resume stand out of the crowd involving the creation of a glitzy marketing pamphlet to sell you and your achievements. Shortly after that, I applied for a position as an area director. Book's suggestion implied getting a professionally produced pamphlet, but in my case, I DIY'd it, doing an amateurish job. It probably got noticed but in a negative way. I was passed over.

An issue that arose before my transfer returned to haunt me: A colleague with a cocaine addiction who filled in during my vacation stole what he thought to be cocaine from my store. It had been switched out with strychnine in a previous theft. When Tim snorted the strychnine at my store, he went into convulsions and nearly died.

Tim's theft provoked an investigation by the RCMP under the narcotics control act. Scrutiny revealed that Tim, doing locums in several company stores, had successfully perpetrated previously unnoticed thefts of cocaine. His accident at my store led to their discovery. It took a while for the investigation to progress, and in the interim, I relocated to Burlington and took on a different store in Hamilton.

On Christmas Eve day, the store observed a holiday schedule to allow employee families to gather during the evening. I was the sole pharmacist on duty. Two burly RCMP officers demanded that I drop everything to accommodate their on-the-spot interrogation. Their investigation centered on my role in the previous theft that substituted strychnine for cocaine. They grilled me for about forty minutes while work piled up in the dispensary. My staff, not understanding the seriousness of the issue, accused me of irresponsibly leaving them on their own.

The officers opened with a question about the effects of strychnine. I wasn't up to date with that drug since it was not in common use, only knowing that it was sometimes used as rat poison. I didn't want to expose my deficiency of knowledge and implied that I was fully aware. The Primary investigator said something about it causing convulsions. I answered in the affirmative, but felt my eyes move to the right. The scope of the investigation widened, with questions about control of access to the narcotics safe. I indicated that the only time it might have been weak was during the relocation to the new premises. Up to eight or nine pharmacists had been involved in the stock transfer.

I told them about the difficulties I had encountered with the joint narcotic inventory conducted with the previous owner and how he had been impeding it's progression so severely that I enlisted Debbie's aid with the process. The three of us had signed the document before the changeover to new premises. The officers responded that the previous owner implicated me during their interview with him regarding that inventory. I said that I noted and questioned the presence of the strychnine before the transfer of inventory but assumed it to be a rat poison. I admitted that I had lost track of it since the move but thought that I returned to the wholesaler to reduce "dead" inventory. They asked if I would submit to a polygraph test. I agreed immediately but then backtracked, saying that I wanted to consult my lawyer first. They seemed to accept that and concluded their questioning.

I immediately called our Chief of Security and asked what was going on and the gravity of my position. He indicated that the final narcotic inventory with Debbie's and my signature figured well in my favor. He advised me to make inquiries about the advisability of the polygraph. My lawyer indicated that I could undergo a polygraph at my own cost and supply it to the police if it went favorably. My staff was upset that I had been unavailable for so long but settled down after I told them that those guys were RCMP and that I had little choice in the matter.

The board conducted an annual Christmas Tour of all the stores. John Giroux asked me to replace a floor mat in preparation for the tour. I ordered the only size available, but with its dimensions being different than the previous one, it would draw attention to the fading of the surrounding floor covering. I recalled that the previous manager ordered the replacement mat before my official takeover but returned the mat with the same reasoning. I followed suit and forgot about it. The day of the annual tour was my day off. Politically, it would have been wise to show up that day, but I didn't go in. When I was absent from the tour, it drew more negative attention. Additionally, John Giroux faced criticism for the state of the floor mat I had sent back, probably with more severity because of my absence. The following day, Giroux asked me about the mat and I said I made an executive decision not to replace it for the reasons already mentioned. He growled, "Well you were wrong!"

On another occasion, John Giroux grilled me in front of my staff about our average cost per prescription. I couldn't answer his question, and he pressed, making me look inept before my staff. In my previous store, I had always made that calculation myself and was at a loss to explanation in this instance since I left that task in the hands of a technician already familiar with reporting that statistic (chosen by the previous manager).

Thankfully, the staff member responsible came to my aid and said, "We just report the figure received from our computer service provider."

From that point on, I could not get ahead. I even commented to John Giroux that I felt like a kid who did everything to gain his father's approval and failed. Every three to six months, I was called to his office for a reprimand. I had over ten years with the company and was due to acquire a sixth week of holiday allotment in recognition of my seniority and management status. I asked about the consequences of stepping down. I would maintain my holiday entitlement at the current level and be placed in the pool of relief pharmacists for a time. I wanted out of the spotlight.

33

Burlington

My motivation to relocate to Burlington had multiple roots. I thought my work problems stemmed from problems working with Jim, the Windsor area director. Relocation to a different area under the supervision of a known entity would solve that. I had a history with John Giroux in Hamilton.

My university friend Jack's parents lived in Burlington. It was a short commute to Hamilton and an attractive choice, being out of the city center. Jack said that if I ever got to live in Burlington, it was a great place to be. It seemed like a guiding hand was showing the way.

Debbie and I were thrilled in our little Bungalow on Reeves Road. It had a substantial yard in a quiet neighborhood and a large deck in the back for private enjoyment. Debbie loved the large, bright, combined kitchen-dining area. I would have kept house hunting because other properties had ticked more boxes for me, but they didn't fulfill the requirement of location, location, location in the same way that Reeves Road did.

We were happy with our choice until toxic Ma-zilla began picking everything apart. She complained that the house was too small and all chopped up because she disapproved of the layout. The closets were too small, and the side slider windows needed replacement. Ma-zilla expected perfection. She felt that our university education guaranteed immediate access to the same financial standing she and her husband attained over three decades. Within a year, we were again looking to move up.

We were fortunate to have a friend, starting out her career as a real estate agent, guiding us through the negotiation for a property on Rankin Drive. We found a perfect three-bedroom side split with a two-car garage. It was two doors away from Jack's parents, on a quiet crescent tucked away from traffic. The yard had a sixty-foot frontage and had previously been a destination on the city garden tour. The current owner was facing relocation with a looming start date. We haggled, sending the offer back and forth several times before making an agreement. When the in-laws saw our new house, they approved, saying, "Well, you've finally got something here." Our satisfaction soared when house values spiked and its value doubled before the closing date.

Jack and Randall helped us with the move. It was the most straightforward move we ever made. We rented a box truck and Randall, who had experience from a summer job with a moving company, took charge of the move to the location we called "home" for the next fifteen years. Jack and Randall complained about the number of boxes of books and children's toys. Of course, at this point, neither of them had children yet.

When we moved to Burlington, we had again been searching for daycare services. We were fortunate to find a woman who treated our kids like family. Hilda and Ted, her husband, had a granddaughter about the same age as Brandan, and the three children were well looked after.

As Brandan got older, we introduced him to sports (encouraging involvement much sooner than in my case). At four years of age, Brandan enrolled in hockey. Kids of that age practiced in the afternoon, so sometimes, we needed to have Ted take Brandan to practice while Debbie and I were at work. Ted helped us out, but told us that Brandan laid on his back on the ice and cried rather than participate. On the occasions we were able to go to practices ourselves, we observed similar behavior. I was miffed because even second-hand hockey equipment is costly, but Brandan refused to try. He expected to play like a pro just because he had the gear on. When reality set in, it was too much effort. We withdrew Brandan from the activity after four practices.

We made a family outing to attend a Toronto Blue Jays game. It was an exciting game that went into overtime. We ordered pizza for lunch in the bleachers. All in all, it was a fine day. On the way home, I asked Brandan if he had a good time. He said yes. I then asked what his favorite part was. He said, "Leaving." I was prepared for a comment about the sunny day, the pizza, or even though it was unlikely, that he might have enjoyed the game. I was unprepared for and disappointed by his actual answer.

Brandan never hit a home run when enrolled in T-ball, but usually got on base. Positioned in the outfield, he mostly chased butterflies flying over the area. The coach announced a unique opportunity to attend a day camp featuring a player from the Blue Jays as a guest coach. When I asked Brandan if he would like to attend the camp, he said something like, " Please, no, Dad. I'll be good!"

Debbie asked me if we should enroll the kids in piano lessons. As a concept, I thought it was sound, so I agreed, thinking we would discuss it in more detail after work. When I got home, Debbie announced that we had to get a piano before Saturday; she had already lined up Brandan and Amber's first lessons. I felt rushed into that decision, but we had the piano in place before Saturday.

Brandan liked Beavers, Cubs and Tai-kwan-do (until they progressed to sparring). He only attended Scouts for two sessions before he quit, saying that all they did was play rough games, in contrast to the crafts and storytelling featured in the Cubs and Beavers. With Debbie guiding him, Brandan qualified for the majority of badges and stars available. I helped him build his first Cub Car, which got as far as the second round of the semi-finals before elimination.

Amber was active too. She had lessons in dance, figure skating and piano. She approached the piano on her own terms, in contrast to Brandan, who could play by ear and had perfect pitch. One of his teachers said Brandan had potential for a career in music. Amber stubbornly insisted on using her unique fingering rather than using the proper form. She felt that it made the piece her own. Neither child liked practicing, and motivation was always a hassle. I wanted them to have the option to pursue music at the university level or as a career choice. A grade six certificate from the Royal Conservatory was a minimum requirement for that. Brandan achieved grade four, and Amber, grade two, before we finally gave up and let them quit.

Amber also attended Tweens and Brownies, as well as voice lessons. At one point, I told Amber that we must limit her activities because she wanted to take dance and figure skating simultaneously. I felt as over-programmed as the kids and set a limit.

When Brandan started school, problems emerged. Because of his November birthday, Brandan began kindergarten at age four but turned five during that year. He was the youngest in the class but was big for his age. His teacher felt Brandan lacked socialization skills because he never attended institutional daycare. He demanded more teacher attention than other kids and moved at his own pace, as if in a separate world. She claimed his clothes made him different from his classmates and recommended velcro closures on his shoes and sweat pants so that he could keep up when dressing to go out for class activities.

Every day, Brandan came home complaining about hating school and being bullied by the other boys. We told him to tell the teacher. Brandan said he did, and the bullying continued. We didn't want to encourage violence, so we advised Brandan to try avoidance. Brandan's bully persisted. From my own experience, I knew that the only thing kids that age understand is an attention- getting show of force. Brandan endured daily intimidation for months. I finally gave Brandan permission to defend himself. I advised him not to be the aggressor but to kick the bully in the shin the next time he bothered Brandan. One of the security staff at work described this as an effective means of gaining control over aggressive, uncooperative clients at the store. He said it worked well, primarily if administered with steel-toed work boots, because the shin bone has no cushion of protective tissue or muscle. It redirects the aggressor's attention from attack to retreat.

The next day, I got a call from Brandan's principal. It seemed that Brandan had taken my advice but ignored the caution about letting the bully make the first move. When asked why he did it, he said, "Daddy told me to." Now, I got called to the principal's office.

Under the third degree, I explained the problem to the principal. The bullying had occurred. We advised Brandan to tell someone in authority. That did not stop the bullying. We suggested avoidance because we understood the zero- tolerance policy that the school claimed to enforce. Our child still got bullied. Finally, in frustration at the lack of action on the part of the school, I had given my son permission to defend himself. I suggested the bully should face expulsion as named under the zero-tolerance policy. My son, having taken the situation in hand, no longer hated to attend school, and the bullying stopped.

Communications from Brandan's teacher continued. We received calls about Brandan proudly exposing his new dinosaur underpants at school, which she found inappropriate for his age. She notified us about Brandan's non-attention in class and the power struggle that seemed to be developing between them. Brandan would not cooperate with her reading program. I suggested that Brandan might be bored in her classes. She responded indignantly that her classes weren't dull. Finally, the school ordered a psychological assessment.

A consultant psychologist observed Brandan during two in-class sessions. He was deemed to be approachable, highly verbal and outgoing. He interacted well with adults. He was compliant with his coursework and performed well on his own. He initiated ten student approaches compared to three approaches to him by others. The other students ignored him. He had a long attention span, often focusing on a concept while the rest of the class moved forward. He told lots of fantasy-based stories.

Over the summer holidays, we noticed that Brandan was able to read every road sign we passed, in contrast to the kindergarten teacher's claim that Brandan couldn't read. At age seven, Brandan was labeled gifted by the school consultant psychologist. I felt proud of my son. Gifted a label I took to mean perfect in every way. How naive I was.

We joined ABC, the Association for Bright Children, for support and ideas aligned with current thinking. The school offered IPRC (Identification Placement Review Committees) each year. IPRCs are more for the optics of the situation and seldom result in substantive action on the part of the schools. Debbie and I attended sessions with the principal and consultants each year to hammer out a plan. We were supposed to act as a team to provide the optimum outcome for the student. One year, I noticed that Brandan's marks were unsatisfactory because he had not been handing in assignments. The teacher informed us, close to the term's end, that Brandan was failing. I asked Brandan regularly about homework assignments, and he indicated that he had completed them or none had been assigned.

In the next IPRC, I suggested that teachers send a note home for Brandan each day with the homework assignment list to give us a chance to be more effectively involved with the process. It was noted and agreed to but never brought about. These sessions seemed pointless, or we misunderstood who was responsible for carrying out which action. Nothing improved and Brandan's marks remained lackluster. When I spoke to Brandan about the issue, he said, I know what I know. I don't see why I have to prove it to anyone else.

We attended sessions with speakers advising how to motivate our children. One, whose delivery was similar to that of a fire and brimstone southern preacher, suggested that you encourage them when they are young. You needed to wake them each morning with a pep talk. He even supplied a script;

"Get up, get up. It's a beautiful morning. I want you to go out today and find one thing, just one thing, that excited you today, and tell me about it this evening!"

It might work, so I woke Brandan the following morning and delivered the speech. That evening, Brandan came home and enthusiastically related his story of the day. Impressed, I performed the same ritual the following morning. Brandan replied, "I did that for you yesterday. I'm not doing it again!" The motivational speaker did not provide an alternative to address this situation. Just like that, my six-year-old had stopped me in my tracks.

On another occasion, I tried to get Brandan to be more flexible. His favorite crossing guard, Onie, had retired, and the replacement guard had different habits. Onie had always stressed that the children should obey traffic lights, and Onie never stopped traffic in a way that contradicted the lights. The replacement was angry at Brandan because he wouldn't enter an intersection if the light was red. The guard was getting frustrated and yelled at Brandan to "go." Brandan has a well-developed sense of right and wrong. Onie said that crossing against the red was wrong. Brandan loved and respected Onie. When I tried to reason with Brandan that the replacement guard wasn't nasty, just different, Brandan burst into tears, feeling that I was being judgemental. What I meant to do was help him adjust to the different situations and "go with the flow." Brandan's difficulty with operation in the gray areas still persists.

My children loved to play "lumpy pillow" with me. It entailed pretending they were a pillow. I tickled them while making adjustments to the "pillow" to prepare the perfect resting place for my head. Sometimes, I gave them rides on my back while on my hands and knees like a horse. Amber especially loved to "punk" my hair. She played hairdresser and sculpted my coif into outlandish arrangements. I reclined my car seat while Amber worked from behind me while we waited for Debbie to shop. When Debbie returned to the car, I'd readjust my seat to upright and drove, sometimes forgetting that Amber had adjusted my hairdo without rearranging it. I'll bet other drivers passing us wondered about the guy with the "shocking" hair.

Inadvertently, I did things that ended with hurt feelings. One Christmas, Amber was very young and enthralled by the magical spirit of the season. I said that if she told me what Debbie got me for Christmas, I would tell her what she was getting. Giggling about our shared misdeed, she gave up the information. When asked about her present, I said, "I'm not telling you." I was using this as a teaching moment to make her more aware of dangers in the world, thinking that this harmless example, played out by a caring father, would prepare and protect her from cruelty. I made the same proposal the following Christmas, but Amber refused to spill the beans. Maybe I hurt her feelings and harmed our trusting relationship, but I thought that was better than possible alternatives.

Brandan also suffered my inadvertent thoughtlessness. He was collecting cards of different animals. One day, he approached me proudly, proclaiming, "Look Dad, I've got toucans!" I offhandedly asked, "Does that mean you can fart in stereo?" I marveled at my wit. Brandan turned and left, highly insulted by my comment.

In her mid-teens, Amber complained that everything came so easy for Brandan. That comment was spurred by sibling rivalry. Brandan had a larger room and seemed to get more of our attention. Amber forgot that Brandan was displaced from his big room to the basement when Mom moved in with us and commandeered Brandan's room.

Brandan claims that putting him in that class was the worst move we could have made because it made him a target. He was marked no matter what we did. At least he developed some long-lasting relationships. His marks, however, did not go up.

Amber, too, encountered issues. She complained that she wished the other kids would stop calling her four eyes. One day she came home and, with a smile, claimed, "I'm fart face!" I wondered how that nickname could bring her joy, so I asked her to explain. She puckered her lips and pushed the sides in with her fingers, forming a figure eight with her lips. She then inhaled, making a loud noise that was an excellent imitation of flatulence. I understood how that made her popular with friends. I guess you accept notoriety in any form that presents.

I was exercising parental responsibility while Debbie worked. The previous night, we had beef stew for supper. I was reheating the stew when Amber bounced down the stairs from his bedroom and asked, "What's for lunch? And if it's that beef stew from last night, I'm not eating it."

Caught out, I thought on my feet. I wanted to present the stew as something exotic and fun. I said, "Well, it's not the stew from last night, it's Penguin stew." Immediately, Amber burst into tears. I could not understand what caused that, so I asked what was wrong. She replied that Penguins were her favorite animal and that she couldn't eat them. She didn't eat the stew that day, no matter what I called it.

34

Pressure Overload

People seemed to act in their own best interest, too. Another pharmacist, being groomed at the same time as me, had been chosen as one of the presenters for our product knowledge session in preparation for the Christmas season. During his session he got asked a tricky question regarding customer service. I wondered how he would handle it, but he said, "Let's get an opinion from someone in the audience, and directed the question to me. I presented an excellent solution to the issue. I felt abused and distrusted him in the future.

On another occasion, during a manager's meeting, I was seated behind the same guy. My front shop manager and I held a quiet discussion on the side regarding an issue before the group. The guy seated in front of us gained the floor and proposed the exact solution my front shop manager and I had been whispering about. There was no doubt in my mind that he had overheard us and used it to his advantage—another backstabber. That was in the past.

I distinguished myself since then, but not in a positive manner. Garth Vinder lurked in the background, pulling strings to hinder my advancement. I had stepped down and was working the relief pool again, a good solution for me. I had maintained my seniority and my vacation entitlement and stepped away from the intense scrutiny that came with a management position. My bosses may have considered that as punishment, but I took the lemon and turned it into lemonade.

Working in different locations daily or for periods of several weeks to cover illness and holidays for other company colleagues required skill and intelligence that I hoped would distinguish me within the company. I was gaining an excellent working knowledge of a wide range of doctors' prescribing habits moving around the city and county, expanding my knowledge base. I hadn't taken a loss in pay, but was on a different pay grid than managers. I focused on the positives.

Debbie was again working in the hospital and introduced me to a resource not typically available to retail pharmacies. It was a drug database called "Grateful Med." Anyone who paid the fee could become a licensed user after passing a CSIS investigation undertaken to reduce the risk of terrorists and cultists gaining access to potentially dangerous information on the Internet. I passed the CSIS investigation and got access. Today, there is no such scrutiny. Grateful Med became Pub Med, freely available on the internet.

At the time, I hoped to prove myself a valued resource for my clients. Along with running the gauntlet of CSIS scrutiny and purchasing the license to use Grateful Med, I also improved my home library to guarantee my access to the information in those books. I purchased guides about herbal products as their use grew in popularity. I gained a broad knowledge base in alternative therapies to evaluate and advise clients. I read medical journals. I took the opportunity to teach one subject in the pharmacy technician course at Sheridan College. I expanded my knowledge of computer technology to keep up with the pace of developments at my placements. I wanted to establish myself as a unique resource to enhance my value as an employee. Garth Vinder actively blocked some opportunities offered to me by using his influence with pharmacists' associations as well as in our company.

Initially, I grew comfortable in my role as a relief specialist. My direct supervision, in the person of John Giroux, remained unchanged. Things proceeded quietly for about six months. At my yearly performance appraisal, Giroux asked me what he could do to make me happy. I surmised he thought I would be keen to change my status from the relief pool, which he considered a demotion. I daresay I surprised him when I said, "Absolutely nothing."

After we purchased the house on Rankin Drive, property values rose rapidly. I invested in property to take advantage of the potential, buying a rental property on George Street in Hamilton containing three apartments. I was unaware of the difference between the demands of property management versus the passive investments I had previously experienced. Rental property requires you to "get your hands dirty" in contrast to a stock purchase. That is what justifies the greater return on investment. The idea seems simple: borrow to buy the place, rent it out, pay your bills with rent collections and see the investment grow over time. Eventually, you own the property, having used other people's money to cover debts and pay your mortgage. This doesn't begin to tell the whole story.

My property investment was structured with no down payment arranged with borrowed money. I arranged a first mortgage through the bank and the vendor held a second mortgage for the remainder. After rents were collected and dispersed, I covered the shortfall with five hundred dollars a month from my other income. It was a stretch, but possible.

Debbie and I were asset-rich but cash-flow-poor. Our lawyer cautioned Debbie not to let me get any deeper in debt. Accounting was getting complex, so we hired an accountant to handle the paperwork and guide us through the maze of tax law.

My rearranged situation brought a source of pressure independent from my professional and family responsibilities. There were the typical worries accompanying a family of four: mortgage and car debts. Debbie and I worked in a profession under significant scrutiny, both from management and from the public. The stress of marriage, jobs, and kids, one of whom was "different," added another dimension before even considering what came with ownership of an income property.

I continued with my usual and customary weekend binge drinking as a pressure valve. Debbie said that I was unpleasant when I drank. I was occupied with the work commute, the demands of ownership of the income property, and my professional responsibilities. Debbie accused me of being a workaholic. When I wasn't working in a store, I was either at the income property, doing repairs and remodels, or involved with the paperwork needed to initiate a rent review process. I further burdened myself with courses for lifelong learning, professional education and reading, or general upkeep around the home. Debbie had different expectations of our marriage, and its fabric stretched to the limit.

In theory, my plan worked. I had successfully reduced the intense scrutiny that accompanied the position of a store manager. I pursued a niche that would differentiate me from the crowd. I also diversified my assets to provide another cash-flow stream. I eventually realized, though, that I had only substituted one kind of pressure with another.

I hadn't fully assessed the depth of loathing my existence had released in Garth Vinder. After telling John Giroux that I was happy under my new circumstances, I noticed that John called me every three to six months with complaints. I was on my back foot again. The renewed uncertainty at work and demands introduced by property management intensified. Debbie was more dissatisfied, straining our marriage. The obscurity I had hoped to attain by stepping down did not materialize. Vinder still had me in his sights. My binge drinking made me unpleasant to be around and wasn't as effective as in the past. I fell into depression, having disturbing dreams and thinking about how it could all end if I drove my speeding car into a brick wall.

Debbie felt anxious about the uncertainty surrounding my job, along with problems of her own stemming from professional and parental demands. She also slipped into depression. I asked for a psychological consult. Wait lists were so long that I got referred to a social worker, the cost of which was not covered by my health care plan. Cash drained away to pay for sessions with social workers, for myself and Brandan, and finally, marriage counseling when pressure threatened implosion.

Debbie and I attended several different marriage councilors over the years. The first one was male. We spent half a session outlining problems from our various points of view. Debbie asked to leave the room to relieve herself, and in her absence, I mentioned to the counselor that I truly loved my wife. I related that she felt I was a workaholic. I characterized myself as just doing what needed to get done to do my job well and deal with chores around the house. I believed those statements. I wasn't talking behind Debbie's back to gain any undue advantage while Debbie was out of the room. I didn't talk about my binge drinking or owning a rental property. When Debbie returned, the counselor said that he felt she was a little "whiney," and he wasn't very supportive of her. I was surprised at his approach. Debbie left the session unsatisfied and complaining that he was just "like a man." She refused to see him again.

We had other sessions over time with different advisers, but the same issues cropped up over again and again. I was upset that Debbie removed an unwanted carpet from the bathroom without discussing it with me before acting. When I got home, she brought me upstairs to see what she had done that day. It felt like I was being railroaded into replacing the floor covering immediately. Our budget was tight then and became even more strained with this unplanned expense; I felt she left me no other choice but to replace the floor covering immediately.

Debbie resented that I imitated her habit of stomping around when upset at work in the presence of people she knew and sometimes worked with. I stomped around, each step landing heavily and I glared around with a frown. The girls laughed and Stook to calling Debbie "Stomper." Some of them forgot Debbie's real name and only remembered her as Stomper. Oh, incidentally my work nickname was Mr. Babble-on. When they first told me that, I mistakenly assumed they were calling me Mr. Babylon, with some religious overtone that I couldn't fathom. I was quickly apprised of my mistake.

With this cauldron on the boil, I finally got a referral to a psychologist. He prescribed Prozac. I know some books and articles criticize this drug and its use, but it worked for me. After eight years of that treatment, I asked my family doctor to prescribe a different antidepressant with fewer side effects. It didn't affect the same brain chemicals as Prozac and claimed to work just as well. Three months after the change, I fell into a major depressive episode. It took me months to realize the coincidence of the drug change and the onset of the depressive episode. I had been "controlled" for about eight years with Prozac (well enough to function but still susceptible to lows and dips into depression), but the switch of medication was ineffective. I requested to return to Prozac and regain control.

I empathize with depressed patients, especially those on the wrong medication because I have experienced the unique hell that this affliction causes. While going through my episode, I commiserated with clients suffering the same ordeal, saying that I, too, had my demons and understood their pain intimately. Thankfully, I had the training to work through the problem and the return to Prozac solved my issue. I feel for those who rely solely on the guidance of doctors, who may have never experienced, and therefore don't fully understand, the condition.

35

Predators

The world can be a hostile place. With the immediacy of information dispersal provided by the internet, there are anxiety triggers galore. Not only do we face anxiety-provoking news, but we also deal with FOMO (the fear of missing out.) Until the internet, which only appeared in the mid-eighties, we were relatively insulated from the weight of world events because information moved more slowly and media controlled it more tightly (print and televised). It was also easier for people in America to isolate themselves using denial if an event occurred remotely. It was more challenging to do in the nineties in Burlington.

Several upsetting crimes took place virtually in our backyards. They went unsolved for a considerable period. I refer to the Paul Bernardo-Karla Homolka story.The fear was more widespread than that. A number of events occurred concurrently. No one knew if one person perpetrated all of the events. Was there more than one individual preying on the community? Initially, we heard reports over several months about the Scarborough rapist. Then the venue seemed to change, and rapes and torture-murders started to occur in Burlington. One victim was taken from her backyard at night. There were reports of girls snatched away in broad daylight, one taken while returning home from school in St. Catharines and the other abducted while on her dusk run near the Burlington Tennis Club. The abductee from the tennis club was taken by a different guy, but that wasn't immediately evident. There were other murders reported, like that of the Hudson's Bay executive who was the victim of a thrill kill at a Burlington gas station. Although this murder did not involve women or girls, it did cause anxiety. Eventually, cement-encased, dismembered bodies were found in Gibson Lake near St. Catharines. Ongoing investigation resulted in the arrest and conviction of Paul Bernardo and his wife, Karla. The duo were even responsible for the death of Karla's younger sister, Tammy.

So many events occurred that it was uncertain who was responsible. Amber expressed concern because her friend down the street waited for her father to come home each night before she'd go to bed. I assured Amber that she didn't have to worry about that because we were installing a home security alarm. Amber wrote about the effect this had on her. She was now afraid to play in the wooded area surrounded by the creek near her schoolyard. She also commented that Debbie and I seemed more cautious, driving her and Brandan everywhere rather than letting them roam alone. Who can blame us?

36

Debbie

Debbie was also having a hard time coping with life stresses. She felt taken advantage of from all sides. She worried about my job stability and my binge drinking. Brandon's issues worried her. My seeming distance from her due to the demands of my job (commute times and shifts) and the attention spent on safeguarding the income property left her feeling abandoned. Her job demands added further to her stress. Then, my Mom came to live with us. I was usually with the family for meals, where Debbie and I rehashed our day, often disagreeing about the decisions we had made in that regard. Debbie found many reasons to be dissatisfied at work, but primarily, these manifested because of burnout from the lack of support on several fronts. She tried to avoid conflicts that arose from this by changing jobs every three to five months, or she might hang on for up to a year.

Once, Audra had suggested a book for the children titled A Child's First Book of Sex. Debbie bought the book when the kids were very young, then worried that the content was too explicit and placed the book at a level that she felt was out of reach. When Brandan was nine or ten, he had grown so much that he was wearing my running shoes when I wasn't home and was tall enough to reach the shelf that Debbie put the book on.

She was preparing the evening meal, and Brandan had been reading the text in the living room, where I, too, was reading. The curiosity engendered by the subject prompted Brandan to ask me, "When you and mom have sex, does it feel good?" I was slightly surprised by the question because I hadn't noticed what he was reading and asked what had prompted his interest. He showed me the book. I was prepared to answer in the affirmative but thought, "Debbie bought that book and left it where he could get it, so, as a joke, I told Brandan to "Go ask your mother." I trusted that she would take the question as a professional and answer her son in a non-judgemental way that would not provoke prurient fixations. Brandan went to the kitchen and made his inquiry. I had sent him into the lion's den, misjudging the type and fierceness of Debbie's response. When she responded with harsh anger, typically referred to today as "Ripping him a new one," I rushed to his aid and told her that I had sent him to her with the question. It had been prompted by the book she had purchased and left in his reach. It would have been better if I had answered, "Yes," when Brandan asked me and then let the matter drop.

Debbie felt taken advantage of at work. When she started at the hospital, they promised that there would be a six-week orientation period on the job. After three weeks of orientation, greater responsibility thrust upon her made her feel unprepared, given her brief exposure. Rather than take this as a compliment, it created work stress for her, and she felt burdened. In addition, her colleagues took unfair liberties. They took extra long breaks or played waste-can basketball rather than work. The pharmacy department director was a nice guy and charming, but he left the day-to-day management in the hands of his assistant director.

Debbie noticed some irregularities that amounted to sexual harassment and bullying by a male colleague directed against one of the other female pharmacists. Debbie spoke up on behalf of the targeted woman. Debbie felt that the action taken to rectify the situation could have been more effective. The action taken only satisfied the optics without addressing the problem. The behavior did not improve, and the harassed woman told Debbie to let the issue drop.

After that, Debbie was given responsibility as the department safety officer. In that capacity, she noticed that the room for preparing oncological medications needed adequate ventilation and informed her supervisors. The deficiency persisted until years after Debbie left. The position fulfilled the optics, but it needed to be more effective, with warnings heeded.

37

Brandan Revisited

When Brandan entered high school, his walking route to school brought him past the primary school where he had been bullied. Some kids in the upper grades still remembered him and, from across the street, made his path a gantlet of bullying each day. Concerned about the consequences, Debbie called the primary school principal to ask for help, hoping to defuse the situation and prevent an unpleasant outcome. The principal said nothing was to be done because the kids were not on school property when the harassment occurred. After months of dealing with it, Brandan was no longer able to handle the abuse. Using techniques learned in tai-kwon-do, he crossed the street at a run and gave the ring leader a running kick to the balls. Given this escalation, Debbie once again called the principal to ask for help. The principal fell back on the same excuse but went further and suggested getting the police involved. Debbie told the principal that she was seeking an ally to prevent any further escalation because negative consequences might arise, with Brandan facing charges. Debbie said that the school must have some influence on the situation. The principal knew which boys were involved, yet didn't act to prevent those students from police charges. Debbie also emphasized that she was concerned that Brandan might be the one who got charged. The principal must have made some effort because the bullying stopped.

Brandan was about six feet tall in grade nine and weighed about two hundred pounds. One of his teachers was on the varsity football coaching staff. He wanted Brandan to join the team. I thought Brandan would get to experience the dream that had been blocked to me. Mr. M. was not the head coach, so Brandan would have to get approved after meeting him. Mr. M was very supportive of Brandan, but my son was not as impressed by the thought of playing football as I had been. Both Mr. M and I encouraged Brandan to go for it. It was a no-brainer. Hand the ball to Brandan, and with his height and weight, all he'd have to do is stumble forward and get a first down. He didn't go to the head coach right away. It was getting down to the wire if he wanted to get a place on the team. The head coach asked him why he hadn't come forward earlier. Was he a pianist, afraid to stub his fingers? That one comment was enough to insult my boy. He was taking piano lessons, and although he was not a prodigy and hated practice, he liked that more than he enjoyed playing football. He vowed that as long as that guy remained head coach, Brandan would not join the team.

With his height and weight, Brandan found that few people challenged him once he got to high school. He told me that being big solved that problem. To add to the effect, Brandan shaved his head and adopted a black wardrobe, work boots and a long duster coat. The day he decided to shave his head, he proceeded on his own without alerting Debbie or me. He had shaved the front and most of the sides of his head but could not finish the back. Suddenly, I heard a mournful call from the bathroom, "Dad, can you come here? I need your help". When I arrived, I found Brandan with half his head shaved and presenting a pitiful spectacle. Although I fully intended to help him complete the task, I teased that I wasn't and would make him go to school in his present state. He almost begged for help, and I quickly relented. He was so tall that I made him kneel so that I could reach the unshorn remainder of his head. Brandan presented a formidable appearance, dressed in black, with a shaved head, standing close to six feet at age fourteen.

Brandan was a mediocre student. If he liked a subject, he excelled at it. If he didn't care for the information, the results were uninspired. He did well with foreign languages, history, and English language studies. Brandan's interest shone here. Math, however, was a great disgrace. SOne year, he failed Math, getting a mark only a few points below a pass. He was allowed to take a summer session at his home school that was only a few weeks long. In the summer session, he got an A. The summer session mark replaced the failure in the official transcript. I told him that was much better and praised his success. I also told him that if he failed again, I would make him take the makeup session. Even with subjects he liked, a familiar teacher complaint was that he only wrote enough to answer the question and never explained his thoughts. Sometimes, if the question's wording allowed a single-word answer, that was all he wrote. Brandan said that he knew what he knew. He didn't feel obliged to prove it to anyone else.

The following year, because of my warning about summer sessions, Brandan failed math with a spectacular forty mark. In this instance, the remedial session was no longer an option. To compensate for the failure, he would have to take an entire summer school course, only available in Milton. Since Debbie and I worked, the logistics were unworkable, and Brandan won the power struggle. We could not force him to pass Math.

I have made great efforts to minimize the use of corporal punishment in child-rearing. The memories I had of Teddy and Dad rolling on the floor, punching at each other, was a stark reminder of the futility of such an approach. It was reinforced with an experience I had with Brandan. I had wanted Brandan to take a nap one day when he was maybe three years old. Brandan didn't want to cooperate and kept getting out of bed, so I decided to try to enforce my will by laying with him and physically holding him in place until he gave in. The more I tried to force the issue, the more he resisted until both of us were deeply upset. I realized that I would never reach my goal in this manner and would only escalate things until one or both of us suffered harm, so I let him win the power struggle.

Once, Brandan was taping a program from the television. Minutes before the program was complete, a visiting friend of Amber's, who had been warned not to change the settings on the TV, changed the station so she and Amber could watch a different program. Brandan charged her and kicked her in the stomach. I worked in my home office that day, so I heard the cry of pain from Amber's friend. When I heard the details of the exchange, I punched Brandan in the chest and pushed him around a bit, asking him how he liked being treated that way. Brandan began to weep and called himself a monster. I held him in a fatherly embrace and told him he wasn't a monster but cautioned him to think about the consequences in future situations. I had acted mostly in fear of repercussions from the girl's parents when they heard about the assault on her. Luckily, nothing arose in the aftermath, but I had broken my resolve to NEVER use force with my children.

38

Amber Revisited

Compared to the problems that followed Brandan, Amber was a delight to deal with. She was intelligent, cute and much more outgoing than her brother. Amber often had friends over and entertained them regularly. To be fair, Brandan did have his weekly group over to play Dungeons and Dragons, but his friends didn't show up as often as Amber's did. Amber felt that Brandan got more attention than she did. Perhaps she felt ignored by me.

Once, I hired College Pro Painters to paint the outside of our house. Amber accompanied me as I inspected the job and redirected the foreman with some observations. I pointed out where the workers had been a bit sloppy with their brushwork and got paint on the downspouts of the evestrough. The foreman asked me how I would have prevented the sloppiness, given the tightness of the space. I suggested that a barrier, like a piece of cardboard or a thin sheet of wood, be placed between the downspout and the painted area. I also pointed out areas that still needed paint. With her short stature and lower point of view, Amber noticed the bottom of an outdoor cupboard needed attention. She tried to tell me, but I put her off with, "Not now, honey, Daddy's busy." Had I listened, that area could have received the proper coat of paint.

As she grew, Amber had typical childhood experiences and run-of-the-mill schoolyard encounters. By the time Mom moved in with us, Amber was in grade three. I was a landlord in addition to being employed as a relief pharmacist with the inherent travel and being affected by the pressures outlined previously.

In the past, while working in the factory, my language had been colored blue to fit in with my colleagues at work. As a pharmacist and parent, I controlled my use of language so that it would not influence the kids.

Once, I built a tiered garden box composed of pressure-treated sixteen-foot-long six-by-six garden ties secured with foot-long spikes. I used a five-pound sledgehammer to drive the spikes into the ties. I was kneeling on top of a tie while hammering, missed the spike, and hit my knee instead. As I limped around, trying to walk it off, I wanted to let loose with a string of expletives beginning with F, but I didn't because Amber would hear me. Amber said, "What's the matter, Daddy?" Limping around the yard, I said, "Oh, Daddy's just hurt his knee." A few days later, Mom told me that Amber had been walking with a friend in the neighborhood and using the F-bomb freely and often. From then on, I resolved not to deny myself the cathartic use of the word.

After an enjoyable shared holiday with Audra, Randall and their kids at a rented cottage on Lake Buckhorn near Peterborough, I looked into purchasing a cottage of our own. Prices were out of my range, so I compromised and purchased a park model trailer at Sherkston Shores on Lake Erie. This became our summer get away spot. It was glorified glamping in an eight by thirty eight three bedroom Mallard that would sleep eight and was equipped with AC for unbearably hot days and a gas furnace for the cooler evenings of later September. On one of our trips to Landgrala (named for Shangrila) Amber wore her rubberized Hallowe'en Troll mask in the back seat of our SUV. I stopped for gas around dusk to top up. After filling, I went into the kiosk to pay. On the way in I saw another customer emerge from the kiosk and he seemed startled as he passed me. I looked around to determine the cause of his reaction. I saw Amber staring out of the back window of our vehicle wearing the Troll mask. In the fading light it was not evident that she was wearing a mask. The guy was probably startled at the appearance of the ugly kid staring out of the window at him.

In the nineties, predators roamed the Golden Horseshoe. As parents, we became overprotective, never letting the kids be unaccompanied. We had an older girl walk with them to school. We drove them to every event or play date. We installed a security alarm.

Debbie remembers finding an entry in Amber's journal describing the effects of our paranoia. Amber wrote that she no longer felt safe playing in the strip of woods that bordered the creek near her schoolyard for fear of lurking danger. We tried to protect our kids from exposure to stranger danger, but maybe we just caused anxiety for them.

Our hyper-alertness could not prevent all unpleasantness. Brandan and Amber were exposed to abuses of the family. Ma-zilla freely harassed Amber about her weight or her choice of clothing. She reduced Amber to tears during one visit by insisting that she change her socks, which Ma-zilla deemed too masculine. Ma-Zilla threw a pair of her own socks at Amber while adding further body shaming comments. She also suggested that Amber was not lady-like. Amber went out to the porch, sat on a deck chair and wept. Debbie and I stood by helplessly, offering no opinion on either side. We failed Amber that day.

Amber was about sixteen by then and, like most teenagers, was asserting her independence. One day, she disobeyed her mother using some blue language. I heard the exchange and stepped in to assert my authority. Amber told me to F.O. Pushed too far, I slapped her cheek with an open hand. I was reenacting an event from an article I read about another parent in a similar situation with his son. Losing his cool, the parent from the article grabbed his son by the shirt collar and pulled him upward, saying something like the world is dangerous. If you want to try it on your own, go ahead.

Amber reacted to the slap by accusing me of child abuse. She said she was going to leave and live with a neighborhood friend. I said, "Go ahead." I even opened the front door for her to leave. By then, Debbie was crying, apologizing to Amber and trying to prevent Amber from leaving. I grabbed Amber's shirt, pulled her upward and said, "Living on your own can be hard. Go ahead, leave. See if a slap in the face is the worst thing you encounter." Amber stomped off to her room, slamming the door. She didn't leave, but her attitude toward me changed. At points, I thought she hated me and I'd lost her forever.

The year before Amber graduated from high school, there was a house party within walking distance from our house, thrown by that year's graduating class. A group of thugs from Hamilton heard about the party and tried to crash it. A couple of the boys from Amber's school ejected the party crashers. About half an hour later, the party crashers returned with baseball bats.

They found one of the boys who had removed them earlier and beat him to death. For Amber's grad year, the school banned any graduation party, given the previous year's events. My warning to Amber when I slapped her for mouthing off proved true, but it neither repaired the damaged father-daughter relationship nor absolved me from my terrible act.

After Debbie's fibromyalgia disabled her, our children became much closer to Debbie and more removed from me. Probably, it was because Debbie became more available to them in her often bedridden state, which meant she was home when the kids returned from school. Amber used to sit at Debbie's bedside and talk about the day's events during this time. Brandan also spent more time in close conversation with Debbie.

Debbie's disability came at a time when financial demands were increasing quickly. Brandan started his first year in linguistics at Brock University. Amber was finishing grade thirteen. Hers was the last cohort in Ontario that attended that grade before it got phased out. Amber wanted to go to the Univerity of Guelph the following year. Debbie's disability increased the stress I felt about finances. To ease some of the pressure, we decided to downsize. A new housing development was under construction in north Burlington, and we took advantage of government grants offered with new home developments to have a home built there that was smaller than the Rankin Drive property and fit our budget. The loss of Debbie's income required that we draw down funds previously contributed to her RRSP. By the time Amber completed her undergraduate degree, most of Debbie's RRSP was gone, except for the portion that was locked in from her hospital employment.

Amber was not happy about the downsizing. More to the point, she was not pleased to be uprooted from the home where she had spent the last sixteen years and moved to a location further from her high school. I suggested Amber take the city bus to school for the next six months, but she steadfastly insisted that she needed me to drive her each morning because it hadn't been her decision to move. She did not make her last months at Nelson High School pass quickly. She spoke out to her teachers about their lack of attention to grade thirteen students, as they often had to cancel classes to attend planning sessions for the impending changeover that eliminated grade thirteen. She also didn't help with our pre-move preparations. The week we moved was incredibly taxing for me because Amber seemed to be intentionally dragging her feet to aggravate me. I asked her if she was consciously trying to drag her heels with each step or if it was because of the design of her sandals. She blamed the sandal design.

We moved into our new home in April. Both Debbie and I were pleased with the results. We chose every aspect of the new home, even the color of our shingles.

Debbie filled her disability-mandated idle time by keeping a journal of each stage of the planning and construction. How can you be disappointed with a custom-built new home? Amber, still in a funk, did not share our pleasure. She had plenty of things to complain about regarding the deteriorating school situation. On her last day of school, she called me in tears to tell me they wouldn't release her report card until she either returned a library book she allegedly had in her possession or paid the overdue fines.

Amber swore that she had returned the book and needed my help. It was my day off, and I was working around the house. I was not dressed appropriately, wearing a Tasmanian Devil T-shirt and jeans, but my daughter needed me, and I responded without delay. When I got to the school office, I asked at the desk about the problem. The secretary provided little clarity, offering the same information that Amber had related by phone. I questioned Amber in the presence of the secretary. Amber adamantly insisted she had returned the book, even naming the person who received it. The secretary said their records showed it missing. I said, "My daughter doesn't lie!" The secretary was unyielding. I demanded to see the principal immediately in a loud voice. It turns out I was dressed appropriately as my inner "Taz" emerged. After a few more exchanges, Amber and I left with her report card.

39

Debbie's Disability Experiences

Debbie started to suffer at work from the effects of her fibromyalgia. Her hips hurt and limited the amount of standing she could endure. Her hands and wrists ached like a repetitive stress injury from working at a keyboard. She saw the doctor about the symptoms, and the doctor encouraged her to keep "moving" because the alternative involved a downward spiral into even more significant pain. The doctor was reluctant to diagnose fibromyalgia because it would potentially be career-ending and push Debbie further into depression (as if the chronic pain and fatigue weren't already doing that.)

The next hurdle was working with her employer to make accommodations, given Debbie's health. Her human resources department recommended solutions to her issues. For a time, Debbie worked in the on-site medical library, a desk job, filing books and answering research requests. It wasn't satisfactory for either side. Her bosses wanted a pharmacist, and Debbie wanted to fulfill the function she was trained to do. The hospital refused to implement any further recommendations made by its own human resources department. We hired a lawyer to try to force the issue. After writing three letters to the hospital, costing six thousand dollars in legal fees, Debbie decided to quit rather than undergo the ordeal.

Over the next five years, Debbie struggled to solve the problem and keep working. She researched alternative treatment regimes. She found employment at other hospitals in the area, but none of those jobs supplied the right "fit." Then Debbie thought that she could handle a reduced, part-time schedule. She freelanced and found part-time placements in retail positions, working only three days a week. Interestingly, the reduction of hours (by replacing a full-time hospital position with part-time work in retail) didn't result in a loss in remuneration. Eventually, even that became untenable. She needed the doctor to help her establish a clear case of disability due to fibromyalgia to apply for her disability insurance.

The doctor was reluctant to spend hours filling out the required documentation because OHIP does not cover the cost of doing paperwork. The situation got so ridiculous that I called and spoke to the doctor on my wife's behalf. The secretary blocked access, saying the doctor didn't want to talk to patients. I replied. "Isn't that interesting, a doctor who doesn't want to speak to her patients?" When the doctor did get back to me, I questioned the delay with the paperwork. The doctor admitted the problem was a lack of remuneration. Eventually, we got the paperwork completed.

Now, the next phase of the ordeal began. The disability insurance denied Debbie's claim. We didn't have the resources for a prolonged legal battle. The six thousand dollars spent previously for three letters indicated the financial burden we faced. My brother, Rod, offered to facilitate negotiations with the insurer, claiming that his experience with the insurance industry would be invaluable. The settlement offer negotiated through Rod was unsatisfactory, and Debbie continued her search for a lawyer who might work on a contingency basis. All of our friends and colleagues told us that contingency arrangements were not allowed in Canada. We were at the end of our rope when Debbie found a legal firm willing to take the case on contingency. I am grateful to those lawyers. They worked on our behalf to get us a reasonable settlement.

Although Debbie could not work beyond the year 2000, we finally reached a settlement in 2003, the day after the Northeast blackout. The final details were negotiated in a parking lot because the blackout forced widespread closures in Toronto, where the negotiation occurred. I told Debbie that we must attend, no matter the conditions, so no one could say we didn't show up. Every traffic light in Toronto was nonfunctional that day, as were all public facilities. Gas stations were unable to function because pumps wouldn't work. But after three years of depositions, Debbie being followed by investigators dedicated to proving fraud and being accused, to our faces, that we were liars, nothing could stop us from pursuing justice that day. Our perseverance brought rewards.

40

Doug - Work Revisited

I have repeatedly stated that I was clueless throughout my life and career. I don't know if it is clear what is meant by that. I will try to illustrate, one final time, with some examples throughout my life and career. Debbie and I were invited to a summer staff party hosted by another manager. I noticed that the team was dividing into cliques and was not mixing very well. The host announced some ice-breaking activities and urged participation. I could help with that to get the party going. I entered the activities hoping to be an example of goodwill and involvement. The opening activity involved partners, picked at random, then tasked with standing face to face on a phone book surrounded by a loop of string. The object was to keep your footing on the phone book while maneuvering the cord upward and over the heads of partners.

My randomly assigned partner was a buxom blond cosmetician. We staved off elimination in the first round, which was not difficult. In the second round, the loop tightened, and we were still in the game. My wife watched closely, hoping that I would clue in and step off the phone book, but my competitive nature took over, and I didn't foresee the game's outcome. After the third round, my partner and I were still in the game, having succeeded in moving the loop over our heads using good balance and many dips and wiggles to get the ever-tightening circle over our heads. I found that my wallet had been an obstacle during that round, so I removed it and brought it to Debbie to hold before attempting the next round. At this point, I found Debbie was upset when she threw my wallet in my face, but I still returned for the elimination round. My partner and I won that competition, being the last couple to squiggle through the even tighter string loop.

I approached Debbie, congratulating myself on my excellent balance, perseverance and sporting nature. My angry wife insisted that we leave the party immediately. As we drove home, I was bewildered at such anger prompted by a simple game. After much discussion (argument) and asking many couples opinion on the issue, I realized that the smart move entailed stepping off the phone book in the first round. Most couples felt that Debbie's anger was justified.

On another occasion, while watching the Stanley Cup Playoffs with my family, I saw a sign that said, "Bring back Stanley." It was the year that Where's Waldo books were popular. I thought that the placard referred to a character, like Waldo, and asked, "Who's Stanley?" I was the butt of goodhearted teasing by the family until the end of that series. I had only ever heard the Stanley Cup referred to as the Cup, never as Stanley, so the sign made no sense until it was explained.

The example of a lousy metaphor describing how busy I was may be more instructive. While serving a friendly client who had a prosthetic leg in reply to his observation that we seemed busy, I said, " Yeah, they've got me hopping like a one-legged man at a butt-kicking contest." When the words left my mouth, I realized I had chosen the wrong metaphor.

Finally, in the Wasaga Beach store I managed, I came across a familiar name as I served a client. He was Amber's classmate from Burlington, working in Wasaga for the summer. He and Amber took photography at Nelson High School, and Amber had mentioned how talented he was and that she admired his photos. After establishing that he was that classmate, I said, "My daughter likes you!" I should have said, "My daughter admires your photography." After that faux pas, Amber, also working on the beach strip that summer, informed me that whenever her classmate spied her, he ran the other way. An excellent example of why you must heed the warning to ensure the brain is engaged before putting the mouth in gear!

Sometimes, I reversed earlier decisions after considering other points of view, or I labored over performance appraisals considering multiple sets of benchmarks.

Instead of seeing this as a strength, management viewed it as indecision and waffling. Some business literature advises against paralysis by analysis, recommending that you make a decision and act on it rather than waiting for certainty; it is better to act and then reevaluate and correct as needed. I tried to keep an open mind and got judged for it. What I felt were my strengths were deemed to be weaknesses. Women claim to face the glass ceiling as an impediment to promotion. I have found that the glass ceiling also exists for men, especially for highly sensitive individuals.

I was called on the carpet by management every three to six months, with one petty issue or another. I was now seeing the psychiatrist at least monthly, trying to deal with the job situation. The psychiatrist suggested that my position as a relief pharmacist denied me the opportunity to forge long-term relationships with staff who might speak on my behalf. He felt that I was perhaps being scapegoated.

I had just returned from a couple of days of sick leave. Halfway through the morning, there was an urgent message from the area office that I was to make my way there ASAP. No further explanation was given, and I wondered what it was about while I drove. When I got there, John Giroux informed me of a termination letter that his secretary had mailed prematurely. He needed to notify me of the letter before its arrival. I don't remember whether that was when John told me (either at this meeting or previously) that Garth Vinder said, "Fire that bastard, I hate his guts." Regardless of the timing, I knew the comment had been made by Garth Vinder.

Ostensibly, my termination was for abusing my sick time. I hadn't used any sick leave in the previous three years, and I only took three days of my yearly limit of seven in the instance in question. I was shocked by the news. I quickly cycled through the stages of anger, denial and acceptance right before Giroux's eyes. I told him that I had only followed the Doctor's orders and asked Giroux if he wanted to speak to my Doctor. He reacted as if I challenged his authority and growled, "Yeah, I'll talk to him." I said I'd set up a joint appointment for us and get back to him. He agreed to this arrangement. I called my psychiatrist and set and subsequently firmed up the meeting. On the appointed day, John arrived slightly before me. When I entered the waiting room, he growled, "You didn't tell me your Doctor was a psychiatrist!" I replied, "You didn't ask." After an embarrassing half hour for John, I heard no more about the intended firing and thought the issue died.

Following that, I received a summons to John's office for a joint meeting of John, Garth Vinder and myself. Vinder told me to sit down and make no comment until he finished his prepared statement. He began with a litany of my alleged failings, dragging in an interview during my failed bid for the area director position. I objected. That did not affect the performance of my actual job-related duties. His hostile reply was that everything was job-related. He continued to list other issues and implied that during my time as manager of my Hamilton store, sales had started to slip dramatically. At this point, I could stay quiet no longer. Upon takeover at that store, I had access to sales records of the seven years previous. A drop in sales in each of those seven years before my tenure was evident. That pulled Vinder up, and he turned to Giroux, asking if there was any truth in that statement. John replied noncommittally that, to some extent, it was true. Vinder was displeased, but again, my spirit guide had put the right words into my mouth at the right time. The interview ended, and I still had a job.

Subsequently, the sale of our corporation was announced. Had I been fired, I would have had to sell all of my shares upon termination and would have missed out on a portion of the profits from my investment. Given the failure of that action, I was able to participate in the benefits. Despite all of the ill will around my treatment at the hands of management, the sale of the company still felt like a significant passing. I shed a few tears about the end of an era and maybe grieved during the changeover. During my time as a manager, I felt micromanaged. I felt like a puppet at each year's Christmas party when managers got summoned to the front of the venue, which seated over a thousand employees to fetch a cake for their table, then paraded around until given the sign to return to our seats. We were glorified gofers. After I stepped down, I became part of the area office staff and felt much more comfortable sitting with the maintenance staff than I ever did with the Big Wigs.

Our new owners did not maintain a stable of relief pharmacists. I must get hired as a staff pharmacist at one of the area stores before the changeover. If placed within the company, my seniority and all benefits would be recognized and continued with the new owners. I was fortunate to find a spot.

During a conversation with one of my female colleagues from the now-disbanded relief pool, she complained that John Giroux had told her that she was the worst employee in the relief pool, the one he got the most complaints about. Recognizing the familiar refrain, I said that it couldn't be. Giroux, using that exact wording, told me I held that honor. We laughed, and I wondered if that was a standard script that Giroux used on all of us.

I was looking for a way to improve my value to the company or a career change, considering some drastic changes. I dabbled with computer imaging, studying programs like Adobe Photoshop and CorelDraw. I drew on knowledge gained from my photography hobby and during my abandoned pursuit of a BFA, in combination with these applications, to forge a career in image manipulation. I invested in sophisticated computer hardware and software, took courses to improve my photo imaging skills and began a hobby business doing photo restorations. After a period of considering enrolment in a prestigious course for computer illustration at Sheraton College, which was sometimes rewarded with employment by the likes of Disney, I admitted that my skills and passion for this path needed to be reassessed.

If I wasn't going to commit to such a drastic career change, what made sense?

To improve my CV, I needed to take an advanced degree, a master's. It should be something that I had the qualifications and passion to pursue. I looked into options and found a distance learning opportunity through Queen's Smith School of Business. I could take an Executive MBA in Hamilton every Friday and Saturday. The course extended over sixteen months while allowing continued employment at my current job. I needed documentation of support from my immediate supervisor and a passing mark on the entrance exam to gain admittance to the course.

I wrote the entrance exam and subsequently got admitted. The representative from Queen's delivering the good news made a bit of a faux pas. When notifying me of my success, she said, "You got the lowest mark you possibly could on the exam and still got in." I shrugged that off, thinking I only prepared for a few weeks after being out of school for twenty-one years, and maintaining a full-time job, so kudos to me.

I arranged a reduced schedule, keeping my full-time status and benefits package. I committed to a sixteen month course that demanded about twenty hours a week of attention, in addition to a reduced work week in my chosen profession; a combined total of fifty-six hours. The program was designed for rising executives in positions that paid the tuition for its enrolled employees. I covered the costs out of pocket.

Over the next two years, I used two weeks of my holiday allotment each August to spend on campus for lectures. During these two weeks, I stayed in the student residence. The days were filled with programmed lessons occupying seven to eight hours each day, similar to a typical day at school. The rest of the course was delivered by distance learning, held in various venues, able to handle the technology that allowed Kingston to communicate between the lecture studio and lecture sites in various across Canada simultaneously.

There were sites in British Columbia, Alberta, Saskatchewan, Manitoba, Ontario, New Brunswick, and Quebec. Participants originated from Washington State, Bermuda, Regina, Calgary, Hamilton, Ottawa and other locales. The groups ranged from four to eight members, depending on their home base and the closest site. I participated at a site based in Hamilton with eight members. My commute was twenty minutes, but some participants flew into the B.C. site from Washington State or commuted from three hours away to attend lectures. We were evaluated on a mix of work submitted as a team and as individuals. Being part of a larger group reduced the individual workload. I was lucky to be in one of the larger groups.

The first year of the program went well and was exhilarating and challenging. Around this time, my sponsor supervisor took a job with one of our competitors, hoping to forge a quicker path to advancement. He was replaced with by my immediate successor as manager at my last management placement. Coincidentally, the fellow who preceded me as manager there got placed in the same store with us. With the reunion of three managers of the same Hamilton Mountain store, one current and two past, I dubbed us the Three Amigos.

I started to experience symptoms of burnout in my full-time job. One day, an elderly disabled amputee in a scooter demanded that I give him an antibiotic immediately for his remaining swollen and painful foot. This demand exceeded my scope of practice. He was being nasty, banging the counter with a cane. I approached him to redirect the situation. I told him that we could not give him anything until the doctor called in his order. Both he and I made several calls to the doctor and had yet to receive an order. Suddenly, the older man burst into tears, explaining that he lived alone, that his wife and son had already passed on, and that he feared another amputation if the infection wasn't eliminated, given his diabetes.

Overwhelmed by the stark realization of his situation, I hugged him. After his departure, I battled to control my emotions. I ran to the office, slammed the door and could no longer hold back the wave of grief washing over me like a tsunami. My wails were audible outside the office. When I felt in control again, I exited to face my somber staff, who had heard everything. My efforts to conceal my depth of feeling had failed. I wondered how much longer I could endure under the circumstances.

Added to these feelings was a sense of loss and grief stemming from Debbie's disability. As professionals, it was our habit to attend meetings and conferences as a team. We always participated together. It was a pattern established over twenty-two years of marriage. Sometimes, we even carpooled to work if our work sites were close together and scheduling coincided. After Debbie became disabled, it felt like I had lost a limb attending these meetings alone. There was a sense of grief as acute as if Debbie had passed away. I felt it most acutely at the annual conferences in Toronto sponsored by our employer.

At one of these conferences, I felt at loose ends and went to my hotel room, skipping some sessions. When I got to the room, I noticed the phone was flashing the indication for a waiting message. The voicemail directed me to call a Burlington police officer regarding a traffic accident that Debbie had been involved in. The officer told me that Debbie was in the hospital and that she would like me to come home. In a rush, I packed and briefly informed the registration desk that I was leaving the conference to attend to a family emergency. On the road, my mind tumbled with possibilities. I drove directly to the hospital, where I met the police officer who provided a more detailed explanation. Debbie had been turning left into the Tim Horton's when she was struck, almost head-on, by a Bronco. Even with seat belts, she was hurled forward and hit the steering wheel with her chest, bruising her heart. The paramedics on the scene had advised her to remain where she was so they could extract her from the car. They strapped her head to the stretcher to keep her neck immobile and transported her to the hospital. The doctors were optimistic about her diagnosis but wanted to keep her overnight for observation. The car, a 1989 Toyota Corolla, was a write-off. Debbie seemed okay and asked me to call her parents to pass on the news. She suggested that I joke about her wanting a new car for her approaching birthday. I did as I was told, including the joke, but got accused by Ma-Zilla of being cold-hearted and rude for making light of such a serious matter.

41

Brandan; Further Education and Jobs

I was surprised when Brandan announced his desire to take linguistics at Brock University. That should have been on the radar had I thought about his study of runes and the elven languages in the appendices of the J.R.R. Tolkien books. Brandan carried a comprehensive knowledge of all gaming that resembled Dungeons and Dragons or role-playing games, including the study of languages and how they developed.

So he decided with little input from us, and we prepared for his first year away from home and in residence. I had mostly positive memories of residence life, so I thought Brandan wouldn't have any issues. I should have known better. His roommate in residence was a jock. The roommate would leave his radio on constantly, leave the room for hours without locking up and rubbed Brandan the wrong way. Brandan got through his first year in the same manner as in previous years.

In the second year, he switched to the Downtown Student Res, an old hotel converted to student housing. He had a single room that year, and we hoped things would go okay. He had several friends from Burlington who resided there to anchor him, but he found the residence noisy and cold. His second-year results were much the same as the previous year. Brandan arranged with the building owner to return to the same room the following year so that, for an added fee, we could leave his stuff in place over the summer to await his return to the third year.

In the third year, Brandan fell into depression. At the end of his third year, he had only successfully accumulated credits equivalent to two years of classes. His depression took its toll. Unimpressed with his marks and unaware of his struggles, I told him to take a year off to work and earn enough to reimburse me for a wasted year.

Brandan didn't say anything about his depression because he didn't want to burden me further.

We had transferred to Wasaga Beach by then, and Brandan worked at the local video store while living with us. Sometimes, I paid him, from my salary, to do filing for me at my store. Warned by my bosses that nepotism was unacceptable, we kept Brandan off the books, but other staff were wary that he was there to spy on conversations. Feeling uncomfortable with that optic, Brandan refused further involvement with my store.

After fourteen months in Wasaga Beach, things weren't working out, and I did not renew the management agreement. I took an overnight shift in a twenty-four-hour store in Barrie. Perhaps that option was offered as an incentive to get me to quit the company, but I had experience with shift work from the factory and didn't feel that I was above working overnight.

We relocated to Barrie, and Brandan got an internship in an IT program at Base Borden. After a year there, he worked part-time at Borden and enrolled at Laurentian College through its satellite affiliation with Georgian College in Barrie. He finally completed a three-year degree majoring in History. Eventually, Brandan gave up his part-time job at Borden because his pay was only covering expenses incurred to travel to and from work. He felt the time could be better spent doing school work.

After his graduation, Brandan's next project was to teach English as a second language in Japan. He took two years of Japanese in high school and wanted to experience life in Japan. Unfortunately, there were no teaching positions available there. Instead, Brandan took a position in and taught English in South Korea for a year.

Although he considered it, he did not accept the contract to teach there for a second year. Brandan got to Japan while in the area, spending his Christmas holidays there. He felt a great sense of accomplishment and enjoyed the interaction with his students. He hoped the experience would give him a leg up teaching in Canada, but his lack of acceptable teachables blocked that.

On return to Canada, Brandan found an apprenticeship program with Georgian College in the IT department. At the end of the apprenticeship, he hoped to find a full-time position. The post did not materialize, so Brandan enrolled in a two-year IT Certificate Program at Georgian College with the option to take a third year of study, ending with an engineering degree. While that would have been my advice, when the third year loomed, Brandan quit school and looked for employment in IT.

Brandan got hired with Bell Canada's IT department in the Orillia call center. He rose to a management position in that job, even when the center changed ownership. After several years there, he became disabled with an anxiety disorder triggered by two car accidents he experienced during his highway commute: once after hitting a patch of black ice and once after hitting two moose blocking both lanes of the highway. In each case, he totaled his vehicles. The panic attacks were the result of these traumatic collisions that prevented his commute, and he applied and got approved for an ODSP disability status.

42

Amber in University

Amber started her first year at Guelph University when Brandan entered his third year at Brock. As you may imagine, my financial burden was at an all-time high. I had finished my MBA by then, but now the loan payments kicked in. Debbie started her Master of Education the previous year at Brock, and her tuition was an immediate debt. I promised both children that I would cover the costs of an undergraduate degree for them. After Debbie's first year of the Masters' degree, she became disabled with fibromyalgia. The financial burden for all the kids' expenses exceeded my single salary. We drew on Debbie's RRSP contributions to compensate. Simultaneously, we initiated the legal wrangling with Debbie's disability insurance, but contingency agreements with the lawyers pushed the debt for that into the future.. In any case, money trickled away, in deviation from my plan. My horizon for retirement went from age fifty-five to at least age sixty-five.

Amber was offered an all-expenses-paid scholarship in the photography program of a University in Michigan. I tried to steer her to that, not only for the apparent financial relief but because I wanted her to have a marketable skill at the completion of her degree. She felt that there were too many struggling, unemployed photographers and preferred a degree in Fine Arts. I argued that there wasn't much difference in future outlook between her options, but she said that she wanted to enjoy her studies. Fine Arts outweighed photography. Interestingly, her Fine Arts Course leaned heavily on mixed media, including photography.

Amber had a more pleasant experience in residence than Brandan's. She enrolled at the Arts House residence, where more students had similar interests to hers.

She met many of her long-term friends in Arts House. She didn't get along with her first-year roommate, though. The girl was untidy, spreading her work all over the floor, hogging space, and was seldom in, as she spent most of her time at her boyfriend's place, often staying there for days at a time.

As Amber was nearing the completion of her fourth year, she wanted to extend her studies for another year, taking a double major in Fine Arts and Philosophy. I reminded her I had only promised to pay for her undergrad degree. She suggested that her double major was still an undergrad degree. Her appeal convinced me, and I agreed to cover the extra year. She graduated with an Honours Bachelor of Arts, with Distinction, in 2007.

After graduation, Amber relocated to Toronto. She found employment as the receptionist in a naturopath's office. Amber found the work uninspiring. She liked the clientele, which included a local celebrity. Still, she thought that her boss had some unrealistic expectations about expanding her practice, given the limited number of examination rooms and the number of hours in a day. The only way to meet the boss's expectation would be to overbook. She remained in that position for over a year, complaining she would rather poke pencils into her eyes than stay longer. In any event, she returned to school to pursue a Master of Fine Arts in Curatorial Studies at the Ontario College of Art and Design University on Queen Street. During that time, she worked as a Teaching Assistant for the maximum term allowed so that the positions were available to more students instead of employing a lucky few. Amber's specialty was performance art, and she had showings in Toronto, San Francisco and Edmonton. She became heavily involved with Nuit Blanche, reading Tarot Cards in association with the Fast Wurms. She also did a stint as an unpaid intern with an Art Magazine, hoping to ease into a full-time position. Eventually, she had the skills to fulfill every task required to publish the magazine, including being a frequent contributor to published content. When the editor post became available, she interviewed for the position, hoping her loyalty as an unpaid intern would pay off. She was devastated when they hired an outsider. The magazine folded within a year of the new editor's installment.

After completing her Masters' degree, Amber found a position as the Director of the Student-run Xpace Gallery, dedicated to showing emerging and student artists in Toronto. It was a one-year contract position that she took in 2011. During that year, the board decided to relocate the gallery to larger premises, removed from the confines of the University but still nearby. During the relocation they extended Amber's contract for a further year and a half. While there, Amber was an advocate for worker's rights, given her experiences as an unpaid intern. She co-founded FEAST (Funding Engaging Actions with Sustainable Tactics) with Deborah Wang, a series of community dinners and micro-funding events to support student artist participants. Her exhibitions explored the collective support of workers as a means for change.

After her contract with Xpace, Amber had hoped to find further employment opportunities in Toronto, but, like many of her generation, she found employment openings limited. After about three months, her savings depleted, and she moved back in with us, now located in Barrie.

While she worked in Toronto, Amber dreamed of eventually owning a home. She had a vision of it that she hoped to bring to fruition, so Amber accumulated many pieces of art and furniture that she hoped to fill it with. Since we had downsized to a house half the size of our typical abode in preparation for retirement, there wasn't enough space to accommodate all of her belongings, so a storage locker got rented to store her things with some of our overflow in anticipation of Amber's future home. She wanted to buy a farm and have many animals, predominantly dogs. When she moved in with us, Tsuki (Moon in Japanese), our Shih Tsu, was her constant companion. It almost seemed like Tsuki was her dog more than ours, but Tsuki slept with Debbie and me each night. Otherwise, Amber cuddled with her and constantly taught her new tricks. It was in keeping with Amber's previous actions as a sponsor for pound dogs that she had taken into her home.

43

Doug's Work Continued

Another year passed. The Three Amigos contributed to the smooth running of our store, but in the time before we were united there, the plaza's tenant mix had changed resulting in decreased foot traffic. The grocery store across the hall relocated, as did the adjacent deli store. With the loss of these tenants, our sales declined. The lease came up for renewal. We stayed on a month to month basis rather than renewing in the long term. Staff and wage cuts were proposed. To prevent my non-professional coworkers from losing wages, I offered to cut my hours sufficiently to offset the proposed wage cuts for the other staff. One of the Three Amigos departed. There were rumblings from management about store closure.

With the departure of one of the Three Amigos, another cost-cutting opportunity was presented and I proposed a cut to our hours of operation to eliminate the need for a third pharmacist. I suggested that we close at six p.m. daily. This pushed the inevitable closure back a few months, but having exhausted all options for further cost-cutting measures, the head office announced the store's impending closure. A store that had been a fixture at that location for over twenty years sadly fell victim to the changing economy. I was guaranteed continued employment, but the rest of the staff had to apply for openings at other locations with no guarantee of success. It marked another end of an era during my career.

Debbie's disability and the cuts to wages accepted in the past affected cash flow. I needed to either get a raise or find a new job. Since graduating from the MBA, I scouted all possibilities. Still, I found that the only career change option available was selling insurance. I didn't want to go that route because there was no evident earnings increase on that path. I now realized that the grass wasn't greener in other professions and reevaluated the wisdom of a career change. I scouted for opportunities in hospital pharmacy or in the developing geriatrics provision sector. I went for many interviews but met with disappointment. I couldn't find a suitable "fit." Eventually, I applied to return to a management position within my current organization. I was rewarded with a spot that required my relocation to Wasaga Beach. Our newly custom-built home in Burlington was sold and we shopped for new lodgings in a new town. My line of credit, financial commitments to my children's education and Debbie's dwindling RRSP savings demanded adjustment. There was partial relief in Wasaga Beach because we were able to purchase a larger house while eliminating part of our debt.

I had a sense of foreboding when the area director showed me to my office on the first day of my new job, recalling all the things I hated about middle management. I was subjected to extreme scrutiny from the moment I arrived in Wasaga Beach. I was an outsider, and upper management trumpeted my MBA status, causing some resistance from the get-go. The previous manager had been fired under a cloud. The secondary pharmacist had management responsibility forced on her for a year with no increase in remuneration. For all I know, she may have even applied for the job in competition with me when it became available, guaranteeing her resentment of being passed over. She was not in any mood to co-operate and documented every failing on my part.

I walked into a store with a staff that was already hostile and resistant to me. The team also encouraged customer dissatisfaction. My boss informed me of his plans to fire the incumbent front shop manager. I had his assurances that it would be done before I took over. A replacement front shop manager was already training at a different store; his wages were allocated to my budget. I stumbled upon this when I requested the staff list to conduct interviews with the team. I made several inquiries about a person on the list who I never encountered. The boss told me that it was a mistaken inclusion on the list.

Although I knew Todd's days were numbered, I was forbidden to say anything. Todd asked me to warn him of any rumblings about his termination. I gave the closest thing to an admission I could without jeopardizing my position. I told him about the wrongful dismissal case my friend had endured. In the court-ordered settlement, which got wide media attention in the business section of papers, the judge had commented that while an employer may dismiss anyone for any reason, even if the stated excuse was that they didn't have the same point of view, the dismissal would only be acceptable if accompanied with adequate separation pay. In my friend's case, the hospital tried to fire her based on incompetence. My friend won the case, but her settlement was only large enough to cover her legal fees. I tried to prepare Todd for the inevitable, alerting him to pursue his rights to separation pay, which the company intended to avoid. In any case, those costs were passed through to my corporation and used as a justification to deny a bonus that year. In spite of significantly better sales following my arrival and the seventy-hour weeks that I worked to turn things around, I had not reached the "cliff" required to earn a bonus.

Todd's termination reeked of unfairness. On my day off, I got called in by the area director because he intended to terminate Todd immediately. Upon his arrival, with no forewarning, the director had a staff member call Todd in from a day off with the purpose of firing Todd upon our respective arrivals. The director also told me that Todd's replacement was waiting in his car to be introduced to staff as soon as the termination was complete. It was not my call, but I had to sign off on the firing because, by the franchise agreement, Todd was my employee, not the company's. It is what I had intended to avoid before my start date. Before my takeover, the head office was responsible for the operation of that store. Upon my installment, all the staff transferred to my corporation as outlined in the franchising agreement. The company passed costs arising from the firing to my corporation with the delay.

During the termination interview, Todd looked at me reproachfully and said, "I asked you!" I reminded him about our discussion about separation pay. After Todd was terminated and marched out, Mason was brought in from the car and introduced as Todd's replacement. During that introduction, the area director said that Mason was his good friend. One of the staff commented that Mason was there to spy on them. I pointed out that it was more likely that Mason was there to spy on me, but that gained no traction. The team judged me complicit in Todd's termination. A staff that had already been wary of me now dug in, uniting to see me fail.

I continued in my role, fulfilling my duties dictated by the franchise agreement. The staff and customers perceived me as the store's owner and assumed that all outcomes and policies enacted were directly attributable to me and were directed by my intent. Given the current situation, I wanted to be sure of my rights and responsibilities according to the franchise agreement. I hired a lawyer and had him review the deal and assess my fiduciary duty, pitfalls,s and options. He said no lawyer would have advised me to sign the agreement as written. He said that the document was written mainly to the benefit of head office and that one clause even stated that a franchisee could be fired on the spot without notice. He pointed out that either party could terminate the agreement with sixty days' written notice.

Before I took over the franchise, I had to form a corporation in my name. A corporation must name a president and secretary in the official filing. I nominated Debbie as my secretary, so she was a member of my board. After the Todd incident, I asked the head office, Big Wig, if I could have the secretary of my corporation attend the sales projections meeting. I wanted a second set of ears there to prevent any misinterpretations that might arise. A member of the board of my corporation should be allowed to attend such meetings. The head office always sent two representatives (with computers ready) to present their point of view. With such double teaming, these meetings weighed in the head office's favor. When I asked if Debbie could attend, the Big Wig implied that I was being childish and that it was not allowed. Every month, I was challenged to meet increasing targets, which I exceeded., only to find the target increased again as a challenge. Micromanagement was the operational standard.

Shortly after I asked about Debbie's attendance at the meetings, I received a summons to Toronto for a meeting with my boss's boss. I was given a time and date with no further details. Because of my past experiences, I felt this would not be a meeting in my favor. I asked my lawyer, Don, to attend with me. He indicated that he could and under the circumstances, he advised that he should. Your legal representative is the only person who can never be turned away.

My boss's boss met us when we got to Toronto, and we were herded upstairs for the meeting. He asked who Don was. I introduced him as my friend, but Don spoke over me, saying he was my lawyer. Immediately, the meeting was called off, with the comment that they needed to prepare to take this meeting with their lawyer present. Don and I drove home knowing we had done the right thing.

It was time for me to start working on financial projections for the following year. I was unaware that it was essential to gain an advantage by lobbying for the earliest meeting possible, as those who waited were seen last and needed more room for negotiation after most of the budget had been allocated to those who met earlier. I was at one of the last scheduled meetings, facing two management representatives who came prepared like a finely tuned machine.

I tackled the project with my usual diligence, considering all of the factors involved. Head office pressed to increase our hours of operation, currently set from nine in the morning to ten p.m. daily. They intended a change to nine to midnight. There was a plan in the works to relocate the store in the face of rising rents. I presented my draft projection. Any discussion based on valid considerations was met with, "This is what the Board decided.

We can't disappoint the Board." I was dumbfounded that valid concerns were swept aside by a decision made in a remote boardroom rather than considering logical concerns.

Hostilities with my staff continued, with several resignations and job abandonment. Any change to the procedure, most of which was of head office initiation, was stonewalled. A whisper campaign against me was started, led by an unspoken partnership between my staff pharmacist and head cosmetician. The damaging thing about whisper campaigns is they don't have to have any integrity. They only need wide dissemination. Once it's out there, the damage is done.

At one point, although everyone on staff indicated they would attend the annual Christmas party, there was an organized movement to boycott the event. After I committed to the costs to host a team of fifty for the event, only one staff member and her husband broke rank to attend the evening with Debbie, Brandan and me. This snub didn't hurt my feelings so much as anger me with the malicious intent to cause inflated costs and harm the company's image.

A visit from the Head of Security for our district seemed to be only routine.

He was new and seemed dedicated to his position. I assumed he made the rounds to acquaint himself with all the stores and management teams. We had a nice conversation; then he went about his inspection. A while later, he asked to speak to me again. He pointed out some areas for improved practices and brought up an irregularity with the purchases made by the cosmetician under the staff discount program. He suggested that she be terminated. He said that he would do the deed. I was not convinced that the action was warranted at that time and asked for more time to observe her purchases over the next little while.

Over the next quarter, I noticed the issues that disturbed him regarding this employee's interpretation of the employee discount program. I called him and revisited the issue. It was decided that the termination should proceed and that he would carry out the act. On the day of her termination, it was again my day off. Since the Security Head said he was going to perform the termination, I did not attend that session. Under the franchisee agreement, I had to sign off on the firing. I didn't think that meant that I had to be there at the actual moment, so I stayed out of it. I did sign the required paperwork and the action proceeded. A month or so later, I received a notice from the cosmetician's lawyer informing me that she was suing me as a co-defendant in a wrongful dismissal suit. Once again, I contacted Don, my lawyer.

I had been in the manager's position for nearly a year. I was informed that my profitability wasn't sufficient to warrant a bonus even though I had exceeded sales targets and met all the continuously increasing challenge targets.

The following summer, the proposed opening til midnight was approaching, and a future relocation loomed. I had done everything expected of me, had endured the hostility of a staff mainly created by past actions of head office, and was named in a lawsuit for wrongful dismissal.

There had been increased pressure from my superiors because of staff complaints, some of which stemmed from Mason's demands for performance improvement. My staff pharmacist had started documenting my perceived wrongdoings, which I discovered while looking for a palm pilot that was supposed to be store property. From the moment I arrived, there had been resistance to change, organized sabotage of efforts to enforce company policy, a whisper campaign of untruths and assumed non-existent motivations spread to the customer base, and efforts to undermine the company's goodwill.

I re-evaluated my commitment to the position and gave my sixty-day written notice of non-renewal of the franchise agreement. The mounting evidence proved that I had nothing more than a job under the arrangement, and I was no longer willing to endure the distortions and muddiness of company portrayals.

Before I stepped down, there was a departure interview with a panel of head office representatives, including the Head of Human Resources. During that interview, they grilled me about my actions and motivations. I did get support and verification from one of the panel. After the discussion, I asked to speak to the Head of Human Resources alone. The other panel members left the room, and I asked him about a managers' meeting about a year ago. I asked him if he remembered the discussion of benchmarks used to weigh performance. He said he remembered that. I asked him if he remembered I asked a specific question regarding staff evaluations of management's inclusion in the benchmarks. He said that it had not. I then, in my typical straightforward, clueless manner, expressed in a raising voice that the recent staff complaints were the direct result of the company culture. I mentioned that the lack of inclusion of that as a benchmark reflected the culture. If head office indicated that there would be no accounting for these considerations, why would they expect any? I also expressed that the lack of that inclusion was attributable to him. I "ripped him a new one," so to speak. I believe my voice carried beyond closed doors. Once again, I stabbed myself in the chest because of my low EQ and my belief in telling it like it is.

44

Moving On

Given my mistrust of the management representatives during the ensuing weeks, I got my lawyer involved in the changeover. There were final inventories to tally and other legalities to work through. I was offered continued employment as an overnight pharmacist in a twenty-four-hour store. Perhaps management hoped this would be so insulting that I would quit, but I accepted the offer. Having worked night shifts during my factory years, I did not feel that it was beneath me. I had to interview for the position.

Coincidentally, the person interviewing me was in the last weeks of her franchise agreement and had little interest in the future of the store she was leaving. There was no collusion involved, but I negotiated three ten-hour shifts a week from Tuesday through Thursday.

On my first day there, I had to remind the departing manager of the paperwork needed to enroll me for staff benefits and in compliance with company policy. Things went fine for about six months. During that time, I put my house in Wasaga Beach on the market and moved to Barrie to eliminate the commute.

A new staff member appeared on the scene. Gabby had two children and her marriage was foundering because of her gambling addiction. Her husband left her and the two kids after the sheriff seized their house to cover her gambling debt at the

Rama Casino. Brandan had friends who had worked the casino and quit after seeing the depth of human suffering that can be brought on by such events. They said you had to be soulless to observe the reality of the effects of such an addiction and continue working there. The new girl spoke to me daily about her situation, asking for advice. She said that she hadn't believed the casino would take her house to cover the debt until the sheriff appeared at her door and accompanied her off the property. Even her parents abandoned her because of the shame she brought to the family's reputation. One shift, she seemed more upset than usual and approached me asking how to "off" herself. She said she had a gun. Another staff member told me that she had seen Gabby on the beach carrying the gun. I asked the witness if she had reported that to anyone. After Gabby approached me a second time that night asking how to end herself, I was genuinely concerned about her well-being. I told her that I could not advise her on the matter of suicide. I said she needed to seek professional help and asked her if she would do that. She said she wouldn't. I told her that if she would not take the matter seriously and get help, then I would force the issue. Having verified that she had a gun with intentions to use it, and knowing she had custody of her children, I felt a moral responsibility for those three lives. I could imagine a double murder-suicide in the offing, so I called the police. They came to the store, interviewed the potential suicide and escorted her out of the store. She left in their custody, saying, "Thanks Doug." One officer took her comment in the wrong way and spoke in my defense, but I never thought she was upset or bitter with me. I accepted her gratitude for my taking charge while she was too confused and lost to act on her own. Six months later she returned to the store, smiling and hugged me. She again thanked me for acting that night. She said her family had forgiven her and she had reestablished connections. My actions saved her life and turned it around.

He Tried

He stood on the corner,

Naked and cold,

And a tailor went by

And said, " Poor man, somebody

Should do something for him."

And he walked on.

He stood on the corner,

Hungry and thirsty,

And a baker went by

And said, " Poor man, somebody

Should do something for him."

And he walked on.

He stood on the corner,

Desperate and in need,

And a beggar went by

And said, " Poor man, somebody

Should do something for him."

And he tried.

Over the next little while, I met the pharmacists who covered the rest of the night shifts. One of them kept asking that I swap days with him. He commuted from Toronto and was self-employed. His sister was also working some of the nights. I held fast to the Tuesday-to-Thursday arrangement that I had negotiated. It became a problem when his sister started to suffer migraines on days that she was supposed to work.

Eventually, I was seen as an obstacle to the smooth running of the store because it was challenging to find coverage on short notice when migraines popped up. The store's current manager approached me and told me that I needed to accept seven consecutive days on, followed by seven days off, or I could become part of the day staff. I opted to move to the day shift.

The day shift schedule consisted of five ten-hour weekly shifts in a high-volume store. I had always worked in high-volume stores, which was not a problem. Eventually, the boss congratulated me on my successful integration into the daytime shift. I greatly respected Jean, the current manager,, for her even-handed treatment. She was the best boss I had ever encountered, giving petty issues the attention they deserved (little to none) and offering encouragement and praise when appropriate. She was not a pushover, but she was consistent.

What became a stumbling block was the ten-hour shifts. About nine months after the changeover, the physical demands of standing ten hours a day asserted themselves. I suffered from numbness in my left heel and foot that was ongoing, and I developed chronic back pain. I began a treatment schedule of weekly appointments with chiropractors, physiotherapists, and massage therapists. The doctor even sent me to a specialist who tested me for nerve conduction issues due to my being a diabetic.

One day, Jean asked if I would help her with a presentation at Georgian College during a weekend diabetes seminar. I agreed, and the feedback on my presentation was favorable. The boss asked me to step up and become a diabetes educator. Jean would cover the cost of the course upon my successful completion and exam results (about one-third of first-time participants fail the exam). I immersed myself in weekly lessons conducted by phone conferencing, determined to succeed. I wanted to take the course while in Wasaga Beach but didn't think I met the entrance requirements. My reservations were unfounded; I got accepted to the class. I may have taken the boss's challenge simply because I thought I would be rejected. After completing the course and passing the three-hour exam, I obtained certification as a diabetes educator, valid for five years. It could only be a plus on my resume.

Meeting the continuing education (CE) requirement to maintain pharmacy licensing and my Diabetes Educator Certification commitment required study above and beyond hours spent at work, increasing my load. Eventually, I began to feel like I was living to work rather than working to live. I asked Jean if there might be an option to decrease the ten-hour shifts in the store. She said no. I worked fifty hours a week dispensing and additional hours devoted to continuing education. The money was good, but I was beginning to fit into Debbie's definition of a workaholic and becoming more depressed with the chronic pain. I was using daily anti-arthritics, but the most effective medication was pulled from the market in the face of growing evidence that it increased the risk of heart attacks.

Something had to give. I needed to reduce my hours; Jean said that was impossible. Fortunately, an option arose. A new store was built in south Barrie, which Jean took on in addition to her current store on a short-term basis. Because this was a new opening, the clientele was growing, and hours of operation were more limited than at the twenty-four-hour store. Jean mentioned having difficulty finding somebody to work the shorter shifts at the new store. I was looking for relief from my blistering pace, so I gladly transferred. It was quite a difference. The pace changed from blistering to tediously slow.

The new store only had five percent of the prescription business compared to my previous placement. I couldn't devote much time to diabetes education there because the client base was lacking. I occupied myself with dusting, vacuuming, paperwork stock checking, and rotation. My income dropped by about thirty percent. On the plus side, the feeling returned to my left heel.

A year later, a replacement manager was found for the new store, ending my association with the best boss I'd ever met. The new boss, Gita, was a go-getter, well-regarded by management. One of her first demands was to ask the pharmacists to present our ideal work schedule. I provided a plan reflecting a long-standing pattern established through my years of service. I knew this schedule worked because it had been utilized in my previous company during my twenty-five years of service there. For some reason, Gita took issue with the proposed schedules, OUR ideal schedules. She requested another submission with the admonishment to be creative. I had already expressed what MY perfect schedule should reflect. I didn't know what she expected with this new request.

Presumably, my ideal schedule did not coincide with her concept. The initial question asked for MY perfect plan. I had provided that. It was a model that had worked for twenty-five years with my previous employer. What else could I say? I made no alternate submission.

A month later, Brenda, the other pharmacist, found another job. I stayed, hoping things would improve. Gita commuted from a city south of Barrie, choosing not to reside here. She preferred morning shifts and ignored my suggested ideal schedule. She placed me on permanent afternoon shifts, starting at three thirty.

To increase our business, Gita introduced a methadone treatment service. It would grow our business because, once established, it guaranteed a prescription a day for each patient enrolled. One hundred patients would raise our prescription count by one hundred daily. I supported the idea but asked to go for methadone training, as this had never been part of my practice. Since then, it has become a requirement for an outlet providing methadone services to have at least one pharmacist with methadone training on staff.

45

Robbery

Noting its location at the intersection of two major arteries in Barrie providing multiple primary highway access going north or south either immediately or within a five to ten-minute drive, my initial impression was that the new store had increased potential for robbery. It was a little isolated, standing in a proposed housing development that had not yet broken ground. Gita experienced the first robbery at the store. It was daytime theft for "Oxy." I asked afterward whether she was okay. She said she was, but told me that during a call to her husband immediately after the robbery, he asked her if she had any "skid marks" in her underwear.

Until then, I hadn't worked in a store that experienced a theft while I was on duty. Most of the targets for robberies were either isolated or not very busy. I usually worked in well-established, busy stores. I remembered an article I had read during my first year of licensure that stated there were more pharmacist deaths on the job in New York State that year than among police officers. I had also heard about a pharmacist who experienced PTSD after being forced to lie face down on the floor; then, the thief discharged his handgun into the floor near the pharmacist's head. I had classmates who had been robbed at gunpoint, some up to six times. There was even the Cowboy

Pharmacist, a name coined by the media, who ran afoul of the law for discharging his legally obtained and licensed handgun in the street at a fleeing vehicle. He tried to shoot out the tires after being robbed. There was a lot of media attention surrounding him (incidentally, he was another graduate from my class).

While working alone in the dispensary one winter night, I noticed a customer bundled up at the counter. He had his coat zipped up to his chin, his hood up and drawn tightly around his head, and he wore gloves, even in the store. The only thing I clearly saw was his glasses peeking out of his hood. I acknowledged him, saying, "I'll be right with you,sir, as soon as I serve this customer." I thought it must be freezing out tonight seeing him so kitted out. When I finished with the previous customer, I approached him, asking, "How can I serve you?" He threw a black cloth bag on the counter and said, "Fill it with Oxy." He seemed nervous, but I saw no evidence of a weapon. Safety and Security meetings always stress that you should be compliant and make no sudden or unexpected moves in these situations. I previously warned staff that it was better to be a live wimp than a dead hero in these situations. I started to move away from him to the narcotics lockup. He yelled, "Don't leave my sight," I went still immediately. I said I had to go to the next room to get it, indicating my destination. He yelled, "No you don't!" I replied, "Yes, I do." and invited him to accompany me to the lock-up. He rushed over to me, and we went to get his "Oxy." The safe was unlocked and swung open smoothly. I dumped all our "Oxy" into his bag, and he fled. I called the police immediately and initiated lockdown procedures to hold all customers in the store as potential witnesses. When the police arrived, they wanted my immediate attention, but as the robber fled, another customer presented a prescription for pain medications. I asked the officers to wait while I offered him a couple of tablets to take for the pain during the delay. After the police left, a female witness complimented me for my dedication concerning the man in pain and my calm control during the robbery.

As part of the police report, you fill out a victim statement. My first impulse was to write that if I had to be robbed, I was glad it was that guy because he presented no weapons, and he was non-violent. I thought that the police would find that answer too cavalier, so my official statement went along the lines that I no longer felt safe in the workplace after the robbery.

46

Next Steps

Gita settled down a bit after that but made snide remarks about my performance now and then. I conducted a diabetes clinic day now that the clientele had grown sufficiently to allow a decent attendance. The number could have been more impressive because we were still in a growth phase, but you must start somewhere. There may have been six attendees. The boss said derisively that she should get her friend in to show me how to conduct a real clinic day. Another time, she planned a bone density clinic without telling me anything about it. The day before it took place, she told me I would be conducting it. I knew she had procured a bone density machine loan from a drug sales rep at least a week previous to the event, but there had been no demonstration of its operation for me or notification that I would be expected to conduct the testing. I had about eight hours (on my own time) to familiarize myself with the machine and to prepare for questions that might arise.

Gita hired a foreign-trained pharmacist intern with a PhD. He would be licensed after four months of training with us. I believe that she planned to terminate me when he became licensed. Her snide remarks became more common and were delivered in the presence of other staff members. I continued my practice of researching answers to customer questions with Pub

Med and in journals, often bringing in printouts and journal articles for the patients to read. I left the information on the counter for easy access when the patient came in. Gita may have interpreted the reading material in the dispensary as malingering on my part, assuming that I was reading on the job. The articles often disappeared when I needed them, only to appear weeks later, tucked into some drawer.

Other times, She approached me with a barrage of questions, giving me no time to answer the first one before asking another, then walking away with a sour look on her face without letting me speak. Additionally, she tried to gaslight me on occasion, removing bottles of medications I had selected to use in completing a prescription while I was retrieving the labels from the printer.

As the time approached for the Ph.D. Intern to be licensed, I asked him about his plans for the future. I expected him to be excited about his approaching licensure. He said he had found a position with a drug company that he would start as soon as his internship was complete. I asked why he didn't want to continue with us. He replied, "I got a PhD. to work in drug companies. I'm not interested in providing methadone treatment." I was surprised but could understand his ambitions. After he left, the boss seemed to change her attitude toward me. I was deemed satisfactory.

On the morning shifts, Gita moved a woman from the front shop into an on- the-job trained tech position working with Gita for her entire shift. She had the tech process as many prescription labels as possible during the day, setting them into baskets for counting, checking, and completion later in the day. Gita only processed prescriptions for waiting customers during the day, leaving me with at least two-thirds of the work to complete in the evening. The tech's shift overlapped mine for an hour and a half. After that, I was responsible for data entry for new prescriptions arriving during my shift and completing preprocessed work. When I asked for more tech help to ease the load, Gita compared the number of prescription labels produced while she worked with the tech, implying that these required no further handling, to the number processed during my shift. It didn't accurately represent a fair comparison of the workload.

Gita indicated I was not pulling my weight. The tech we had was untrained and receiving on-the-job instruction. Having trained techs for years, some with no previous training, like the one offered now, I knew it would be challenging. The new "tech" had the will to succeed and was extremely pleasant and genuine. I taught a portion of the tech course at Sheridan College for a term. I trained at least fifty to one hundred newly graduated or from-the-floor techs in the past, and I realized that this woman would need at least six months of job training before she was of any use and would increase my load until then. Even a fully trained, newly graduated college technician needs to adjust to the demands of the specific operation that eventually employed her. How helpful is an untrained person who doesn't even know the drug names she must select to process the prescription using the drug identification number on the bottle? How practical is a person unexposed to Latin-based short forms used on prescription orders? Julia did her best, as did I, but she finally asked to return to the front shop as she felt out of her depth in the dispensary. A certified tech eventually got hired. During the time Anna worked there, things improved to a degree. She was knowledgeable and efficient. It relieved a lot of stress.

Eventually, Gita found Anna unsatisfactory and let her go, replacing her with a more pliable new grad. Lea was pleasant and efficient but held no loyalty to me and reported back to Gita regarding my performance. In one case, Lea heard me comment that I did not know a particular fact about reporting requirements for methadone prescriptions that were prepared and not picked up or lost due to spillage. It got reported back to Gita. Since the beginning of the methadone treatment program at our store, I found that Gita had done a poor job communicating what she knew about the program requirements, even though she was very familiar with the procedure from previous experience. She also failed to communicate critical information like patient dosing changes. Gita's lack of communication became a problem when adverse outcomes arose because she'd blame me. She claimed I was negligent for not knowing information that hadn't been passed on. I received a probationary notice and was told that if my performance did not improve one hundred percent over the ensuing month, I would be terminated. I asked Gita what the odds were that I might pass this hurdle, and she answered, "None," suggesting that her mind was already made up. She further suggested that I take a short-term leave of absence for "health issues."

The health issues Gita referred to were my chronic back and knee pain. When Gita took charge, I presented her with the result of an X-ray assessing the bulging discs in my back. The condition was diagnosed as progressive. She barely took notice, grunted, and did not take a copy for for my employee file. Since that day, I have attended appointments with chiropractors, massage therapists, osteopaths and physiotherapists. These professionals recommended that I sit during my shifts to ease the pain in my back. I had passed these recommendations on to Gita, but they got vetoed.

It is difficult, but possible, to do the job while sitting because of the need to move to different workstations. I began to wear a back support brace on shift. Soon after that, chronic pain in my right knee prompted me to wear a knee brace. Once, Gita suggested that I pursue disability through the company's group insurance, saying that she and the head office would help me obtain the coverage. With my distrust of management and experience fighting with Debbie's insurer, I rejected the idea, saying, "I won't get disability." I had little faith that she or the head office could influence the insurer's decision. During Debbie's disability struggles, our lawyers warned us that some insurers provide coverage for a short term and then cut you off, suggesting you work in a different job, any job, as long as they can get away with it. I remembered this when I rejected Gita's suggestion. I took her advice to take a short paid leave of absence. I booked off for two weeks.

Given the short period I was presented with to improve my performance, I did not take the total sick leave arranged and returned after a week. I expected that the period for improvement would kick in from the date of my return, but the day I showed up for work, Gita took me into her office, with Lea as a witness and presented two forms to consider for my signature. One of the forms was an admission and acceptance of termination for cause that would be immediate and deny any severance pay. The other was a termination document that would be immediate but did not rule out my pursuit of legal recourse. Gita pushed the first form forward, expecting me to sign it. I told her I could not sign that document and asked for the second form, launching me into legal action.

During my sick leave, I consulted a lawyer regarding constructive dismissal.

Gita took pains to document my alleged incompetence. Her evidence appeared hastily put together, written long after the fact, with sparse details provided. Each of her claims was reasonably disputed. The day that I attended the lawyer's office, I arrived home to the news that Teddy had succumbed to his lung cancer that day. There was also a call from Gita in search of information about a situation at the store that I had no involvement in. I returned her call but was unable to clear up her problem. Shortly after my termination, a fire in the store caused extensive smoke damage to inventory. I heard that the store was closed while they sorted through and cleaned salvageable items. I felt that may have been a sign of retributive Karma and was glad I didn't get called upon during the salvage operation. A mouse nibbled through electrical or computer wiring, initiating the blaze.

While on sick leave, I attended Teddy's funeral and one interview for a planned start-up for a methadone clinic in Kingston. I got a second interview for the job, but it didn't work out. I also attended two interviews for an opening at a hospital in Orilla that passed me over. I scouted for jobs in other Barrie stores and, by the fifth week post- termination, got a shift at a methadone clinic that provided some much-needed income and several follow-up shifts. I decided to go the self-employed route and put my name in at an agency to improve my success with the hunt for shifts. By the sixth week post- termination, the agency worked to my benefit, resulting in steady employment over the next year. The only problem was that the agency jobs booked me for remote jobs requiring travel and prolonged motel stays. Debbie and our dog Tsuki could accompany me during some of these jobs, which took me to Chapleau, Sudbury, Owen Sound, Espanola and Terrace Bay.

47

Terrace Bay

In February 2013, I was scheduled for a week at a store in Terrace Bay.

Usually, I drove to my assignments, but this was so far north that the drive would exceed ten hours, so I took a plane into Thunder Bay. I was picked up there by the store owner's stepson, and we began the two-hour drive to Terrace Bay. The boy told me his parents were vacationing somewhere in the Caribbean. I arrived on a Saturday. My first shift was scheduled for Monday. I was housed in an apartment that usually was occupied by my chauffeur, the owner's stepson. I spent the Sunday relaxing alone and feeling drained.

After my first shift on Monday, I needed some groceries, so I asked to be chauffeured to shop. While there, I suffered extreme shortness of breath. I felt like I just ran a marathon but couldn't catch my breath. I considered laying down on the floor to ease my breathing, but I thought that was too drastic, so I headed to the checkout. My chauffeur, the owner's stepson was waiting at the end of the counter with eyes as big as saucers. He asked me if I was okay. He had witnessed his father's fatal heart attack and was fearful that I was experiencing one. I said I was okay but still struggled for breath. As we entered the car, he asked if he should take me to the hospital. I said no, I was okay, but I still struggled to catch my breath. Then, I considered that I would be alone in the apartment when he dropped me off. If things did not improve, I would be vulnerable, so I agreed to go to the emergency room.

With his eyes still wide, my chauffeur hurried to the ER to get help. The nursing staff rushed out with a gurney and started the protocol for a heart attack. They administered oxygen along with chewable aspirin. My breathing began to ease, and they admitted me for observation. Still receiving oxygen, I was warned not to get out of bed, even to use the bathroom. I was hungry and asked for something to eat. The nurse brought me a sandwich. By now, it was about seven p.m. I fell asleep and slept soundly through to the late morning hours.

When I awoke the following day, the nurse said the doctor would be in shortly to see me. He brought me up to date with his findings. He said that I was a mystery man. I hadn't had a heart attack, and the usual blood tests were non-conclusive. A later X-ray revealed that I had a partially collapsed lung. He scheduled me for a heart angiogram the following day in Thunder Bay.

I had an angiogram a few years previously. Then, the procedure entered the groin and wound into the heart. That was ordered after a routine stress test seemed to indicate a serious blockage in my heart. Coming so suddenly, accompanied by the warning not to do anything until the results of the angiogram were known, I suffered extreme anxiety waiting the eight-day delay until the procedure. Jack had received emergency heart bypass surgery as a result of his angiogram. That thought brought the fear of my chest being cracked open with rib spreaders and the painful recovery period that followed. I was not secure enough financially to endure the prolonged recovery period. My mind was swamped during the delay with an overwhelming fixation on an uncertain future. I was so worked up before the procedure that the prep nurse asked Debbie if I was always so skittish.

The approach through the groin required a two-hour recovery time with clamps immobilizing the area. I was secured between the gurney and a square of plywood to provide adequate pressure to prevent a possible serious hemorrhage. Given my chronic back issue, this positioning was agonizing. When I was told that the results of the test showed no blockage, the same nurse commented on the drastic change in my demeanor post-testing. Until the all-clear, I had been consumed by negative thoughts overpowering anything else.

The Terrace Bay hospital transported me to Thunder Bay for an angiogram—the distance from our destination required transferring from one ambulance after another because we kept crossing service boundaries. Our trip required the use of five ambulances. One of the transfers occurred in a frigid parking lot during an early February cold snap. I was only covered with a thin sheet and maybe a blanket. It was so cold that I told the accompanying nurse that my nipples were hard enough to cut glass. She obliged me with a chuckle.

I was assured that the angiogram in Thunder Bay would approach through the wrist, the risk of hemorrhage being controlled by an inflatable wrist cuff, so I was relaxed before the procedure. At one point during the process, the doctor asked me urgently if I was okay because my blood pressure had dropped significantly, but that was the only hitch. We made the return to Terrace Bay, again doing multiple transfers. The whole day was occupied by the time at the hospital and the round trip.

That night, I again slept soundly through to the morning. I had been in touch with my chauffeur, who was concerned about my ability to complete my contract. As I had understood the situation, the blood markers diagnostic of a heart attack were not present upon admission, so I mistakenly reassured him that upon release from the hospital, I would complete the assignment. That day passed with me calling my agency and home and indulging myself with several naps. Debbie wanted to fly to be with me. I said that wouldn't be necessary because I did not yet understand the severity of my condition.

I couldn't believe how tired I felt. Late that day, the doctor graced me with another visit. He was concerned about my expectations of completing my contract. He said that I was mistaken that my blood levels were absent of any indicators of a heart attack but that the levels were low and non-conclusive. He told me that I most likely wouldn't be fulfilling my assignment and said he would give me more information the next day after he got the angiogram results.

The following day, the doctor informed me that the angiogram was not conclusive, but there was no evidence of blockage. I most likely had a pulmonary embolism (PE). He said he would release me later that day and that I should use the fastest method to return home and see my doctor when I arrived. I had flown in, so I had to fly out. I paid extra fees to move my departure date forward in spite of having a prepaid return ticket. I flew into Pearson International Airport, where Debbie met me.

Surprisingly, my Terrace Bay doctor was also returning to Toronto on that flight. I was already seated when he boarded, and he stopped and said, "I didn't expect to see you here." I replied, "Well, ya told me to go home."

On landing I was drained and weak. The walk to the departure lounge was a formidable task, and I was the last passenger through the gate. Debbie wondered if I'd missed the flight because of the lapse of time and my arrival twenty minutes later than all the other passengers from my flight. When we got home, I was grateful to crawl into bed.

The next day, I called my GP to get an appointment regarding the potential pulmonary embolism. He was on a weekend getaway, taking advantage of the Family Day long weekend. He was unavailable until the following Tuesday. Instead of going to a walk-in clinic for more immediate attention, I waited for my doctor's return.

A CT scan ordered by my GP on his return indicated that I had several clots in my lungs and a partially collapsed lung. The treatment with anticoagulants initiated in Terrace Bay continued, and I was thankful that I had survived the encounter.

My shortness of breath continued. After seven months of anticoagulant treatment, I asked the doctor when he would attempt to discontinue the anticoagulant. Liver function tests indicated a concerning elevation of enzymes. He discontinued the anticoagulant.

Two weeks later, I was back in the hospital for a CT that revealed a recurrence of pulmonary embolism in both lungs. The anticoagulant therapy was resumed using warfarin, a different medication than previously prescribed, to allow elevated enzymes to fall. Further pulmonary function testing conducted that day resulted in a diagnosis of Chronic Obstructive Pulmonary Disease (COPD).

During the months after the initial PE, I was unable to work. I applied for EI sick benefits but got denied. That got reversed with aid from my member of Parliament.

Simultaneous applications were made for early CPP benefits and CPP Disability. The first application for CPP Disability was denied, but I got coverage on appeal. These manipulations left my future financial situation in question for the duration but eventually reached a favorable conclusion. At the same time, I proceeded with legal action. I faced scrutiny from the College of Pharmacists with one action and filed a wrongful dismissal lawsuit with the other.

My lawyer negotiated a solution that saved my license, whereby I signed an indefinite undertaking to submit to a period of supervision at my own cost and to participate in an awareness seminar. Considering the big picture, I finally opted for early retirement. I was no longer up to the job's physical demands.

48

Retirement

I entered a period of adjustment. My situation was still not settled because the wrongful dismissal suit remained ongoing. Anxiety about our uncertain financial stability colored every day. I tried to appear accepting and calm, moving on with my life by indulging in long-postponed pursuits. I occupied myself with guitar lessons. I persisted for about six months before frustration with arthritic fingers and poor coordination called a halt. I became aware of other physical limitations after the Terrace Bay incident. I felt limited by shortness of breath that had not been evident previously. During that hospitalization, the doctors asked if any symptoms might have alerted me to the pending PE. I had denied any warnings, but upon reflection, I realized that I had noticed my strength waning with exertion for about three months before the incident. I had also been short of breath on exertion, but not to the extreme that emerged in Terrace Bay. Night awakening with excruciating cramping in my calves may have been indicative of developing deep vein thrombosis that usually precedes PE's. In any case, I concluded that I had ignored some of the symptoms, mistaking them for signs of aging or being part of my pre-existing condition. Now, I had to adjust to physical changes that limited my abilities. Just a year ago, I walked for forty minutes a day. Now, I couldn't endure for ten minutes.

Multiplying that frustration was the prolonged legal action, with delays and repeated depositions over the next two years. I needed a successful outcome for this case to allow for certainty. Events that foretold a secure, but not extravagant, existence increased with each favorable result concerning EI sick benefits and Disability CPP. A definite outcome to the dismissal case would allow a more accurate assessment of the future. The waiting exacerbated my frustration. My legal advisers urged me to remain steadfast and calm because they were making progress. Finally, a significant offer was offered. The lawyer said I should wait, hoping for more. My frustration with delays and uncertainty prompted me to direct an acceptance of the offer in the interest of closure.

In 2015, we experienced an event that had long-lasting consequences for the whole family.

49

Coming Out

After suffering years of gender dysphoria, combined with his depression. Brandan revealed feelings that could no longer be tamped down and denied. Brandan had not revealed his level of depression at school and had never openly discussed his mental agony. It was a contributing factor to the poor performance at Brock. Instead of opening a dialogue about his mental state, he hid behind the role of a mediocre student. Finally, he revealed deeply hidden feelings that could no longer be denied. What had been deemed attention-seeking when his sister was born (claiming to be Eileen), revealed itself as an early attempt to express her inner struggle.

Without involving the family, Brandan announced that he would no longer respond to the pronoun he, nor would she respond to her dead name, Brandan." She was Molly Amelia Landgraff, a transgender woman, and wished to acknowledge her identity. As her father, this took time to understand. Did Molly not understand the care we took choosing her given name? Why were Debbie and I not invited to choose her new name? Her coming out was understandable. Her abrupt announcement made us feel that she doubted our support during her journey to self-acceptance.

Could she not appreciate the hurt that would arise by rejecting her given name and labeling it a "dead name? That it represented a virtual death? That, as parents, we would need time to grieve? These were issues we grappled with on our own. Molly had a non-inclusive point of view in this regard. A path had been chosen and Molly boldly set out upon it. My "antiquated" attitude was not going to hold her back.

Amber accepted and supported Molly's decision. In school and as the director of the Xspace Gallery, she had dealings and close relationships with the LGBTQI community, so maybe she was more prepared than Debbie and me. In fact, Amber abandoned organized religion in reaction to their condemnation of the LGBTQI community.

I have taken great pains to support Molly since she came out. I have also worried about the bigotry directed at the LGBTQI community. Molly's censure of lack of acceptance by society and certain celebrity figures has caused my concern.

50

Amber In Barrie

Amber returned to the family home in 2014 when her contract with Xspace ended, and she could not find a replacement job in Toronto. Having two adult children return to the nest was stressful, especially with the uncertainty of our own future security.

Many of our friends and acquaintances did not understand why we didn't insist on our children's return to independence. What was I supposed to do, throw them into the street? My friend's kids seemed to have no trouble getting jobs, but I encountered many news reports of the growing phenomena of return-to-nesters. Many of Amber's friends were having similar difficulties finding employment.

Parents from our book club dealt with similar situations. I wondered if I was being too indulgent or just unaware of reality. My kids said jobs were unavailable. Other friend's kids had business or engineering degrees and relocated to find employment. Overall prospects for millennials and Gen-Xers were not as hopeful as for the Baby Boomers. The later generations were adopting new attitudes, many abandoning hope of home ownership and turning to more immediate gratification, treating themselves with creature comforts and self-pampering.

After months of searching, Amber got hired part-time at the LCBO in a store in Cookstown, a twenty-minute ride from home. Unfortunately, Amber had not progressed through the graduated licensing milestones yet. She'd lived in Toronto without access to a car but with access to excellent public transport. I became her dedicated chauffeur. Debbie and I thought that the LCBO would offer a secure position, being a government agency with union benefits.

Although hired part-time, Amber's schedule was more like a full-time position. She worked about forty hours a week, often with no time off to allow downtime.

The LCBO's expectations of commitment were reminiscent of my experience in retail pharmacy. I tried to soothe Amber's frustration by making comparisons to my career, prompting accusations of fixating on my past. I would let it go to avoid an argument. I should have realized that Amber wasn't asking for solutions but just wanted to vent. I felt incapable of offering solutions anyway because her problem was identical to my experience, and I had just endured.

Her friends from Toronto were cut off because Amber was too tired to host visitors. She also felt that her creativity was stifled by her mundane cashier position. She applied for other jobs, some within the LCBO influence within their union. Other options existed out of the province or in different locations in Ontario. She made several applications to courses she was interested in. Still, she either was unsuccessful in finding an advisory professor willing to engage with her thesis proposal or was wary of increasing her student debt, chasing another degree with limited marketability. Eventually, she settled on becoming a paralegal, enrolled, was accepted, and would start lessons in September.

In the face of my platitudes and given the close relationship developed during Debbie's disability, Amber communicated more openly with her mother. I learned of Amber's isolation from friends, her aspirations for the future and her physical downturn, including her prolonged lack of sleep due to pain through Debbie. This secondhand communication left gaps or provided incomplete information after undergoing Debbie's unconscious filters.

I should have expected Amber to confide in her mother rather than me because it involved an intimate feminine issue. Amber endured menstrual bleeding for a duration of a month to six weeks. Eventually, I became as alarmed as Debbie when Amber experienced an extreme bleed that gushed onto the seat of the dining room chair. That, coupled with the length of time her problem lingered, got my attention. A trip to the ER resulted in a prescription for a clotting aid. Debbie requested a gynecological consultation, but no one was based in Barrie then. A gynecologist was relocating to Barrie but hadn't arrived yet. I still had faith in the medical community and remained calm.

Debbie started to panic, researching cancer in young women. I felt that Debbie was catastrophizing, drawing extreme conclusions and jumping to worst-case scenarios.

Amber's problem continued beyond the first prescription for the clotting aid.

A second trip to the ER resulted in a renewal of the treatment. After that course of treatment ended, the problem persisted. Amber began to suffer shortness of breath. A call to her GP sent Amber to the ER after being advised that her GP was booked solid for a month. The GP directed her to the emergency room. The doctor shortage had emerged and was evident even then.

At triage in the ER, Amber was asked why she was there. She told the nurse about the shortness of breath and her prolonged bleeding issue. The nurse pressed Amber to select the most pressing problem, which Amber verified was her bleeding. Her shortness of breath was not severe yet. When Amber saw the doctor, Debbie was with her and intended to bring up the breathing issue. After a six-hour wait, Amber finally saw a doctor. He angrily told Amber that many women shared her situation and that she should never have come to the emergency room for such a common problem; it was diverting services away from actual sick people. He told Amber to get used to it and that it was within everyday experience. After that cursory dismissal, Debbie was so incensed by the ER doctor's cavalier dismissal that she forgot to mention the breathing issue.

Another ER trip in an attempt to get proper medical attention for Amber's shortness of breath resulted in a blurry CT scan judged to be evidence of infiltrates to Amber's lung. A consultant lung specialist diagnosed Sarcoidosis. He tried to take a biopsy in the ICU to be sure. During the procedure, he encountered a problem that prevented the biopsy but prompted his accusatory comment to tell her GP that Amber had sleep apnea. Amber was admitted and treated with oxygen and a steroid to ease her breathing. She stayed for about a week. During that stay, we witnessed a dissatisfied family arguing with staff about their relative's treatment. The woman in question had agreed to a DNR after an extreme resuscitation. When her daughter discovered that, she accused the hospital staff of bullying her mother into acceptance. Later, the woman's husband came in, threatening legal action and involvement of the media. He took out his Health Card, pointed at it and yelled, "This says health card, it means that you have to return my wife to perfect health." In defense of the staff, a private place to discuss the issue was offered but rejected because the man wanted to create a disturbance. He failed to consider the effects of his actions on his wife and the three other patients sharing her ward room, Amber included. Debbie requested that Amber be removed from the room and moved to the sitting room in case of another altercation. Instead, they moved Amber to a private room. In preparation for the Canada Day weekend, they released her; neither oxygen nor pain medications were prescribed.

In response to Debbie's repeated request for a gynecological consult, she and Amber presented at the newly arrived specialist's office. The doctor didn't have admitting privileges, so she attempted a biopsy in her office. Amber was in so much pain that the doctor abandoned the attempt. No further provisions were made.

Another lung biopsy, with a preventive breathing apparatus on hand, was ordered for mid-July at Southlake Hospital in Newmarket. A week before the test, attending a pre-op appointment, Debbie noticed Amber's extreme shortness of breath at receiving and alerted the nurses. They dropped all the bureaucracy, got Amber in a wheelchair and admitted her to the ER, providing the paperwork after the fact.

Now, we entered genuinely dire straits. I have to admit that Debbie bore the brunt of this because she stayed in the hospital with Amber for the duration while I traveled home each day to check on Molly and monitor the home front. I spent about eight hours daily in the hospital, though. During that time, we met with numerous doctors. They worked in teams, monitoring Amber's situation. We saw internists, oncologists and other specialists. One of our classmates from the pharmacy department even came up when he saw Amber's order. Doctors would suddenly appear and conduct complete body examinations, trying to find any blemish or mark, like melanoma, to explain Amber's condition. I admit that the reason for the various doctors might be shift changes and specialists called in for consults, but for the most part, we never saw the same doctor more than once. They tried different pain regimens to increase effectiveness or decrease side effects. In a trial of ketamine, Amber went for eight hours with no pain relief to allow a complete washout of other medications for an accurate assessment of the ketamine. She pleaded with the doctor to put her back on morphine so she could get some relief.

Eventually, an oncologist visited, apologized to Amber and told her that she had cancer. It had metastasized to the lungs, liver, bones and brain, as well as her reproductive organs. Debbie and I knew it was serious because of our medical background, but Amber asked about the prognosis. The doctor could not be more specific about the origin of the cancer, whether it was ovarian or something else, other than to say that it was an aggressive carcinoma that had spread quickly. Amber expected a few months and was devastated when the doctor spoke in terms of weeks. Amber asked me what would happen to her now. Facing death, she needed assurances of an afterlife. I fell back on my religious explanations, which Amber protested. Eventually, she found some peace in the indigenous imagery of the final journey related by the hospital chaplain.

Amber had rejected any affiliations with organized religious. When I suggested that Amber receive the sacrament of the sick, just in case, Amber's vehement rejection of the ritual stopped me. When Debbie's Catholic friends suggested that we go through with the ritual after Amber became comatose, Debbie resolved to honor Amber's wishes. The scene witnessed during Amber's previous hospital stay made a discussion about a DNR unnecessary, as Amber told us her preference soon after her diagnosis.

My life turned into a surreal experience. I felt flattened, as if I had been hit by a steamroller. I carried on but just went through the motions. Debbie alerted friends and family to come quickly if they wanted a last visit with Amber. That began a flood of visitors, some making multiple visits. Through these visits, I learned that Amber had been refusing friend visits because she felt so tired.

Those who couldn't make it in person phoned from as far away as Boston.

Some brought flowers; others brought crafts they had created. A long-term friend arrived from British Columbia with a frog he had crocheted. Amber's days were filled with visits and calls over the next week. Amber hid her pain and presented her friends with a positive, upbeat appearance. They joked about her abandoned diagnosis of Sarcoidosis, saying that on the medical series, House, Sarcoidosis was never the proper diagnosis but predominantly a misdiagnosis for cancer.

Although Amber appeared upbeat and competent throughout the score of friend visits, the strain revealed itself by shortening her window of clarity a little each day. Debbie witnessed all of it, staying with Amber in the hospital, and sleeping on a fold-out couch in the room. She witnessed Amber's night terrors and held Amber's hand through the night to calm her and let her know she was not alone. Debbie related Amber's hallucinations about "bad people trying to get her to do bad things. and phantoms making faces at her. In many of her ramblings Amber told of her efforts to save the world, so much in keeping with her life outlook. The crocheted frog was removed because it said nasty things to Amber. Debbie watched helplessly as the disease progressed, causing a significant, noticeable, daily decline in Amber's status. We contacted a lawyer friend to prepare Amber's will. Three days after Syl came, Amber was non-compos mentis, having slipped into a coma.

I began to stay over at the hospital with Debbie. After two nights, I returned home to check with and update Molly. On the morning of August 1, 2018, Debbie called extremely early to ask me to return to the hospital. When I arrived, Debbie told me that my thirty-four-year-old daughter had passed on shortly before Debbie's call. I looked upon the shell of my baby girl, who departed only ten days after my sixty-fifth birthday. Until her death, no origin had been determined for her cancer. Because Amber died in the hospital, no autopsy was ordered. It was only two weeks since the oncologist had informed us of Amber's diagnosis. We were drained but numb, always on the verge of tears, but there was more to come.

Why

To what purpose

Do we strive?

For success and fame,

Why must we drive?

For in the end

We all must die.

And a dead man,

Is a dead man,

Is a dead man,

And that's to cry!

And if we do

Attain our goal;

SELF ACTUALIZATION,

Is it all for naught?

Our greater knowledge

Will be lost

When we have died.

And a dead man,

Is a dead man,

Is a dead man,

Is he not?

51

Celebration of Life

Debbie and Amber had discussed her last wishes during my absence at the hospital. Amber envisioned her Celebration of Life Event. She planned to leave her friends with keepsakes from her personal belongings. Perhaps that was why Debbie was named executor of Amber's will. Following the will, it seemed that probate was not necessary because Amber had a negative net worth. That only shortened the list of duties required of the executor.

We went with an undertaker more in tune with Amber's vision of her Celebration of life. They guided us through the legal requirements of the process and handled the details in preparation for the Celebration. Amber requested cremation, and her remains rest in a vase that she received from her staff and friends at Xspace, not a traditional urn. It shares space in our dining room hutch beside the remains of our Shih Tsus Zoe and Tsuki in a place of honor always available to the family. Amber shares space with the dogs she loved so much during her time with us. We may purchase a niche somewhere in the future where Debbie and I will rest with them. Choosing a final resting spot after moving around so much is difficult. We have many connections but no forever ties.

During her hospitalization, Amber started paperwork requesting EI sick benefits. The government had not declared that, so Debbie went to the Service Canada Offices. The bureaucrat speaking to Debbie said, "They haven't decided whether she's sick enough to warrant benefits." Debbie replied, "She's dead! Is that sick enough for you?" The stress and Debbie's grief were taking a toll.

The day of the Celebration of Amber's Life arrived. I was gratified with the attendance of over fifty friends and relatives. Her friends rented a bus in Toronto to allow as many attendees as possible. There were many condolences on Facebook and several moving tributes from her friends and coworkers. The official notice from Xspace spoke of her accomplishments and urged Amber to rest in Power as she had done in life.

The entrance and celebration room were set up as we requested. The entrance had photos of Amber's childhood and life that we shared as her family. It was not what I desired as I provided a digital slide show prepared to cycle on a projector. Still, the program I used to create the presentation was incompatible with the banquet hall software, so the photo array was used instead. Many celebrants commented on the pictures, asking us to explain them in more detail. The celebration room was spotlighted with hopeful green lighting, as Amber had requested, and an area with labeled gifts for the appropriate recipient was set up.

I spoke first, opening with, "All Amber wanted in life was to love and be loved," moving on to a Quebecois reference, "Nous nous souvenirs." I screwed up the pronunciation but received forgiveness under the circumstances and quickly carried on, saying, "Each of us has a souvenir of Amber in the form of memories. I then related a few stories from her childhood, referring to "Penguin Stew" and a vignette from our family trip to Disney World when she was in her terrible twos. I spoke of when Debbie tried to dress her for the day, only to have Amber reject every outfit brought with us. In tears, Debbie retreated to the bathroom, telling me, "You can dress her." I wondered what Debbie expected me to do since Amber turned down all the outfits. I picked one up and asked Amber, "Will you wear this?" Her response was, "Yes, Daddy," accompanied with a wide smile. My rendition met with comments of "Daddy's girl" from the celebrants. At one point, my shaking hands and swaying balance due to back pain prompted the undertaker to approach, asking if I was okay. I reassured her and carried on, finally inviting others to the podium to share their souvenirs. Speakers came one by one to share their experiences with Amber. College roommates, past neighbors, friends, relatives and coworkers each shared. The room was filled with peace.

After the presentations, we shared sandwiches and drinks. At the conclusion, we offered everyone some leftovers to go. In the end, about half of the prepped food remained. The banquet hall staff told us they could donate the food to the homeless shelter on our behalf. It felt in keeping with Amber's desires. So were Amber's wishes. So it was done.

52

Molly's Path

Molly walked her chosen path, seeing multiple doctors and psychologists to evaluate her commitment and suitability to the process. These evaluations established that Molly had made an informed decision, and a course of estrogen therapy began.

Additional support for Molly was provided by a specialist GP who was familiar with and had treated all of the family members during a trying period bracketed by major life stresses. Our specialist GP adviser helped each family member through individual situations.

At that time, Molly was deemed to be on the autistic spectrum. Autism spectrum disorders were not recognized because of the association with Asperger's Syndrome, first described by the Nazi, Dr. Asperger, in WW2 and termed Asperger's Syndrome. Shunned, given the negative association with an unpopular political regime, it didn't get widespread recognition until the mid-eighties. The diagnosis was renamed and became mainstream in 1994.

I finally understood why Molly responded to life with such a narrow viewpoint, unable to navigate the gray areas. Molly was gifted with coexisting conditions left unexplored. I was also diagnosed to be on the autism scale. It explained my past "cluelessness," marked by my missing cues and low EQ. It also explained why I could keep focused on tasks (school) in the face of distractions. Perhaps it was even the reason that I came to a career in a scientific field because I had a predisposition to the scientific method I followed throughout my life: observation, hypothesis, and conclusion.

Molly's coming out forced reevaluation of my professed acceptance of religious education. I had doubts since my first exposure to mythology. I read books that presented evidence that all religions had similar creation and great flood stories, observations of the same astronomical phenomenon, and descriptions of the afterlife and armageddon. Even after studying alternative beliefs, I clung to what was familiar. I tried to follow the teachings of Jesus as related in the New Testament, and I continue to do so. What I question are the actions of organized religion. Through the ages, every sect has perpetrated heinous acts: crusades, sexual abuse, forced conversions and genocide. None of these are in the New Testament. I imagine that if Jesus viewed the world today, he would condemn the behavior in the same way he condemned the Pharisees. I told myself not to abandon religion because of the actions of weak, flawed sinners, as C. S. Lewis advises in Mere Christianity. I convinced myself that an adherence to ritual provided meaning in life.

The attitudes of religious organizations around the LGBTQI community became a decision point when Molly came out. I had been steadfast before that, but Molly and Amber forced me face to face with the extreme inhumanity arising from legislation and religious attitudes. When I revealed Molly's chosen pathway at church, their lack of support pushed me away. I now identify myself as an agnostic. I accept that there may be a higher power or a unifying force in the universe, but I'm not sure. I am unsure whether there is an afterlife. On the other hand, scientists accept theories supported by statistical data analysis but not proven by direct observation. In either case, it remains a matter of faith.

53

Life Changes but Continues

Throughout my life, I've seen many things, made observations and drawn conclusions:

Bad things happen to good people and vice versa. Existence doesn't ensure the concept of fairness.

You will encounter people that dislike you, mistreat you, and may even repulse you. There will be bullies and backstabbers. Unless you become a hermit you must find a way to coexist.

Be like water; when it encounters an obstacle it always finds a way around it. Water is very relentless. Over time it can wear down mountains. Adopt this behavior in all of your dealings.

Past decisions made will seem to have "painted you into a corner." Don't dwell on the limitations of choice, rather exploit the opportunities presented by your choices.

An article I read in a business magazine before the millennium suggested the next great war would erupt along religious differences. On September 11, 2001, I witnessed the fall of the Twin Towers, along with the rest of humanity, experiencing the trauma over and over on the news as footage of the event replayed endlessly. The Western Allies engaged with Iraq and Afghanistan, declaring a war on terrorism.

Strangely, Afghanistan has been a repeated center of turbulence through the centuries. In the nineteenth century, Britain warred with Afghanis. In the twentieth century, Russia and the Western allies engaged there. No one has eliminated the rebellion of fundamentalists; it only slowed them down. Regional confrontations with genocide arose in Bosnia, Rwanda, Syria and now in Gaza. The U.S. and Russia, among others, stand accused of criminal acts arising from war. ISIS and a new Caliphate rose and fell. But life continues. The new millennium marked a turning point for humanity.

Added to that are the Global Warming phenomena and the COVID-19 pandemic, which resulted in a crisis of personal isolation and economic downturn, reawakening inflation fears. There is widespread refugee migration, feeding humanitarian crises and general food and housing shortages. Housing prices have soared, dashing the hope of home ownership in our younger generations. The world changes, but life goes on.

Debbie and I have endured further losses concerning our economic well-being and the passing of our dog, Tsuki, on December 29, 2022. I continue as an observer, making hypotheses and drawing conclusions. Over time, I recognized myself as a striver or Type A personality. My disability forced me to accept limitations and make adjustments. I have discovered alternate life paths. Once, I felt depressed for months after reading a biography of Lee Iacocca. It derailed me because I wasn't making a million dollars a year. I later read about the value of accepting changes from fluid intelligence exhibited post-graduation to crystallized intelligence that comes with aging. I stepped off of the treadmill. I learned that we are okay as we are. We must accept ourselves and our strengths as we find confidence and comfort in being ourselves rather than seeking approval from others. Another self-destructive behavior is measuring our worth by our ability to consume. Be satisfied with enough. The pursuit of amassing possessions creates a unique hell where even abundance beyond need does not bring satisfaction. Cultivate an acceptance of release from striving to reach specific benchmarks and seek a work/life balance. Finally, love and be loved, as Amber desired to be. Learn from the younger generation's vision and build on the foundation of the past. Discoveries with technological advances like the James Webb Space Telescope will present an expanded understanding of the universe. Instead of mourning the loss of Pluto as a planet, celebrate the addition of Ceres and Pluto as dwarf planets. Don't dwell on lost potential resulting from past decisions; take advantage of the enhanced potential offered by change. The only guarantee in life is change. Roll with it.

Made in United States
North Haven, CT
01 December 2024

60549303R00192